A Glitch In Time

By
Carmen Peregrim

PublishAmerica
Baltimore

ISBN: 1-4241-3329-7
PUBLISHED BY PUBLISHAMERICA, LLLP
www.publishamerica.com
Baltimore

Printed in the United States of America

Chapter 1

Studying her image in the mirror on the dresser, Laura began thinking about how she never had time for her private life, anymore. The gravity of her impending journey to that other reality had placed her in this introspective mood. Just thinking about what she and Lola would be facing in a few days was frightening and she was trying to focus on something pleasant for a while. At forty-seven, she was still quite pretty. Some even said she was beautiful, with her blond hair and deep blue eyes. Her eyelashes were dark and curled upward a little at the ends. Her dark brows, which had a slightly high arc to them, made her blue eyes appear even more striking. These facial features contrasted nicely with her fair skin. She had a fine figure that was evident even in the military fatigues she wore. Fatigues were the standard leisure clothes for both men and women in the society to which she belonged. Laura cut her hair short in the fashion of the day and her make-up, if worn at all, was just lipstick and a touch of rouge. In spite of her appeal to the opposite sex, her love life was all but nonexistent. As an adult, she was too busy for anything but casual relationships with the men she met while in the military. Now, the project she was heading precluded involvement with anyone on long or short-term basis. This was not abnormal in a society that was constantly preparing for war, especially for women of her status.

Gazing at her reflection in the mirror made her recall that she was born in New Jersey and her full name was Marie Laura Claremont. She was an only child because her mother could not have any more children after being exposed to radiation fallout in 1962. She recalled her mother telling her about her French Canadian heritage and that her ancestors fought on the Plains of Abraham trying to prevent the English from capturing the walled city of Quebec. The things her mother told her about their family were precious to her and made her feel unique in a militaristic society, which made everyone appear the same.

As she continued to study herself in the mirror, she wondered what things would be like if there was no threat of war and the world was at peace. Often in her life, she became exasperated with the state of emergency that existed since 1962. At these times, she would fantasize about being married and leading a life about which her parents would so often talk. However, she would dismiss these thoughts as foolish childhood fantasies that were not in the realm of possibilities. A physicist of her stature should not waste time on such trivial thoughts. Military service and the constant threat of war hardened life in this reality. Love and marriage were the ruminations of the older members of society. In this society one served in the military, in one capacity or another, until the age of fifty-five. Although Laura had spent only four years in the Army, she was now a colonel in the Army's Special Forces Reserve. Going back to her family to start a different life was impossible now, even if she wanted to. Her parents had passed away several years ago due to the long-term effects of exposure to nuclear radiation.

The thoughts about her parents' death caused her mind to refocus on the real possibility of perishing in that fiery aperture. What was she doing, she thought. The thing she and Lola were about to do would not matter in least to this war-maddened world. Whom would they impress, that bean counting lab manager, Farnsworth? He could not even understand how the Synthesizer worked, even after she explained it to him in one-syllable words. Maybe, she should simply abandon this absurd mission and take a meaningful assignment in the Advanced Nuclear Laboratory. This would make more sense because it is a very secure facility buried deep in the ground outside Los Alamos. Perhaps, she should just pack it all in and go to a part of South America that would be unaffected by the nuclear devastation. Nevertheless, she could not do any of these things because of her loyalty to her country. The ringing phone startled Laura out of her thoughts. It was Lola calling to update her on the status of the next experiment.

"Lola, what was the problem? Did the Bifurcation Locator malfunction?"

"No, the Synthesizer's field generator wasn't ramping up. We found that the field coils weren't being energized; heat had caused a power lead to burnout. We have replaced all the power leads with heavy-duty versions and everything seems to be functioning within specs, now. We will be ready to start tomorrow, Team Leader."

Moving away from the mirror and sitting on the sofa, Laura began thinking about the consequences of the series of experiments they had just performed. Again, fear began to gnaw at her insides as she tried to sort things out in her mind. Her thoughts quickly went back to the events that lead up to her involvement with the Time Crease Project. Because of her academic prowess, they allowed her to take her doctorate at Harvard before they inducted into the Army. When they finally inducted her, they trained her in all types of military combat. Her outstanding physical condition and intelligence qualified her for the prestigious field commander's school in Virginia. However, because of her accomplishments in science, they assigned her to Chronometry Laboratory deep in Cheyenne Mountain, near Colorado Springs.

Arriving at the Chronometry Laboratory, they offered her a choice of positions. One particularly far out project intrigued her. They called the project Time Crease. Its members were trying to find a way out of the abysmal mess the world had gotten into since the nuclear debacle back in 1962. Since then, NATO and the Soviet Bloc countries were systematically placing nuclear tipped missiles in various locations around the world. One could easily see that the situation was developing into a confrontation that would dwarf the Cuban Missile Crisis in comparison. The scientists on the Time Crease Project were trying to find a time anomaly that would permit them to return to 1962 and alter the course events that had occurred since then. Laura did not realistically expect the group would discover a way to travel in time. She felt, however, joining them allowed her to protest the lethal arms race and the world destruction it promised. Every newscast she heard now seemed to say nuclear war was, again, the only solution. The Time Crease Project appeared to be the only glimmer of hope left, so she started the project with considerable enthusiasm. As implausible as it seemed, her intuition told her that the research might lead to some useful discoveries that could change things for the better in her world.

Sitting in her dingy little apartment, with her feet now on a makeshift desk, her mind began to focus on the theory of time travel she had discovered.

She recalled the thoughts she had when she first studied the work of the other scientists on the Time Crease Project. She had decided very quickly that their efforts were futile because they were violating the principle of causality. That is, going back in time and changing even the slightest thing, changes one's own future, which to her way of thinking violates the causality principle. To avoid the causality difficulties she postulated that bifurcations in time had occurred in the past. These bifurcations were points in space-time at which the timeline had split into two segments. From the instant of bifurcation, things were free to evolve differently along each timeline, causing the futures in each reality to diverge.

After several years of grueling experimentation, and many ridiculous time-consuming suggestions by Dr. Farnsworth, the laboratory manager, Laura developed a device called the Bifurcation Locator in 2007. Soon afterwards, she discovered that a bifurcation had occurred in October of 1962, just before the launch of the Soviet missile against Washington. This discovery was puzzling because they had detected only one bifurcation point. A detailed analysis of the instrumentation suggested that its sensitivity was too low to detect other bifurcations that may have occurred further in the past. At this point, they realized they had discovered another reality, which they began calling the Alternate Reality.

In a desperate quest to find a portal to that other reality, the Time Crease Team began a series of critical experiments. These experiments led, ultimately, to the development of the Space-Time Transitional Synthesizer, or just Synthesizer, as they called it, informally. Carefully contrived experiments with the Synthesizer led to a disturbing discovery. It implied that space-time travelers must have a cellular DNA compatible with the reality they enter. Further study of the data indicated that when they are synthesized in the Alternate Reality their counterparts in that reality must not exist. In Laura's case, the experimental data seemed to indicate that they could not synthesize her on the bifurcated timeline before 1983. This further implied that her counterpart in the Alternate Reality ceased to exist by that time. By the same reasoning, all those conceived after 1962 had, in all probability, no counterparts in the Alternate Reality. This was the true because the odds against the same egg and sperm meeting in both realities were astronomical. People conceived and born after 1962 could be placed anywhere on the bifurcated timeline, but could go back only as far as 1962. Going back further would violate the causality principle because the timelines were one in the same.

Because of the strange constraints placed on space-time travelers, they qualified only one other member of Laura's group, Dr. Lola Gonzalez, for time travel. Lola met the required boundary conditions of the Synthesizer's portal because she was born in 1964. For these reasons and other qualifications, they selected her as Laura's space-time travel mate. The hope was that the women, once in the Alternate Reality, could design and fabricate a two-way Synthesizer. Then, with the aid of the new Synthesizer, find a way to save this doomed reality, which the Laboratory staff now dubbed the "Fated Reality."

———————————

As Laura entered the chamber that housed the Synthesizer apparatus, Lola clamped down the headgear on the specially designed lab suit that the team had prepared for the experiment. They designed the suit to prevent proximity forces from sucking her into the Synthesizer's multicolored aperture. The design of the suit and tethers were such that they would hold Laura just close enough to the aperture created by the Synthesizer to measure any incipient cell changes. The lab team was still trying to collect data on how the Synthesizer transformed living tissue, when going from one reality to another. It was mandatory they have this information before subjecting Laura and then Lola to the transforming fields of the Synthesizer. The same experiment performed on mice with monitoring sensors attached to them resulted in the mice being sucked into the multicolored aperture by the proximity forces. The data collected was inconclusive, but seemed to suggest that going back to a point on the bifurcated timeline would cause the cells of a living creature to grow younger. They reached this conclusion by studying the tails on the chromosomes of a few cells ripped off the mice, as the proximity forces pulled them into the aperture.

As the field energy ramped up in the Synthesizer, the aperture it created glowed in colored light. The light was so brilliant that its intensity would have blinded Laura; if it were not for the special visor shield in the helmet, she wore. In addition, the high temperature of the aperture made wearing an insulated helmet and suit a requirement for any space-time traveler. Laura's heart was pounding as she approached the brilliant aperture. Her back stiffened as she felt the pull of the proximity forces. She tried to make her body ridged to resist the strange forces, which were now very evident. Her fears began to mount as the proximity forces pulled her tightly against the front of her suit. She felt a strange tingling sensation in her body and she began to lose consciousness. The team seeing her stagger grabbed the tethers and pulled her out of the grip of the proximity forces. They quickly removed her helmet; her face was ashen but quickly regained its color and she was now fully conscious. She hid her fears from the team because it was not fitting in her world for the Team Leader to show such emotions. She did this in spite of knowing that going into that aperture might very well kill her.

The experimental data from the suit's sensors showed that the intensity of the light and heat in the aperture increased many-fold as one approached the fiery portal. This increase was much more in Laura's case than observed with the mice, leading the team to believe that it is proportional to the amount of living tissue passing through the aperture. The sensor data, obtained by measuring Laura's initial and almost infinitesimal cell changes, was far from conclusive. However, it did show that there was, indeed, an age reversal process taking place in the portal. This phenomenon was baffling, but even more baffling was the apparent lack of change in her neural cells. They also noted that samples of her blood, held near the portal, began to disintegrate when the date to enter the other reality was set before 1983. With the entrance date set after 1983, the blood samples showed no signs of disintegration only evidence of age reversal. This again supported the supposition that her DNA was compatible for synthesizing in the Alternate Reality after 1983.

Time was running out in this doomed world and there were precious few days left. Laura, feeling the sense of urgency, decided to test the time travel equipment by using herself as a guinea pig. She would go through the aperture generated by the Synthesizer and take her chances. When the Time Crease team objected, she rationalized her decision the following way.

"People, as you know this project was replete with pitfalls from the start and frankly, I didn't think we would get this far, but we did. And, yes, we really haven't taken enough data to ensure any real measure of safety to anyone who goes into the aperture. But, as you know an impending nuclear disaster is imminent. It would be foolish to let this opportunity go by and not test the one thing that could ultimately save us all."

"Dr. Claremont, going through that aperture would probably result in your death. You are more likely to survive a nuclear war here, than walking into that hot aperture, suit or no suit. We are a mile under ground in this Cheyenne Mountain facility and relatively safe here," a colleague pointed out.

"Survive for what? To live in a hole in the ground for many years and probably die there. No thanks," Laura responded with determination. Most Time Crease members were shock by her seemingly reckless perseverance.

"You don't expect others to follow you to your death in that aperture, do you?" remarked Claude Harris. Harris was a young man who had recently joined the team and was compatible with the boundary conditions imposed by the aperture.

"No, you are released from the agreement you signed when you volunteered to participate in this experiment. That also includes Dr. Gonzalez. I can't expect any of you to risk you lives based on incomplete experimental evidence and untested equipment."

"Laura, I didn't spend all this time working on the Time Crease Project just to abandon it for life in a hole in the ground," Lola quickly injected.

"Lola, we don't know what will happen to us with our cells going through a reverse aging process. Even if we manage to survive the transition through the aperture and are synthesized in the Alternate Reality, we might be in some kind of coma. You know my body cells experienced a slightly favorable mutation when I was in fetal development, consequently, I have a greater chance of survival than most people."

"My cells also experienced a similar mutation, because, as you know, my mother was subjected to residual radiation fallout in '63. For chrissake, Laura, I also excelled in academics and survived rigorous endurance training in the Army just like you. I'm the only other one on the Time Crease Project that is as qualified as you to go through that aperture, and I'm willing to take my chances, too."

Laura was pleased that Lola still intended to remain her time travel mate. She was extremely intelligent and was quite capable in a combative situation. She would be a real asset if they survived in the Alternate Reality. She would definitely increase the chance that, once in the Alternate Reality, they could build a Synthesizer, and with it establish a two-way linkage with the Fated Reality. Over the past few years, she had learned to admire Lola and had come to appreciate her capabilities. She liked the discipline Lola exercised when they confronted her with a difficult task. Laura was certain they would make an excellent time travel team and quickly accepted Lola's request to see the project through to its conclusion.

Over the next few days, the lab technicians fabricated space-time travel suits that incorporated all the safety features that the Time Crease Team could imagine. The items the women were to carry on their persons into the Alternate Reality were of concern. They decided after much deliberation that they would carry their military survival kits, which contained, among other things, the new compact, hand-held laser weapons. The next decision was to select the place and date to enter the Alternate Reality. Further analysis of the experimental data confirmed that they could not synthesize Laura on the bifurcated timeline before 1983. It also confirmed their previous conclusion that her counterpart in the Alternate Reality had ceased to exist by that time. Lola, on the other hand, was conceived after 1962. This meant that her DNA was compatible with the aperture's boundary conditions from the time of her birth in June of '64 to the present. However, they determined that she should not go back to a date within fifteen years of her birth because theory indicated the de-aging process was very nonlinear in that region. It was not necessary, anyway, because Laura could not go back that far, either. Still, the women wanted to go back as far as safety permitted to give them enough time to design and develop a new version of the Synthesizer.

Given all the constraints imposed upon the space-time travelers, the Time Crease Team selected the Garden of the Gods in Colorado Springs as the point of entry. This was not far from the Chronometry Laboratory's location and it was within the Synthesizer's limited range of operation. The Garden of the Gods would not likely have military personnel wandering about when they synthesized the women there. They were not sure, of course, that there was a military base in the Alternate Reality at their Cheyenne Mountain location. On the other hand, they did not want to take the chance of synthesizing there because one did exist at that location in 1962. The time of entry on the bifurcated timeline was to be just past midnight in a secluded part of the Garden of the Gods. The point of entry would be behind a large formation of red boulders that was likely still to exist in the Alternate Reality. It would take place the Monday after the Fourth of July weekend in 1984; a year after Laura's counterpart in the Alternate Reality had ceased to exist. Tomorrow, the Laura and Lola would take that fateful step through the portal leading to the Alternate Reality.

Lola had gone to Albuquerque to spend the evening with her aunt before her historic journey into the unknown. Her parents were exposed to nuclear radiation when the Soviets targeted the Air Base near Alamogordo. It was where, they thought, the US hid a large stockpile of nuclear warheads. Her aunt had raised her since she was twelve and now lived alone in Albuquerque. At that time, her mother had died of complications cause by the nuclear blast; her father had died several years earlier of similar complications.

Lola's aunt, Carmen Zaragoza de Saucedo, was her mother's twin sister, who had married a man from Spain. She was living there with him when he died suddenly in the aftermath of the 1962 nuclear war. Her aunt's family name was Zaragoza. She had kept that name because Spanish women did not give up their family name when they married; they just appended their husband's to it. Lola's name was actually Dolores, but her aunt always called by the diminutive Lola and the name stuck. Her aunt told her she came from a family of military men and that she was a descendant of Ignacio Zaragoza, a courageous Mexican general. Her aunt's stories of her heritage made her strive to be a model officer, when she was in the Army, and live her life, even now, by the ridged code of military ethics. Although Laura had offered her the option of backing out of the Time Crease Mission, her adherence to military ethics made that option unacceptable. She was as aware of the risks involved in the mission as Laura, and the thought of entering that fiery aperture was making her very apprehensive. However, there was no way she was going to let Laura face the risks of that mission alone.

Arriving at aunt Carmen's house in Albuquerque, Lola hugged her aunt so tightly that it caused her to gasp for breath.

"My god, Lola, you'd think you hadn't seen me for several years. Let me look at you, child."

Lola was a woman with dark brown hair and beautiful dark eyes, which at times seemed as black as night. Her long black eyelashes and her delicately arched brows gave her eyes a certain unforgettable look, especially, when she smiled. Her slim silhouette, delicate face, and light olive skin were reminiscent of Spanish aristocracy. Carmen had often thought about Lola's fair looks, but something puzzled her.

"Lola, why have you never married? You are such a pretty woman. You must have had many offers."

13

"Aunt Carmen, no one came along that interested me, and my career as an electrical engineer and an army officer never left much time for men in my life."

"You mean to tell me you never found anyone that met your expectations," Carmen asked in disbelief.

"Oh, there were a few quick romances that never amounted to anything. If I wasn't so wrapped up in the defense effort I guess I might have found someone, but it wasn't in the cards. I'm forty six now and too involved in a highly classified project for romance to enter my life."

"I know it's hard to live a normal life in these frightening times, but you must make time to find a husband," Carmen told her in serious tones.

"I'm never going to find anyone in that hole in the ground I work in. Even if I did, I couldn't get involved because I'm starting on an important assignment tomorrow that will take me very far from here. The journey is going to be very risky and I may never get back."

Her niece's last remark stunned Carmen and she thought, Mother of God, what is she saying.

"Lola, you're scaring me. What are you trying to tell me? Are you going on a dangerous mission? Do you think you may never return?"

"Aunt Carmen, I didn't mean to alarm you, but you know there are many dangerous aspects to what many of us do in these trying times. All that I am saying is one can never tell anything about one's future. We could all be wiped out if another nuclear confrontation occurred; you read the papers and can see the gravity of the situation."

"I know all that, but I'm still concerned about you. Maybe we should go to South America and get away from this frightening place."

"Oh, Aunt Carmen, there is no security there. The Soviets will even clean out the brush with nuclear weapons because they think we have nuclear bombs hidden there; you heard those accusations by the Soviets."

"Can't you give me some idea about what you're involved in, something that will give me some hope?"

Lola could not tell her aunt about space-time travel or their plans to enter the Alternate Reality. It would just confuse and frighten her even more. It might even sound as if she had taken leave of her senses if she mentioned that stuff.

"Dear Aunt Carmen, the project I'm involved in is highly classified, and to divulge its nature at this time would only serve to further confuse and frighten you. But, I think it's safe to tell you this. If my mission is successful, a better world may result from my team's efforts."

With that final remark, Lola hugged her aunt and kissed her good-by, then left for the airport to catch a military helicopter back to Colorado Springs. Tomorrow was her last day in this reality and she wanted to get at least a little sleep, if she could, before for stepping into that awesome looking aperture. The idea of entering that fiery aperture was still causing her to have some second thoughts. Maybe Aunt Carmen was right. There must be somewhere in the godforsaken world where she and Carmen could live out their lives in peace. Maybe the southern tip of Chile would be safe. She quickly got hold of herself and put those thoughts out of her mind. She did this because going to the Alternate Reality seemed like the only way to save this miserable world from self-destruction.

Laura walked briskly as she made her way down the long, damp corridor to the Chronometry Laboratory. The sounds of her heels echoing through the passageway seemed to amplify the anxiety she already felt, and were forcing her to think about the imminent danger her and Lola were facing. The thought of what she was about to embark upon was sending shivers down her spine and was forcing her to have second thoughts, again. Reaching the Chronometry Laboratory brought Laura's disturbing train of thoughts to an end, as she focused on clearing herself for entry. She accomplished this by looking into a retina-scanning device that could uniquely identify her through the retina's rod and cone patterns. Before gaining admittance to the inner office, however, another device scanned her body for passive radiation emitted by objects hidden under her clothes. This scanning device always irked her. It not only determined whether she was concealing any type of weapon or explosive device on her person. It also displayed on a monitor, a passive image of her private parts to the gawking security guard behind the partition.

Passing all these tests, they allowed her to enter the inner office. Once inside, she went directly to the dressing room and found Lola waiting there for her. Lola told her that the Time Crease Team was making some last minute adjustments to the Synthesizer and would notify them when things were ready. As they began donning their space-time suits, they began to discuss the nature of their relationship to each other while on the Time Crease Mission.

Laura was the designated leader of the Alternate Reality Team and the Chron Lab scientists began using the acronym ART when referring to them. Laura was designated ART1 and Lola ART2.

"Lola, I want you to dispense with the formalities of military rank and call me Laura on this mission. I also want you to know that I'm very pleased you volunteered to join me, although you could have refused without prejudice. With you at my side this mission, clearly, has a much greater chance of success. Thank you. OK, now I want to go over something before we go to the space-time chamber. I want to test the microchip communicators that they surgically implanted behind our left ears. They're advanced versions of the ones developed for the Army and have many useful new features."

"Laura, I was reading the literature the communications officer gave us and it says they have a range of one mile in the talk mode and five miles in the signal mode."

"They're activated by pressing in the space-pause sequence, given in the manual, behind your left ear. When we hear the other's modulated signal tone, we activate the unit by pressing the in the same sequence and then speak in low clear tones. The microchip communicators can transmit and receive our words, simultaneously. With the older units, we had to alternate the conversation because they couldn't transmit and receive at the same time. These new units permit simultaneous communication and have several other features that make them extremely useful. OK, now let's give them a try."

Laura went down the long hall outside the lab and activated her unit. Hearing the modulated tone Lola activated hers and carried on a conversation from a hundred yards away through the walls of the Chron Lab's outer office. They decided to use their code names, ART1 and ART2, in any microchip communication between them. This was essential because the link was not secure, and could be monitored by anyone tuned to the frequency they were using. They also tested the S.O.S mode, which they could activate, in an emergency, by pressing in a short activation sequence with the tongue behind the left upper molar. Once satisfied that their microchip communications system was working, properly, Laura went back to the dressing room. They, then, began completing their countdown together.

"Laura, do you really think we will need these new Laser hand-held weapons. We're supposed to be going in peace and be inconspicuous in the Alternate Reality, not blast our way in."

"Your right of course, but suppose the Alternate Reality is more hostile than here and we have to get ourselves out of a difficult situation. This weapon is an advanced application of the pulse-coded, maser technology under development by the Armament Laboratory and is not in general a killing weapon. When its pulsed coherent radiation impinges upon the skin or enters the eye of a perpetrator, it induces a signal in the nerve endings that is transmitted to the brain. Upon which, it induces a state of profound sleep."

"Still, do we really need these weapons? You and I are extremely capable in a combat situation and could handle almost anyone."

"Yes, but not against a squad of men trying to get control of us. Besides, these appear quite innocuous and look like ordinary pocket pens. The safety is here; press it; then turn the clip and it's armed. Here put it in that slot in your uniform and hope that we never have to use them."

"OK. Are we finished?"

"Oh, one more thing, Lola, I want to say, again, how pleased I am that you volunteered for this mission. I can't think of anyone I'd rather have than you as my time travel mate, thanks again."

"I can't think of anyone I'd rather have as Team Leader on this mission. You are a constant source of inspiration to me. Thank you for having me."

With those final remarks the women ended their mission checkout procedure and left the dressing room. As Laura and Lola entered the facility that housed the Space-Time Transitional Synthesizer, they clamped down each other's helmets onto the specially designed space-time suits. The team had carefully prepared the clamps on those helmets so that the women could quickly release them after they entered the Alternate Reality. Standing a safe distance from the Synthesizer, the women paused while the chief technician announced that he had imputed the coordinates into the space-time computer. They would be synthesized at the specified location in the Garden of the Gods, behind the huge red rock formation. The time of entry on the bifurcated timeline would be just past midnight, July 7, 1984.

When ART1 and ART2 finally took their designated positions in front of the aperture, the chief technician commenced the countdown. As the field energy ramped up in the Synthesizer, the aperture that it created glowed in blinding colored light. Laura and Lola would have definitely suffered eye damage if it were not for those specially designed visor shields in their helmets. Even the monitoring crew in their remote locations had to wear special glasses. When the energy field reached its peak, Laura stepped toward the glowing aperture and was immediately drawn into the brilliant chasm by the proximity forces. Lola hesitated a moment, then stepped forward and was similarly drawn into the glowing aperture.

Chapter 2

The Garden of the Gods' maintenance supervisor and his assistant began to make their daily rounds on the morning of July 7, 1984. Their first task was to see that the grounds were ready for viewing when the park opened to the public at 9:00 a.m. As they walked among the red rock formations, they notice something metallic looking sticking out from behind a rock formation that was about a hundred feet away.

"Jack, you better go over there and see what that is. Maybe some kids got in here last night and left some garbage behind those rocks," the maintenance supervisor directed his subordinate.

When Jack got to the other side of the red boulders, what he saw had startled him.

"Bill, you better come over and look at this."

"What the hell do you want? We have to get this damn place checked out before the crowd gets here. Now just pick up whatever it is and throw it out."

"Bill, you better get over here, it looks like we've been invaded by aliens from outer space."

"What the hell are you talking about?" the supervisor shouted out as he walked over to where Jack was standing.

"What the hell do you want me…?" The supervisor stopped in the middle of his sentence as he viewed the site in front of him.

"Geez, what the hell are they? We better call the police."

The supervisor told Jack to wait there in case they moved and ran back to the maintenance shed and called the Colorado Springs police department. He told them that he had found two men, in strange looking spacesuits, behind a rock formation in the Garden of the Gods and they seemed unconscious. They told him not to touch anything until they arrive. They said they would also be sending an ambulance.

When the police and the paramedics arrived, they saw two unconscious figures in pale green metallic spacesuits with strange looking helmets on them. The helmets had dark blue visors imbedded in them.

"We better get those helmets off them and see if they're still breathing," one paramedic shouted to the other.

The police were standing there staring at the two figures lying motionless on the ground; they looked as stunned as the park custodians did.

When they got the helmets off, what they saw further stunned them. Lying there was two very young women in the space suits, one blond and the other brown-haired.

"They are breathing. We better get those suits off so we can check their vitals," said one paramedic.

As they unzipped the suits down the front, they could see that the women were wearing some kind of military fatigues under the space suits. When the paramedics unbuttoned the fronts of the women's shirts to put stethoscopes against their chests, they saw the women were wearing chains with plastic identification tags on them.

"This one says, Col. L. Claremont, US Special Forces. This other one says Lt. Col. L. Gonzalez, US Special Forces. There are also serial numbers on them," a paramedic said, reading the tags to the police.

"This just took on another level of significance. You guys get them to the hospital and we'll notify the authorities at the SAC NORAD Base in Cheyenne Mountain," one police officer said.

As Laura began to regain consciousness things seemed to be spinning so fast that focusing on anything was impossible. Then the room seemed to rotate slower and slower until it finally stopped. She thought, what the hell happened, where was she. Her head ached, but her mind was beginning to clear. Looking around, as things came into focus, the strange surroundings startled her. She soon realized she was in some kind of hospital room when she noticed they were giving fluid, intravenously. She wondered how she got here. Then, she remembered she had been working on the Time Crease Project in the Chronometry Laboratory. As time went on the intensity of the pain in her head began to subside. She now recalled that Time Crease was the project she elected to work on when she joined the Chron Lab. The project was engaged in a serious study of time and was looking into the possibility of some type of time travel. She recalled taking the project along way toward that goal by inventing the Space-Time Transitional Synthesizer. Things were rapidly coming back to her, now.

She remembered that she and Lola Gonzalez had been in the Synthesizer Chamber. The chief technician had informed them that he had imputed, into the Synthesizer's computer, the coordinates at which they were to enter the Alternate Reality. They were going to be synthesized at a specified location in the Garden of the Gods. She remembered stepping toward the glowing aperture and recalled a strange feeling of being compressed, then nothing. What had happened? This was not the Garden of the Gods. Did the mission fail? Why was she in this hospital room? All these thoughts were running through her mind as a nurse entered the room.

"Colonel Claremont how are you feeling? When I saw you move on the monitor I knew you had regained consciousness."

"You have me on a monitor? Not much privacy in here, is there?"

"We had to place you on it by General Philips orders."

"Where am I and who is General Philips?"

"You are in the hospital on the SAC NORAD Base in Colorado. General Philips is the Base Commander."

Laura thought for a moment, trying to understand what they had just told her. The name of the Base was not quite the same, and the Commander of the Base was not Philips. Something was wrong. Had her memory been damaged by her attempt to enter the Alternate Reality, she wondered. Then a thought occurred to her: *could I actually be in the Alternate Reality? Is this really a different world?* With those thoughts running through her mind, she decided to ask the nurse a set of questions. She contrived the questions to learn whether she was in the Alternate Reality without revealing that she was from the Fated Reality. She called out to the nurse.

"Nurse, how long have I been here?"

"You were in a coma for four days."

My god, four days, she thought, what the hell happened to me?

"How did I get here?"

"By ambulance from Colorado Springs Hospital."

Her situation was still ambiguous. So, she continued to ask the nurse questions.

"Apparently I suffered some kind of trauma and it may be playing tricks on my memory. Just to make sure I have everything straight, who is the President of the United States?"

Laura knew that if she were in the Alternate Reality it was not likely that the same president would exist simultaneously on both timelines. She was not ready for what the nurse was about to tell her.

"Colonel Claremont, Ronald Reagan is the President."

The nurse's answer dumbfounded Laura. *She must be putting me on*, she thought. Then she decided to try to find out if the nurse was serious.

"Wasn't he in all those war movies a few years back?"

Laura meant during the late sixties and seventies because Reagan became very popular making war movies in her world.

"A few years back? You mean forty to fifty years back, don't you? He hasn't acted in a movie since the fifties."

That answer just about convinced her that she was in the Alternate Reality.

"Another question before you leave. My mind is still a little foggy. I don't recall being brought to the Colorado Springs hospital. Do you know how I got there?"

"All I know is that someone said you and the other one were found unconscious in the Garden of the Gods."

"The other one? What other one?"

Laura asked those questions pretending to be surprised because she did not want to let them know how cognizant she was of the situation. That video camera and the hidden bugs, she now surmised, were monitoring everything that she said and every gesture she made.

"Lt. Colonel Gonzalez was found with you."

"One more thing before you go. Could bring me a newspaper?"

"OK, but if you're looking to find your picture in the papers don't waste your time, it's not there."

When the nurse left, Laura thought about what had just happened. She thought: *The portal did lead to the Alternate Reality and my theories were essentially correct. However, it didn't work out as we planned and we are going to have a lot to explain to the military authorities. I must try to contact Lola.* The nurse's last comment gave Laura the germ of an idea for a cover story.

Laura inconspicuously activated the microchip circuits behind her left ear and sent the modulated activation signal to Lola. There was no response, she wondered if Lola was still unconscious. She tried again.

"ART2 this is ART1 one, respond."

"This is ART2 responding."

"Speak, softly, they are monitoring us," Laura admonished.

"Where the hell are we? I just came out of some kind of stupor and my head hurts. Are we in some kind of hospital? Did the mission fail?"

"Relax ART2, you're going to be all right, your head will clear in a few minutes. I just came out of it, too, about fifteen minutes ago. We were in some kind of space-time coma. We are in the Alternate Reality."

"You mean we actually made it."

"Yes, but we've been discovered. I questioned the nurse, being careful not to reveal anything about time travel. It appears they found us in the Garden of the Gods four days ago and they turned us over to the military authorities. We are in the hospital on the SAC NORAD Cheyenne Mountain Base in Colorado."

"That's not exactly its name in our reality."

"I know, and when the nurse said that name, it was my first clue that we were in the Alternate Reality. The problem is, they have taken our clothes and even our dog tags. They're calling us by our reserve ranks. I feel we're going to have some really tall explaining to do."

"Why do you suppose we were in a coma so long?" Lola asked.

"My guess is that our cells needed that time to age reverse. Did you notice how young you look?"

"My nurse remarked to me a few minutes ago, when I just came out of that coma, that I seemed a little too young to be a Lieutenant Colonel. I told her some women don't show their age."

"When we left the Fated Reality I was forty-seven and you were a year younger. In this reality you're physically twenty and I'm twenty-one, but our neural cells did not regress. We still have all the knowledge we gained in our reality. However, we may not be able to get away with the 'some women don't show their age' pretense for long. My counterpart did exist in this reality until about a year ago. They probably have her fingerprints on file somewhere. You don't have the same problem because you never existed here. By the way, my nurse made an interesting remark when I asked to see a newspaper. She said, I shouldn't waste my time looking for my picture in the paper because it's not going to be there. They're suspicious of us and I think we should reinforce their suspicions. We should let them believe we were pulling off some kind of college girl stunt and it backfired."

"Sounds complicated, but plausible."

"We can take that ruse as far as we have to. It may still be useful even if they identify me through my counterpart's fingerprints. By the way, I bet you can never guess who's President in this reality."

"No, who?"

"Ronald Reagan."

"You're kidding."

"No, I'm not. It's Ronald Reagan. The nurse is coming back with the newspapers for which I asked. ART1 out."

"Whom are you taking to?" The nurse asked as she entered the room.

"Oh, no one, I'm just reciting a poem to myself. Thanks for the papers."

"When you have recovered sufficiently, the General has requested you be brought to Colonel Thompson's office. He'll find out who you really are. You and the other one are young enough to be his daughters not military officers."

"Who is Colonel Thompson?"

"Never mind, you'll find out."

"Well, I guess you found us out," Laura remarked, smiling.

Laura's smile reinforced the nurse's suspicion. Laura knew suspicions spread quickly at military bases in her reality and that was probably true at this one, too. She suspected that the conjectures of the nursing staff would reach the General. He would probably conclude they were part of some kind of prank and dismiss the whole thing. At least she hoped they would. However, if they discovered the pocket pens in their space-time suits were some kind of weapon, the whole cover story she was weaving would blow up in their faces. Her happiness over making it safely to the Alternate Reality was fading rapidly and concern about their precarious position in this reality was beginning to mount.

Over the next few days, Laura and Lola read as many newspapers as they could get their hands on. After three days they gave them their clothes, that is, only the fatigues they had on when they arrived at the hospital, but no spacesuits. They then released them from the hospital the next day and gave them quarters in a building near the Base library, pending the outcome of an investigation that they were conducting. They restricted them to the library, mess hall and their room. The women were pleased with those orders because in their reality they would have taken this situation a lot more seriously. They would have been spending their time locked up in a cell somewhere on the Base. Instead, they spent their time in the library reading and browsing through as many periodicals and books as time permitted. The women found a book on the 1962 Cuban Missile Crisis and read it cover to cover, finally understanding what event caused the timeline to bifurcate.

They found that eleven days into the crisis the blockade appeared to have failed, and the Soviets had completed the deployment of their missiles in Cuba. Soon afterwards, a surface-to-air missile shot down a U2 spy plane over Cuba, killing the pilot and escalating the crisis. The generals during the crisis had recommended a military response to the military action taken by the Soviets. Kennedy's decision was to either invade Cuba, as recommended by the generals, or attempt to broker a face-saving deal with the Soviets. The face-saving deal required that the Soviets dismantle and remove the missiles from Cuba. In return, the US would recognize the integrity of the Castro regime in Cuba. The decision to take out the missile sites in Cuba caused the timeline to bifurcate. The Fated Reality followed the doomsday scenario and the Alternate Reality followed the path that led to a face-saving compromise.

The new understanding the women had gained from their studies, made them believe that they could probably broker a deal between the antagonists in the Fated Reality. However, it, now, appeared to the women that such a lofty goal might take many years and many innovations to accomplish. If they intended to succeed, they should take one step at a time and solve the problems as they come along. In particular, how do they get out of the situation they were in now?

During the second week of August, Laura and Lola were ordered to report to the Colonel D. Thompson's office, Laura at 0800 hours and Lola at 1500 hours.

"Well, it looks like they're finally ready to debrief us," Laura remarked, as she and Lola examined the papers they had received that morning.

"Come on, let's take a walk outside and talk about it," Lola remarked, as she pointed to her ears and then the walls.

When they got outside Laura acknowledged that the walls could have ears and agreed that they might have bugged them.

"Well, Team Leader, we better get our act together and come up with a good cover story. Our first thoughts, a month ago, were to admit to some kind of ruse, but after all our reading and discussions, I don't think we know enough about this culture to pull it off."

"You're right, Lola, we're going to get tripped up explaining where we got those suits from. We don't even know where to find suits like that in this reality, even if our lives depended on it."

"Those pens, if they find out they're weapons we'll never explain how we got them."

"I've been thinking about that. Here, take a couple of these pens I found in the library, they look a lot like ours, maybe we can switch them if the opportunity arises. I figure our best strategy at the debriefings will be to feign amnesia, claiming we suffered some kind of trauma that caused those comas."

"That sounds more plausible, Laura. We could still acknowledge that it obviously was some kind prank, but we can't recall the circumstances."

"OK, we'll play it that way, but let me repeat the strategy so we clearly understand the plan. We feign amnesia when they ask about the suits. Let's ask to see the suits and tell them they might help jog our memories. Then acknowledge it may be a prank of some kind, but we can't remember. For the rest, however, we'll have to play it by ear. Oh yes, don't forget we have to leave our microchip communication systems activated. I figure they're questioning us separately so they can look for some discrepancies in our stories. If we keep the comlinks activated, we can hear at least what the other says during the questioning."

Having developed a cover story that was flexible enough to handle almost any situation, the women relaxed and went to the library to gather more information about the Alternate Reality.

At 0800 hours, 17 August, they escorted Laura to Colonel Thompson's office for interrogation and debriefing. As she entered the office, she noticed another man was sitting next to Colonel Thompson at the conference table. After they seated her at the table across from them, Colonel Thompson spoke.

"Ms. Claremont, we are no longer going to address you as Colonel Claremont because we don't believe you're associated with the military. Before we begin, however, let me introduce you to Agent Hartwell, the FBI agent assigned to the case."

Before Laura could respond, Lola transmitted a quick message over their micro comlink.

"ART1, I can hear what he is saying. The micro receiver must be picking up your eardrum vibrations when he speaks, just like it does when you speak. So, don't risk repeating anything for my benefit. ART2 out."

"Your probably right, Colonel Thompson, but I can't recall how or why I was in that spacesuit or in of all places, the Garden of the Gods. It certainly appears like I was involved in some kind of prank," Laura responded.

"Well, we're glad you're not going to embarrass yourself by pretending you were on some secret military assignment. I agree you were probably involved in some kind of prank or perhaps a publicity stunt," agent Hartwell commented.

"Publicity Stunt?" Laura questioned, she didn't quite understand. They didn't use that term in her reality.

"You know, some kind of advertisement for the movies, but something bothers me; those space suits look too authentic to be props. Where do you suppose they came from?" Colonel Thompson asked.

Laura knew they were not telling her everything, so she played along.

"Actually, I never saw them, I only heard from the nurses that I was in one when they found me. Maybe if I looked at them, I would remember."

"All right, the suits are, over there, in that box in the corner; go have a look. Agent Hartwell, I have to make a call, will you tell my secretary we'll be down in a few minutes."

While the colonel was on the phone, Laura took the suits out of the box and examined them. She quickly found out the laser pens were still in the concealed pocket inside the jackets' flap. She hurriedly exchanged them with the pens she had in the inside pocket of her fatigues. Then, she noticed they had confiscated the survival packs attached to the hip clips. She thought, it was a good thing they removed those pens from the kits because they would be gone, too.

"ART2, I got the pens. ART1 out."

While Laura pretended to study the suits, the FBI agent came back into the office and walked over to her. By that time, the Colonel was off the phone and walked over to join them.

"Remember anything?" the Agent asked.

"They're a funny green color, aren't they? No, nothing looks familiar. However, the nurses did say we had helmets on. Where are they?"

"They're studying them in our labs along with what appears to be survival kits." The agent answered.

"Why?" Laura asked, pretending to be puzzled.

"We can't tell you that, except to say they're certainly not props. Maybe what we tell you next might help clarify our position. Let's go back to the table."

The last remark puzzled Laura and Lola.

"ART1, be careful, don't let them trip you up. ART2 out."

"Ms. Claremont, what we are about to tell you is going to shock you, but there is no other way to say it. So, I'll get directly to the point. Your apparent amnesia may not be cause by a trauma received in the Garden of the Gods, but may be caused by a memory-wiping drug you were given. The FBI Lab has identified you through your fingerprints. You're a twenty one year old college woman who disappeared last summer while touring Europe with your friends. The FBI has been on the case since then. Your friends said you and another woman crossed into East Germany on a dare one evening, and never returned. You were missing until last month, when they discovered you in the Garden of the Gods."

"Was the other woman you mentioned I was traveling with, Colonel Gonzalez?" Laura asked, genuinely surprised by what they just told her.

"Probably not. We don't know who she is. Her fingerprints don't match any we have on file. We suspect she is part of whatever was going down, but we won't know until we question her. Did you know her in the past?"

"I'm not sure because everything in the past year is a blank? However, she does seem familiar to me. It seems like I knew her a long time ago, but just can't remember where I met her."

"ART1, excellent sidestep, it leaves me several options to think about. ART2 out."

"That's OK, Ms. Claremont, we have another surprise for you. We have gotten in touch with your parents and have flown them here to meet you."

Laura sat there stunned, her face showing bafflement. Her parents died of radiation effects many years ago in the Fated Reality, but here in the Alternate Reality they are alive. She could see them once again. That revelation almost blew her mind.

"Oh, my god, they're here, what can I say to them?" Laura responded, now showing genuine evidence of shock.

The Colonel and the Agent could see that revelation nearly traumatized her. She also appeared very confused.

"Don't worry Ms. Claremont. Everything will work out all right. We have informed your parents about the coma you were in when we found you. Come, let's go down stairs, they're in the conference room waiting to see you."

"ART1, wow, that is a surprise. It looks like this mission will really have some unexpected pluses. ART2 out."

As Laura followed the men downstairs, many thoughts raced through her mind. What would she say? What if she did not recognize them?

Entering the conference room, two people stood up. They were her mother and father. They looked so good, so healthy, she could not contain herself, and she started to cry. She could see they recognized her and soon they were all hugging each other. Then her mother said, "Marie, it's so wonderful to see you. My baby we missed you so."

That was her first name, a name she never used in the Fated Reality. Laura was so overwhelmed at the sight of her parents that her tears kept flowing, though she was now smiling broadly. She never dreamed she could exhibit such emotions. In the Fated Reality, she had never shed a tear, even when a good friend died in her arms. Suddenly at the sight of her long, dead parents, she was crying like a baby.

"You look so surprised, I know, the Colonel told us you call yourself Laura, now. We don't care what you call yourself, do we Roland?" her mother said.

"Anything she wants, Joan. Honey, we don't care what name you want to use, all that matters is that you are safe and back with us," her father responded.

"Mom and Dad, you'll never know how good it is to see you. I never thought I would see you again. However, you'll have to bear with me for a while; my short-term memory is very cloudy. Colonel Thompson thinks I've been drugged."

"I know he told us, dear, never mind that now, we can talk about it when we get home. I'm sure Helen can help jog your memory. You two were very close."

"Helen?" Laura said, her face showing puzzlement.

"ART1, I know this must be overwhelming but don't lose it, she's probably your sister or best friend from home. Don't say anything, let your mother respond. ART2 out."

Laura paused for a moment to try to comprehend what was happening. Her mother, seeing her confusion, quickly took a picture out of her pocketbook.

"Look, dear, this is the family picture we took a year ago in our backyard, before you left. That's your sister Helen and that guy is your kid brother Rheal."

"Of course I remember them, but when you said Helen, something disturbed me; I must know someone else by that name.

Laura thought she would throw that in for Colonel Thompson and Agent Hartwell, who were listening intently to her every word. Maybe it would allay some of her parents' concerns, too.

The reunion went on for the next hour and by noon the group went to lunch at the officer's club. The FBI Agent and the Colonel excused themselves at one p.m. to attend to some pressing matters. Before they left, they told Laura's parents that they would need her later that afternoon. They further said, she could not go home until about the first week in September, after their investigation was completed. They said they would fly her back to New Jersey, then. The Colonel said, he did not think there would be any problems because they were completely satisfied that she was their daughter. However, they did recommend that her parents send her a few changes of clothes and some money to cover incidental expenses.

After her parents left, Laura contacted Lola. They met in front of the library and then went for a long walk around the drill field at the Base.

"Laura, meeting your parents again in this reality, after they had been dead for many years in ours, must have been wonderful."

"Lola, you cannot imagine how wonderful and moving it felt to see them, again. They are alive and looking so well. However, I won't elaborate further because you'll have a similar experience when you finally meet your parents."

"I would love to but it's going to be tricky; I didn't exist at anytime in this reality. Even if I can find them; they won't accept me with open arms as their long lost daughter."

"Lola, why don't we use these investigators to find them for you? Besides, if you don't, they might conclude you are an illegal alien and deport you or worse put you in jail. We could never let that happen; I would have to break you out of here and then we would both be on the run. If that ever happened, I doubt we could ever achieve our goals. So, developing your family connection is crucial."

"I agree, and have been giving it much thought over lunch. My family was living in Alamogordo, New Mexico when the 1962 missile crisis happened. I was thinking that I could represent myself as my mother's twin sister's daughter and pretend to be her niece."

"Your mother had a twin sister?"

"Yes, she did. But, as you know, in our reality my mother died and my aunt raised me. That aunt was her twin sister."

"Well, I guess that ruse might work, Lola, but your surname is Gonzalez, and if I remember correctly your aunt's name is Carmen Saucedo. How do you explain that?"

"My aunt told me that a few years before she married Saucedo; she and my mother dated the Gonzalez brothers, Francisco and Pedro. My father is Pedro Gonzalez and my aunt was his brother Francisco's fiancée. Francisco was killed in an automobile accident and my aunt was so distraught that she left home and went to New York. There, she found a job and in time recovered from the tragedy. She met Saucedo; they married and his job eventually took him to Spain. I guess I could say my aunt was pregnant when she left and I was born in New York. I could further say that she gave me my father's name."

"But, your aunt may be still alive in this reality."

"If she is, maybe she's still in Spain. In the other reality, she came back to the United States and was reunited with my mother after nuclear war ended. She might not have done the same thing here because the motivating factor, the war, did not occur in this reality."

"Well, time is running out and your meeting is at three o'clock. You know the more I think about it, it's not a bad cover story, use it. Only one thing, do not tell those men anything about your aunt getting pregnant and running to New York. If they ask about the name difference, say your real father died in an auto accident and your mother later married Saucedo. Consider the 'secret pregnancy' a private family matter they don't have to know about, but your family, no doubt, will have many questions about it. Now, if or when you meet your parents play the 'aunt raising you ploy' very carefully by ear until you find out if they know of her whereabouts. If you get tripped up, feign memory loss, like I did, at the appropriate point in your conversation with them."

"My god, Laura, I hope I can pull it off. This could get very complicated and I don't know how I will react if I ever see my parents alive in this reality."

"Cross that bridge when you come to it, and don't worry, you will handle the situation just fine. I have the utmost confidence in you," Laura said, putting her arm around Lola to assure her.

At 1500 hours, they escorted Lola to Colonel Thompson's office for her interrogation and debriefing. Entering the office she noticed the FBI agent was sitting next to Colonel Thompson at the conference table. After they seated her at the table across from them, Colonel Thompson spoke.

"Ms. Gonzalez, we are no longer going to address you as Lieutenant

Colonel Gonzalez because we are sure you are not in the military. Before we begin let me introduce you to Agent Hartwell, the FBI agent assigned to the case."

Lola nodded her head to acknowledged the introduction.

"Ms. Gonzalez, let me be brief, we don't have any idea who you are or where you come from. However, we are sure you are not in any of the armed services or their reserves. You are going to have to tell us who you are. We know you were in a coma like Ms. Claremont and cannot remember much about your recent past. Nevertheless, maybe you could tell us where your parents live."

"Well, gentlemen, I remember we lived in New York City, but we had moved and I do not remember where."

"We checked the address you gave one of the nurses and no one remembers you in that New York neighborhood. We checked the phone directories in the New York metropolitan area, but they list many Saucedos and it would take months to track down all of them. Even after all that work, your parents may not be living in that area. Do you remember anything else that might help?" Agent Hartwell asked.

"I recall something that my mother once told me. She said that her sister María lived in Alamogordo, New Mexico."

"What is her married name?"

"Gonzalez, she was married to a man named Pedro Gonzalez. That's about all I know."

"That may be our best lead yet. Tell me, do you know your biological father's first name." The agent asked.

"Francisco," Lola replied.

After giving the Colonel and the FBI agent that information, they sent her back to her quarters and said they would let her know when the session would resume. They said, maybe with this new information they could wrap this case up in a week or so. Laura had heard Lola's conversation over their private comlink and later met Lola in the library to discuss what had transpired. After discussing the situation for a while they concluded that things were progressing as planned. The FBI could, now, find Lola's true parents if they were still alive in this reality.

When the FBI contacted María and Pedro Gonzalez, a few days later in Alamogordo, they informed them they had in custody a young woman who claimed to be their niece. That revelation astonished them. They said they never heard of her, but when shown her picture they said that she did resemble their eldest daughter, Lupe. When they heard her name was Gonzalez, it did not surprise them because Gonzalez was a common Hispanic surname. The FBI agents were about to leave when one of them asked if they knew a man by the name of Francisco Gonzalez or a woman called Carmen Zaragoza de Saucedo. The question flabbergasted them and looked at each other in disbelief. Finally, recovering from that revelation they told the agents that Francisco was Pedro's deceased brother and Carmen was María's sister. The FBI agent then informed them that Lola had claimed Carmen and Francisco were her parents.

"Agent Hartwell, you have completely astounded us, we haven't seen my sister for twenty-two years and have lost touch with her. The last we heard she was living in New York and that was twenty years ago. We never knew she had a child or knew she was married to a man named Saucedo. All we knew at that time was that she left here brokenhearted, after Francisco was killed in an auto accident. She was a very private person and didn't say much. We guessed she had been in love with him and couldn't bare to remain here after he died," María informed the agents.

"Mrs. Gonzalez, we found her, under strange circumstances, in the Garden of the Gods up in Colorado. She was in a coma. We'll go into more details later, but for now we must make a positive identification. If she is not who she claims to be; she may be a part of something that is unlawful. Will the two of you come to Colorado Springs and confirm that she is your niece?"

"Mr. Hartwell, if she were in a coma and does not know us, we probably could not confirm anything," Pedro responded.

"We have a way that we can use to get proof positive that she is your relative. It's something we just started using; it's called DNA testing. If you and your wife would give us a sample of your blood, we would have it compared with hers and tell you for certain if she's your niece."

Pedro and Maria had seen something about that new identification procedure on television, and consented to having blood samples taken. They did this because they did not want to put the young woman or themselves through an emotional ordeal that proved in the end to be unfounded.

Time passed quickly over the next few weeks. The women planned many "what if" strategies, if the authorities tried to accuse Lola of being an illegal alien and then attempted to deport her. Laura had given Lola back her Laser weapon, just in case they had to fight their way out of the Base. Laura had received a package from her parents containing several changes of clothes and a hundred dollars spending money. They were her counterpart's clothing in this reality, they fit her quite well, and in addition, they fit Lola, who was the same size. She gave Lola a few changes of clothes and half the money because she would need them no matter what course things took.

After the Labor Day weekend passed, they informed Lola that she was to report to Colonel Thompson's office at 0900 hours, Wednesday morning.

"Well, I wonder if the FBI has found my parents."

"Lola, I don't think they would be calling you in if they had no new information. However, just go to the meeting and improvise. Remember, I'll be listening and if I detect something is awry I'll give you the benefit of my thoughts."

Walking to the Colonel's office Lola activated the micro communication chip imbedded behind her left ear. She then made contact with Laura whom the Colonel had asked to wait in her room until needed.

When she entered the office, she noticed Agent Hartwell was present and sitting next to the Colonel at the conference table. After initial greetings, they sat her at the table and the Colonel began relating their findings.

"Ms. Gonzalez, Agent Hartwell went to Alamogordo and spoke to your aunt and uncle. At first they didn't think you were a relative of theirs, but after he mentioned your mother and father's names they began to think you were their niece, but needed more proof."

"Needed more proof?" Lola responded, puzzled by what that meant.

"They wanted more proof because they didn't want to raise your hopes or theirs. We told them we could get the proof they and we wanted, if they would permit us to do a new procedure called DNA analysis. They agreed and gave us samples of their blood to compare with yours and we are now certain you are their niece. In fact the test shows you could even be their daughter," the FBI agent informed her.

"I don't like what you're implying. Why didn't you inform me of this? You had no right to do this without my permission," Lola said, indignantly.

"ART2, calm down, I know what you're concerned about. It will look like your father, not Francisco, had an affair with your aunt Carmen. From what I read in the library, their technology isn't advanced enough, yet, to decide whether your father or your uncle mated with your mother's identical twin. ART1 out.

"I wasn't trying to imply anything. I was merely repeating what the DNA experts told me."

"What did they say exactly?" Lola asked, a little calmer, now.

"They said they couldn't tell which brother had mated with the identical twin because the state of the art in DNA identification isn't advanced enough at this time. Consequently, they cannot say for certain that you are their niece or their daughter," the agent informed her.

"Did you tell my aunt and uncle that?"

"No, not exactly that way, I just told them you're certainly their niece," the Agent responded.

"Look, Hartwell, I think I see where she's coming from. She doesn't want you to make the aunt think that her husband was involved with her mother. I think the aunt and uncle can figure out that she is much closer than just a niece, because she has the blood of a brother and a twin sister. Now, enough said."

"Thank you, Colonel," Lola responded, relieved that he understood her concerns.

"We have a surprise for you, your aunt and uncle are down stairs waiting for you in the conference room."

"Oh, my god."

"Take it easy ART2. I know from experience that seeing one's parents alive and well can be quite overpowering. So, get hold of yourself," Laura said, as Lola followed the Colonel and the Agent to the conference room.

Entering the conference room, Lola could see her long dead parents were very much alive in this reality and seated at the table. They were smiling and looking her over very carefully. The scene brought tears to Lola's eyes and the tears kept flowing as she stared in stunned silence at their smiling faces. She never in her life had felt such a flood of emotions. When she regained her composure, she went over and sat across from them.

"Please excuse my outburst of emotion, Aunt María and Uncle Pedro. Aunt María looks so much like my mother, and Uncle Pedro looks like the pictures my mother showed me of my father."

"Lola, you look so much like my daughter, Lupe, that the two of you could be almost taken for twins. But, of course you should, you're my twin sister's daughter and your father is my husband's brother. Isn't that amazing, your mother named you Dolores."

"That's not so amazing, your mother's name was Dolores and both daughters named their daughters Dolores," uncle Pedro commented.

"Do you have a daughter named Dolores, too?"

"I had one by that name but she died in infancy," María explained.

"We know you been in a coma and can't remember where your mother lived in New York, but you do recall she was married to a man named Saucedo. Is there anything else you can recall about her?"

"It's my short term memory that seems to be gone. However, I do remember things she told me when I was a little girl. She told me stories about her family in Mexico. She told me I came from a family of military men and was a decedent of Ignacio Zaragoza; the Mexican general, whose bravery incited the Mexicans finally to expel the French from Mexico."

When Lola related that information about her family, María got up, came around the table, and kissed her.

"Now, I know she's ours, and I don't need those DNA experts to tell me who she is," María said, as she and Pedro hugged Lola tightly.

"I guess we really don't need those DNA experts either, right Hartwell, come on let's get out of here and let them spend some time together."

Lola's reunion with her parents went on for another hour and a half. Lola related to them as much as she could remember about her family's history, before they finally broke for lunch. During lunch, they told her all about her cousins, who, of course, were her siblings in the Alternate Reality, and how much they wanted her to meet them. When her parents were finally leaving that afternoon, they insisted that she come and stay with them in Alamogordo after the investigation was completed.

Given the way things were evolving in this reality, the Team's plans to fabricate a Synthesizer that could establish a link with the Fated Reality would have to be postponed. That project would have to wait until they could get themselves into a realistic position to do the required work. At this point on the timeline in the Alternate Reality, they were only in their early twenties and unable to work on the project. The knowledge they had gained in the other reality was intact in their brains, but they had no resources or the respect of the scientific community to take any advantage of it. They knew they would need both of those things to achieve their goals. It appeared that the best approach would be to go back to their families in the Alternate Reality and start establishing their credentials. They needed to get into a position that would enable them to accomplish their objectives. The only way they could think of doing this would be to go back to college and fast forward through the degrees they would need. Once they accomplished this, they could then start working on their objectives in some well-equipped laboratory. This was the only way they could realistically hope to fabricate a device that would allow them to establish a linkage with the Fated Reality.

They agreed that the best strategy for achieving all their goals would be to somehow get into schools like CALTECH OR MIT. Even from their limited exposure to the Alternate Reality, they knew those places had the resources they required. After much discussion, the women finally decided to rendezvous at MIT in Cambridge, Massachusetts a year from this September. They knew that getting into that school would be difficult, given the circumstances they were in, but they felt their special gifts would enable them to accomplish that preliminary task.

Chapter 3

As the plane entered the landing pattern over Newark Airport, Laura's heart began to beat rapidly in anticipation of being reunited with her family. Staring out the window, she watched the buildings and vehicles loom larger and larger. Amid thoughts of family, it suddenly occurred to her that the scene below lacked the military vehicles she was accustomed to seeing in the Fated Reality. How different things were here, there was no national emergency and consumer product advertisements filled the pages of magazines and newspapers. As she looked about the airplane, she marveled at the variety of clothing styles the passengers were wearing. Another thing that struck her was the lack of people in military uniforms on the plane. She wondered what other strange things she would encounter in this reality. The things she had already experienced had begun to change her outlook on life. However, she was the team leader and had to keep focused on the goals of her mission.

Descending the gate ramp, her heart pounding with expectation, she clutched tightly the carry on bag her mother had sent her. Her family was meeting her at the airport but, now, she wondered exactly where they would be waiting for her. They said, follow the signs and the crowd toward the exit to street transportation. Walking with the other passengers onto the escalator, she saw her mother and father, below, waving to her. Along side of them were the siblings that were in the picture her mother gave her. As she stepped off the escalator, they rushed over and started hugging her. She was overwhelmed with joy and tears started flowing down her cheeks. She never in her militaristic world experienced a surge of emotion like this. In fact, she could not recall ever shedding a tear in her life, even when her parents had died in the other reality. She wondered if it was because there was no joy in her world, only the kind of humor that is based on sadness.

After the hugging and kissing was over the family quickly exited the airport and found the family car in the huge airport-parking garage. The need for such large parking facilities in this reality amazed Laura. In the Fated Reality so few of the people owned cars that only curbside parking spaces were required.

On the way home, Laura's brother and sister started firing questions at her. Although she did not have any siblings in the other reality, she felt a bond forming between her and them. She could not explain why this bonding was occurring. She thought, maybe the old adage still applies. Blood is thicker than water and it even transcends bifurcated realities. Her sister, Helen, was nineteen, her brother Rheal was seventeen, and both appeared to be much younger than their physical ages would indicate. She then realized it was because she was mentally forty-seven years old and they were teenagers. She would have to try to view things from their perspective if any meaningful relationship between her and them were to develop.

"Marie, why do you want people to call you Laura, now?" her brother Rheal asked.

Laura thought for a moment that she would just give him some plausible answer. However, thinking again, she realized the whole family deserved a reasonable explanation.

"When I was in college, a few years ago, I became very aware of our French heritage and wanted to follow at least one of our traditions. As you are all aware, my full name is Marie Laura Monique Claremont. Some French families in this country still follow the old practice of giving the girls in the family, the first name Marie, after the Holy Mother. The second name is the one they will call her by and the third is the name of her patron saint. I guess I wanted to honor this ancient tradition and be called Laura, rather than Marie."

That justification for using her second name surprised everyone in the car, including her mother.

"Mother. You never told us that. Why didn't you name me the same way?" Helen asked, feeling a little putout because her big sister had that option.

"Frankly, I'm surprised she remembered that, because I don't recall explaining that custom to her. I stopped following that tradition after she was born and called her Marie because it sounded more sophisticated and I liked it better. When you were born, I dispensed with it all together because it seemed irrelevant in this modern society," Joan responded.

Her mother's explanation caused Laura to reflect upon her thoughts on the subject in the other reality. The things her mother told her, about her heritage in that reality, were dear to her. They made her feel unique in a military society that made everyone the look the same. In this world, she thought, with the only threat being a cold war that might become hot, maybe that tradition did not have any relevance here.

"Enough of this talk about names, if she wants to be called Laura, we'll call her Laura," her father said.

"Family, I know some things I say may sound strange to you, but bear with me I'm still a little hazy about recent events."

As her father drove, Laura thought the road he was on looked familiar. In fact it looked like they were on Bloomfield Avenue, but there were so many new buildings and signs that she could not be sure. The whole scene she was observing from the window of the car prompted her to ask a question that might seem strange to her family.

"Where do we live now?"

"Gee, big sister, you really don't remember, do you?" her brother remarked.

"I do remember living in Bloomfield, a long time ago," Laura remarked, recalling that from her life in the other reality.

"Laura, we still live there. Boy, what did they do to you?" her sister asked.

"Come guys, you know Laura has suffered some kind of trauma, we must take every opportunity to help her recall," her father said.

After that reminder by their father, Laura's siblings filled her in on many interesting things about her counterpart's life in the Alternate Reality. They told her about her friends and what they were doing now and about the boyfriend she had dropped. Apparently, her counterpart's friends and the ex-boyfriend were away at colleges in other states. As a result, she would not have to worry about the awkward problem of interfacing with them at this time.

Arriving at their home in Bloomfield, her mother took Laura to her counterpart's room and said to rest a bit before dinner. Looking around the room she quickly noticed it was quite disorderly. Papers and make-up containers were all over the dresser. The draws were a jumbled mix of underwear and clothes. Apparently, her parents or her siblings did not straighten it up. Who knows, maybe her counterpart didn't want them to touch anything, Laura thought. In any case, her counterpart no longer existed and she felt free to organize things to her liking. She was a model officer when she was in the army and carried the discipline learned there over to her personal life. She was a neat and orderly person and could never perpetuate the messy lifestyle of her counterpart.

Laura spent the next day cleaning and organizing her room. Cleaning the dresser, she found a year-old transcript from the college her counterpart was attending. She was attending Rutgers University in Newark and was an English major. Laura could see from the report that her counterpart was a "B" student overall and only a "C" student in math and science. This was very different from Laura's achievements in the physical sciences. Amazing, she thought, what a slight mutation of ones genes in the right places could bring about. Studying her counterpart's grades started her thinking about her own agenda. She was supposed to rendezvous with Lola at MIT a year from now. The grade report had just given her an idea about how to accomplish that goal.

Laura was sitting on the bed in deep thought when her mother entered the room.

"My god, what hit this place? Everything is so neat and clean. What got into you, I had to remind you every day just to get you to fix your bed?"

"Maybe what you said finally sunk in, Mom," Laura said, smiling.

"My god, you even straightened your closet and dresser draws," her mother remarked, as she peeked into the closet and a few draws.

"Mother, I was thinking, the fall term will be starting soon at Rutgers and I better go over there to register."

"Dear, you just got home from a traumatic experience, don't you think you should take a semester off and rest?"

"Oh, Mother, only some of my recent memories are missing, other than that I feel fine. I missed enough school and wanted to get back as soon as possible."

"Well, if you feel up to it, I guess you might as well get back into the swing of things. Your sister is going there to register Monday, why don't you go with her and find out what you have to do to enroll in classes this term."

"Thanks, Mom. Are you sure that you and Dad can handle the expense of two daughters in college at the same time?"

"We'll manage, and next summer you, your sister and your brother can find summer jobs and help out."

Laura knew she needed a birth certificate and a picture ID. So, she asked her mother if she had her birth certificate.

"Mother, one more thing, do you have a copy of my birth certificate? I'll need it to get a new driver' license and I'll also need to get a copy of my Social Security Card. The authorities in Europe never recovered my original license or passport."

"That will be no problem, dear. I have your Birth Certificate and your Social Security Card. But, you'll have to take them to the New Jersey Registry of Motor Vehicles and have them issue you a duplicate copy of your driver's license. On second thought, ask your brother to drive you to the Registry, later this week."

Monday morning Laura and Helen took a bus to Bloomfield Avenue and then took another to Newark. Laura took with her the copy of her counterpart's transcript; it contained her student number and other information she would need. At the registration building, the sisters went separate ways but arranged to meet for lunch in the student lounge.

Laura went to the Registrar's office to start the registration process. The office staff knew her; they said the FBI last year interviewed them and asked many questions about her. They took her transcript and gave her the necessary forms to fill out. After finishing the paper work she returned it to them and they were about ready to send her to her advisor when they noticed she had changed her major.

"Ms. Claremont, I see here you have changed your major from English to Physics, is that correct?" the clerk asked.

"Yes, my experiences over the last year made me reevaluate my career goals," Laura responded, in serious tones.

"Well, I don't know whether they'll let you do that. You had better speak with an advisor from the Physics Department. Why don't you go over and speak to Professor Peyser, he's in the registration hall now? I'll call and let him know your coming," the clerk advised, rolling her eyes at the clerk next to her.

Arriving at the registration hall Laura found Professor Peyser sitting at a table signing students' registration cards.

"Well, Ms. Claremont, the Registrar's office informs me you that want to register as a physics major. May I see your transcript?"

Laura handed him her counterpart's transcript, knowing the courses her counterpart took in math and science did not qualify her to major in Physics. Therefore, she would have to find a way to make him let her study the physical sciences.

"Ms. Claremont, you're an English major, you don't have the prerequisites to take these advanced physics courses."

"I don't need them. I already have a complete knowledge of what is required."

"How did you acquire that knowledge, there's no record of that in this transcript?" he asked, somewhat amused by her temerity.

"I studied the required subjects myself and mastered the fundamental principles."

"Please, Ms. Claremont, a casual reading of the elementary principles of physics can hardly qualify you to take advanced courses."

"Professor, isn't there some kind of test I can take to demonstrate my knowledge?"

The professor took a long look at this determined young woman, thinking he should disqualify her, officially. He certainly did not want her to claim he was biased against women wanting to enter the physical sciences. He did not like bursting the bubble of such a determined young lady and he would not have to. He had just the battery of tests that would bring Ms. Claremont down to reality and in turn remove any suggestion of bias on his part.

"There is an advanced placement test we give physics students transferring from other colleges to determine where they fit into our curriculum. If you wish to take it, they are giving it this afternoon at 1:00 p.m. in the Physics Building."

"I most certainly would."

"All right, take this slip, you'll need it to take the exam?" the Professor replied, as he signed the permission slip smiling, smugly.

Laura met with her sister Helen for lunch, and suggested that she go home without her; she had to take a placement exam before they would let her register. Her sister thought it was odd that they would require that sort of thing of a student who had missed only one year of school. Laura did not tell her that she was trying to change majors, because she did not want to go into a long explanation at that time.

After lunch, she went to the physics building and took the advanced placement examination. The exam was trivial for her and she completed the tests, on each subject of physics, in a fraction of the time allotted.

Laura and Helen were out shopping for clothes the next day and Joan was in the kitchen having a cup of coffee. She sat there contemplating what Helen had told her about Laura having to take a placement exam. She wondered why Laura had to do that. Why didn't they just simply let her resume her studies, her grades were better than average and she was only gone one year? She was thinking about calling the school and asking for an explanation when the phone rang. Joan answered, still in a quandary over that exam.

"Hello, may I speak to Ms. Claremont?"

"Which one? There are three of us."

"Ms. M. Laura Claremont, please."

"She's not here now, may I take a message? This is her mother."

"This is Professor Peyser from the Physics department at the Rutgers, Newark campus. Tell her we would be pleased to enroll her as a physics major; she passed the placement exam with very high scores."

That revelation dumbfounded Joan.

"Are you sure, we thought she was an English major? She has no aptitude for science."

"No aptitude for science? My dear Mrs. Claremont, your daughter had perfect scores in all the subjects of physics on which we tested her. Tell her to see me in the registration hall tomorrow afternoon so we can get her properly registered."

When Laura arrived home later that afternoon, her mother confronted her with the message Professor Peyser had left. Her mother was expecting some kind of explanation, but Laura just thanked her for taking the message and went about went about her business, leaving her mother standing there speechless.

At the dinner table, Joan brought the subject up again.

"Laura, we never realized you had any aptitude for physics, we thought you wanted to major in English."

"Oh, Mother, I read all the texts associated with that curriculum a few years ago and wanted to move on."

"The professor said you made perfect scores in the physics subjects they tested you on. Why weren't we aware of that talent when you were young?" her father asked.

Laura thought for a moment, she did not want to reveal anything about existing in the Fated Reality, so she answered.

"I guess I had a latent talent no one realized I had. I found a physics book, a while ago, in the library at the base in Colorado and began to read it. I grasped the subject so easily that I started to the read separate books on the various subjects of physics and I fell in love with that science."

"How could you just read a book and pass an advanced physics exam? I'm an experienced graduate engineer and I would have a hard time doing that. Daughter, that is amazing. In fact I don't know of anyone who could that," her father responded. He wondered if that coma she was in somehow affected her brain. She did seem more lucid now than she did a year ago. Maybe, he thought, she was some kind of latent genius and it took the trauma she had suffered to awaken it. Perhaps, it was there all along and he never recognized it.

"Oh, Dad, they gave me easy questions, they don't make those tests very hard," Laura replied, trying to minimize her achievement.

"If she wants to study physics, let her. Now, can we talk about something else, this is getting boring," her brother Rheal replied.

"Rheal's right. Laura, why don't you come with Helen and me and have your hair done Friday, it looks like it could use a little shaping," Joan said, changing the subject.

The men took that remark as an excuse to leave the table, leaving Laura, Helen and their mother to chat about hairstyles.

As the semester progressed, Laura's reputation in the physics and math departments was fast becoming legendary. She was taking what might be considered a heavy load, but still maintained a perfect average in each course. She joined the tennis team and became the one to beat in competition. She also joined the martial arts team and soon demonstrated that no one was her equal. When she realized she was attracting too much attention, she dropped out of those activities claiming her science studies were demanding more of her time. This was not true, of course, but that excuse did get the spotlight off her.

The Christmas Cotillion was the social event of the year at the school and several young men had asked Laura if she would like to go with them. She declined their offers for several reasons, not the least of which was their immaturity. Not only was she superior to them academically, but also because she was at least twenty-five years their senior, mentally. One day a surprising offer came from the least expected person, Professor Peyser. Peyser was a tall, handsome, distinguished looking man of thirty-four years. He had dark wavy hair and a very athletic build. Not only was he her physics advisor but also a tennis opponent on many occasions.

Laura was in the Radiation Laboratory in early December finishing an experiment she was conducting, when Professor Peyser walked over to where she was working. He had been watching her from the doorway of the laboratory for the past ten minutes and she was aware of his presence.

"Ms. Claremont, I have never asked a student out before. However, I have to chaperone the Cotillion and would like to brighten up the evening by asking someone to accompany me who is capable of carrying on a serious conversation."

Laura did not think that invitation for an evening out was unusual. She had associated with scientists all her adult life and they were usually quite blunt, speaking their minds, take it or leave it. She paused for a moment to evaluate the invitation and thought: *He is quite handsome and I haven't been on a date for years, maybe I should relax a little and enjoy some of the latitude this reality affords.* She pondered his invitation a little longer, thinking, he did have the kind of mind with which she was comfortable. He also had a maturity level that was a better match to hers than the students trying to date her did.

"Professor Peyser, before I decide if I am available that evening; I would like to ask you a personal question. What is your marital status?"

That question caught him a little off guard. He thought: *She certainly can cut to the chase, can't she? She has a level of maturity that doesn't seem to exist in other women her age.*

"I'm not married and have never been."

"Then, Professor Peyser, I will be delighted to have you escort me to the Christmas Cotillion. I, too, would like to spend an evening with someone who can challenge me mentally."

That was hardly what one would expect from a woman in her early twenties, but it was what he might expect from someone of her caliber. He normally would not have considered dating someone in her age group, but she had overwhelmed him from the day he first spoke to her. He thought, how could one so young and pretty have such an incisive mind. He knew such thoughts were chauvinistic, but he was having a hard time suppressing that chauvinistic thinking while studying her physical attributes.

"Thank you for so graciously accepting my invitation. I have one more request, would you mind terribly if we dispensed with the formalities and got on a first name basis? I would like to call you Laura and would you please call me Kurt?"

"I would be happy to, Kurt."

After they exchanged a few more remarks, Kurt asked Laura for her address and phone number and told her he would pick her up at seven on December twentieth. Then he excused himself because he said he did not want to disturb "science in progress" any more than he already had.

After he left, Laura pondered the pluses of a society that is not perpetually in a state of emergency. In the other reality she did not have time for dates, but here, things were moving at a much more relaxed pace, allowing time for some pleasant social interaction.

The weekend before the Cotillion, Joan Claremont was driving to Macy's in the Willow Brook Mall. She had her younger daughter, Helen, with her and was planning to pickup the dresses she had bought her daughters for the Cotillion. Laura could not go with them because she had to go to the Library to do some research for a project on which she was working. Helen was somewhat miffed over her sister's lack of interest in shopping at the mall.

"What's wrong, dear? You look so glum. It's the Christmas season and your going to a beautiful ball at the Marriot Hotel. You should be in a festive mood."

"I guess you're right. But, Mom, it's not easy being Laura Claremont's little sister."

"Why, has she done anything to you?"

"No, it's not what she is doing to me directly. It's what's happening indirectly."

"I don't understand."

"Everybody at school is in awe of her. Do you know that she is considered some kind of super brain? Everybody is talking about how smart she is. As if that isn't enough, she is also considered the best tennis player on campus. The damn guys are hanging around me on the outside chance she might come along and I'll introduce them to her. Mom, it's very annoying and embarrassing to have to live in her shadow at school. Even the jocks respect her; they say she's the star of their Marital Arts team. Mom, why is she so damn competent at everything she tries and I'm so mediocre at everything? We're sisters aren't we?"

"Of course you are, and you're not mediocre, either; you have good grades and are very good at skiing. But, I have to admit she surprises me, too, a few years ago she seemed like a normal girl and now her talents are certainly amazing and even formidable. Dad thinks she was an underachiever before she disappeared last year and somehow that experience caused her to become intensely focused, thereby allowing her natural abilities to surface. It's not fair to compare yourself with her. I hope you have noticed that Dad and I have been very careful not to make comparisons between her accomplishments and those of you and your brother.

"I guess so."

"Come on, let's love her for what she is and not hold her achievements against her?"

That explanation went a long way in helping Helen deal with her sister's remarkable accomplishments.

Chapter 4

Kurt Peyser was picking up Laura at seven, so they could be at the Cotillion before eight. He had explained to Laura that chaperoning this event required that he be there before the festivities got underway. When he mentioned this to her, a few days ago she seemed distant and nodded her head, continuing to be absorbed in whatever she was thinking about. Something about the way she looked made him feel she was hiding something. Nonsense, he thought, she is just a brilliant science student with her mind focused on something and, besides, he caught her in that pensive mood many times before. Yet, there seemed to be a lot more going on behind those striking blue eyes than appeared on the surface, but what could it be? Was she covering something up? These thoughts and others about her kept circulating in his mind as he drove, but he was unable to conclude anything from them.

When Kurt arrived at the Claremont house in Bloomfield, Joan Claremont him brought into the living room to meet Laura's father. She had already introduced herself to him at the front door.

"Roland, this is Kurt Peyser, Laura's date for the evening and this is Roland Claremont, Laura's father."

After the customary handshake, Joan offered Kurt a seat and said Laura would be down in a few minutes.

"Dr. Peyser, I'm told you're my daughter's advisor in the Physics Department."

"Yes, I am. I guess you are wondering what I would have in common with a woman in her early twenties. Well, Sir, she is more interesting than any other woman I know. Your daughter has the whole physics department enthralled by her thorough grasp of even the most advanced principles in the physical sciences. Her instructors find it a pleasure teaching a student with such a keen mind, although at times they are not sure who is teaching whom. I thought she would brighten up what might be a rather dull evening for a faculty chaperone, if she allowed me to escort her to the Cotillion. I am honored that she has consented to accompany me."

Mr. Claremont did not know how to respond to that commentary. He wondered, could Peyser be telling him that his daughter is the mental equivalent to a full professor of physics. As he was pondering this thought, he heard someone start down the stairs.

As Laura came down the stairs, her beautiful blond hair bounced softly on her shoulders and her blue eyes sparkled in the reflected light from the lamp in the hall. She had on a stunning blue gown that perfectly complemented her eyes and the color of her hair. Kurt watched as Joan pinned the corsage, he had brought, on Laura. He suddenly wished this beautiful, brilliant young woman were actually interested in him, instead of just accompanying him to the Cotillion out of respect for the position he held. Still, the way she was smiling at him made him think, perhaps, she was interested in him. When she glanced at him again, as she came into the living room, he noticed her blue eyes appeared even more striking than he remembered. What was it about those eyes that captivated him so? Scrutinizing her face more closely, as she continued to approach, he thought he discovered the secret; it was the curl in her dark eyelashes. They seemed to point upward at her dark brows like star bursts. Her brows obliquely slanted up and then gently arched down, gradually disappearing into smooth skin of her temples. He thought, being such an observant scientist does not make him any less susceptible to her charms.

Kurt and Laura's father were standing there in the living room as Laura approached and Kurt could not help remarking.

"My, the lady looks so beautiful that I will be the envy of ever man at the ball."

"Thank you, Professor Peyser, for your kind compliment. But, I think we should leave now, if we are to arrive at the ball in time for you to do your duties as chaperone. Otherwise, you will quickly lose your status as the most envied man at the ball and turn into a pumpkin."

Everyone in the room laughed at her remark, except Kurt, who wondered what she really meant by it. Did she think in some droll way he was a male Cinderella or something? The problem with dating such an intelligent woman, a student or not, he thought, was that he was always looking for the hidden meaning in everything she said. These thoughts, annoyingly, kept circulating in Kurt's mind as he helped Laura on with her coat, which her mother had just brought. However, he smiled at her, anyway, thinking he was just lucky to be her escort. The couple, then, bid her parents, good-by, and left for the Cotillion.

A short while after Laura left, the doorbell rang, again, at the Claremont home and her parents knew it must be their daughter Helen's escort. Helen was in her room touching up the makeup she had been applying for the last half hour. The sound of the bell made Roland say, "I'll bet she doesn't have a college professor as her escort."

"You better not tell her that, either. She's having a hard enough time coping with the attention her sister is getting, without you exacerbating the situation," Joan admonished her husband.

The Christmas Cotillion at the Marriot was getting underway and Laura was listening carefully to the music the band was playing. The students were gyrating to the unfamiliar and offensive sounds of a group of creepy looking guys banging on guitars. Hearing this cacophony of sounds, made her long for the music that had evolved in the Fated Reality. It was the revival of the big band sounds of the forties combined with new patriotic music. Even classical music was quite popular. In that reality, people spent their time preparing for the next nuclear war, and would have responded negatively to the music they played here. There was no Vietnam War to bring on the resistive, rebellious music of the youthful generation in the sixties. Rock had died quickly after the nuclear debacle and its derivatives never occurred.

Kurt could see Laura was not enjoying the music; there was a faint look of disgust on her face.

"The band is not up to your expectations?" Kurt asked.

"I guess they're not my cup of tea. I'm a fan of classical music and I also enjoy the big band sound of the forties," she replied candidly.

That remark impressed Kurt. He thought: *She's not like the other students, she thinks for herself and has developed a taste for quality music.*

"I can appreciate your sentiments because mine are similar, however, I do like some soft rock sounds that have evolve out of the music of the sixties."

"I haven't heard any of those sounds tonight," Laura responded, tersely.

"Let me see what we can do about that."

Kurt, at that point, went to speak to the bandleader who had just taken a break. He had a short discussion with him and then returned.

When the band came back, they started playing and singing some popular soft rock tunes.

As couples started to slow dance, Kurt asked Laura to join him on the dance floor.

"Is that better?" Kurt asked, as he and Laura danced slowly to the rhythm of the music.

"Much better," Laura responded, as the music eased her into a dreamy mood.

As they danced, they would occasionally look into each other's eyes and romantic thoughts passed through their minds. The place began to take on a mystical ambiance and Laura began to feel comfortable in the arms of this tall, dark and handsome professor. Her cheek brushed lightly against his, he pulled her close and they danced the next few soft rock numbers in a close embrace. The smell of his aftershave lotion mingled pleasantly with the manly scent that his hair seemed to give off and she felt herself becoming very interested in him. The whole experience was confusing her; was she sensing the male hormones that some magazines claimed women sensed, subliminally? Soon, the music stopped and the mood was broken. She quickly warned herself: *You had better stop this romantic nonsense, you are the Team Leader and your mission should be first on your mind.*

Later that evening after he drove her home, he parked his car in front of her house and they talked for a short while. It was a nippy December night, and he preferred to say their good-bys in the warmth of the car, rather than on her door step.

"Laura, I had a wonderful evening and thoroughly enjoyed your company."

"I enjoyed the evening, too, and also enjoyed our discussion on the cold war."

He appeared a little nervous and seemed to linger for a moment before he spoke his next thought.

"Laura, I would like very much to see you again. The College of Arts and Sciences Faculty is having a New Year's party at the Hilton in Paramus and I would like you to be my date for that evening."

Laura thought for a moment: *I guess he is interested in more than my views on the cold war, or my analysis of the research trends in physics.* He did, she thought, stir something inside her that had all but died a long time ago in the other reality.

"I think I would like that," she answered softly, gazing deeply into his eyes.

Then he did something unexpected. He took her into his arms and kissed her tenderly, holding her tightly. She pulled back slowly a bit surprised by his sudden embrace and looked at him closely; making him wonder if he should not have done that. Suddenly, without warning, she kissed him back her tongue plunging into the depths of his mouth, then gently pulled away shocked herself by the way she responded. She could tell his passion was building and so was hers. She was confused, again, why did she kiss him that way, what was wrong with her?

"Wonderful, I'll call about seven, New Year's Eve," he responded.

The way she kissed him made him think she was interested in him. Her gentle pull away, at first, probably meant she was a little tired and wanted to go in. After exchanging smiles, they got out of his car and he walked her to her door. On the doorstep, he kissed her briefly and they said good night.

While Laura was getting ready for bed that evening, her mind was on Kurt Peyser. She had always liked his type, a man with intellectual prowess that had an athletic anatomy. She thought that his avid interest in tennis and handball had served to keep him in good condition. She also told herself that she had another agenda, and she had better be careful. He was bringing out feelings in her that she had not felt since her college days in the other reality. Still, even during that period she never had a relationship with a man like him, only fantasized about it.

Driving home, Kurt thought about what had just happened. What the hell was he doing kissing one of his students. He was a full professor of physics. This could cost him his career if not handled properly. Why was he so attracted to her? In the next breath, he answered his own question. She was the most intelligent person he had ever met and a very beautiful woman; that

52

combination was lethal, he thought. He wondered if he had taken advantage of her, after all he was twelve years her senior. However, he soon dismissed that thought because she was too smart to let anyone take advantage of her.

Christmas break was flying by fast, and Laura was busy writing a paper on a new topic in quantum mechanics. They had given her credit for the intermediate physics courses, based on the results of the advanced placement exams she had taken. Quantum mechanics was one of the graduate courses she was taking. However, they allowed her to write a paper, instead of having to sit through lectures on material with which she was already familiar.

The afternoon before the New Years Eve party, Laura decided to take a nap so she would be fresh for the evening ahead. Awaking from her nap at six, she now had to rush through her shower and dress for the evening because Kurt was calling for her about seven. After her shower, she dressed and then sat in front of her dresser mirror to apply her makeup. She was extra careful to make her eyes up properly. The make-up advisor, at Macy's in the Willow Brook Mall, had admonished her to do her eyes carefully. The cosmetologist said, paying attention to detail there could make an ordinary face pretty and a pretty face, beautiful. Laura usually did not pay much attention to those people because she was not very concerned about her looks. Her mother and sister insisted that she listen to the cosmetologist and do her eyes properly. With their prodding, and because of Kurt's interest in her, she decided to use the make-up technique that the cosmetologist had formulated for her. When she had finished, she was pleased with the results because the technique seemed to work well on a person with her facial structure.

As she descended the stairs, she saw Kurt standing in the living room. He looked so handsome in that dark blue suit that she blinked her eyes when she first saw him. His dark wavy hair was neatly combed and nicely complemented his high intelligent looking forehead. He was there studying the mural on the wall over the sofa. She saw Kurt's eyes light up when he caught sight of her. She had on a long powder blue evening dress that had on a pretty blue and white waistband. She was beautiful, he thought. Her swept back blond hair gave her an elegant look, before which he had not noticed. Those blue eyes were so pretty they astounded him. As she drew near, he paused for a moment drinking in her beauty, and then embraced her lightly. They studied each other for a moment longer, then bid her parents, good-by, and left for the evening.

During their drive on the Garden State Parkway, Laura and Kurt engaged in light conversation.

"Laura, what are your plans after you graduate from Rutgers?"

"I plan to do graduate work at MIT or CALTECH. I want to do research in solid state physics."

"Why don't you apply to Columbia University? They have a fine physics department. I'm sure you can do solid-state research there and in addition you would be close to your family," Kurt suggested. He was thinking he would also like to keep her in this area because he was interested in her, and knew if she attended graduate school in another state they would drift apart.

"Kurt, I would like to, but Columbia doesn't have the facilities I require."

"With all the graduate schools in the metropolitan area one must have the facilities you think you need."

Laura was not ready to reveal her real reason for seeking admission to MIT's graduate school, so she changed the subject.

"Let's not debate the merits of graduate schools this evening, lets just enjoy the festivities. Look, it's starting to snow, do you think it will stop by midnight?"

"I don't know, but if it doesn't let up I'll get us rooms at the hotel. Better yet, I'll reserve rooms when we arrive, if the weather report says we're in for a heavy storm."

When they arrived at the Hilton hotel in Paramus, Kurt rented rooms for them, immediately, because it was snowing hard and the weather reports were negative. It certainly did not look like they could make it back to Bloomfield after the New Years party. Laura called her parents and informed them of the situation, and told them not to expect her until the next day.

It was about eleven forty five and the crowd at the party was getting ready to ring in the New Year. Laura and Kurt were dancing to the sounds of the big band orchestra the faculty committee had hired for the party. As the New Year arrived to the strains of the Auld Lang Syne, Kurt kissed Laura long and passionately. She thought: *That custom is one thing that is still the same in both realities.* Kurt had the bandleader play a medley of old tunes from the bygone big band era. Laura enjoyed the selection they played because it reminded her of the music from the Fated Reality and the music put her in a sentimental mood.

As the party moved into its final stages, Laura observed that Kurt seemed to know many people at the party, apart from the faculty. They all listened carefully to him when he spoke, and it was apparent they had a great deal of admiration for him. Some women told her, it was a great honor to be invited to this affair by a man held in such high esteem. Though her mental maturity and academic achievements were actually greater than his were, the praise they were bestowing upon him was causing her to look up to him with admiration. She could not explain the feelings she was experiencing, maybe it was her physical age in this reality or maybe it was simply that she was falling for him. As these things past through her mind, she quickly reminded herself that she was in this reality on serious business and should not be even entertaining such thoughts.

The party finally ended, and Kurt and Laura they took the elevator to their rooms. When they reached her room, he stood there looking at her for a moment. After he kissed her good night, she paused at the open door, thinking, perhaps, she should invite him in for a drink. Forgetting for the moment that she was supposed to be an innocent college girl, she opened the door, peeked in, and saw there was a guest bar in the room. What the hell, she thought, from what she had observed in this reality, the college girls here are not naive at all.

"Kurt, look, they have a little bar in these rooms, would you like to come in and have a night cap or a cup of coffee with me?"

That remark was more indicative of a mature woman than a college girl, he thought. Then again, nothing she does is indicative of a college girl.

"Sounds like a great idea," he responded, looking grateful for the offer.

"Wonderful, we can unwind a bit and finish that discussion we started on Reagan's inflammatory 'evil empire' remarks."

When they got into the room, both opted for a cup of decaf coffee. While the water was heating on the hotplate, they sat on the little love seat in the corner of the room. Laura playfully loosened Kurt's tie to make him more comfortable. She thought: *I could really go for this guy if he wasn't my physics advisor and I wasn't in this reality on a serious mission.*

Kurt was having similar thoughts, wishing he were not her physics advisor so he would not feel so guilty about being in her room. He thought: *My god, she is so intelligent, looks so fabulous, and acts so mature; I wish there wasn't a twelve-year difference between us.* Their attraction for each other soon over came their better judgment, and the next thing they knew they were hopelessly locked in a passionate embrace. The hotplate turned itself off and they forgot the cup of coffee for which they were waiting.

He feels so good, she thought, as her arms went around his neck and he pressed her tightly to his chest. She felt so small and delicate in his arms. As their mutual desire crested, they began rapidly removing each other's clothes. Laura could not believe she was doing that, for chrissake, she thought, she was supposed to be here on an important mission not on a romantic interlude. Still, she could not think about anything else but him; she was pulsating with desire. He had removed her dress, and was unfastening her bra. After he had completed that task he began kissing her shoulders and breasts, then she helped remove his shirt, undershirt and trousers. As he looked at her beautiful youthful breasts and figure, he was overcome with desire. He was on his knees slipping down her panty hose and then helping her remove them. He kicked off his shoes and slipped off his briefs. She looked at him, standing there in front of her and thought his body was even in better condition than she had imagined. He was so desirable she felt herself quiver.

She pulled the spread off the bed and pulled down the blanket and the sheet. She watched as he slipped on a prophylactic. Then thought, after breathing a sigh of relief, at least she didn't have to remind him about that. Kurt pulled her on top of him, as he lay on the bed. She kissed him gently, rubbing her nipples back and forth across his hairy chest, sending their mutual desire to its pinnacle. They could not think of anything but gratifying each other. Kissing him excitedly, she mounted his manhood and started rocking back and forth. As their excitement reached an extreme height, he quickly slipped himself out from under her. Kissing her tenderly, he then gently laid her back and mounted her. He carefully pushed into her, thrusting slowly at first and then steadily increasing the tempo. Laura never felt anything like this moment in her whole life; all she could do was to groan with him in blissful ecstasy. When at last they lay exhausted side by side, she thought, *He's a physicist, all right, and doesn't want to waste time on nonessentials.* Finally, after one last fond embrace, they drifted contentedly off to sleep in each other's arms.

Kurt was still sleeping the next morning as Laura was taking a shower. As she washed, she could not help making comparisons between making love with him and the few moments of sexual gratification she had in the other reality. Making love back then had to be squeezed between grueling military training and the scientific demands of a nation constantly in a state of national emergency. The sexual gratification she managed to achieve was so fleeting that it was hardly worth the effort. Making love with Kurt was very intense, explosive and thrilling, unlike anything she had experienced in the Fated Reality.

As the experience she just enjoyed cycled through her mind, she realized the price people were paying in the Fated Reality by living constantly on the brink of nuclear war. Even simple pleasures were muted in that society, or maybe it was just her sensitivities that were muted, but she thought not. She now wished her mission would cease to exist and she did not have an obligation to design and fabricate a Synthesizer in this reality. She wished she could let her relationship with Kurt continue its natural course, but in all probability that was not feasible. She would have to follow her original schedule and get accepted to MIT for the fall semester, as planned. As she pondered these things, she wondered if Lola was on schedule.

When the next semester got underway Laura was taking twenty-two credit hours of advanced math and science courses. She did not find it difficult, but it was time consuming, and she told Kurt she had to limit their dates to twice a month. She could have easily handled one or two dates a week. However, she did not want to accelerate their romance because she would only have to break it off when she left for Cambridge. She was really quite fond of him and did not want to hurt him, but her obligations superseded any personal feelings she might have had. In March, she took the Graduate Record Exams in Physics and scored the highest level of anyone ever taking those examinations. When her letters of recommendation, GRE scores and grade transcripts reached the MIT Physics Department, they immediately admitted for the fall semester. She graduated with her counterpart's class in June obtaining a bachelor degree in physics. This was so because they gave her credit for the required intermediate science courses based on her advance placements test scores.

During the summer of '85, Kurt dated Laura several times. He was falling deeply in love with her and wanted to marry her. She found herself developing similar feelings, but refused to let those feelings deter her from the mission she vowed to complete. The night before she was to leave for Cambridge, they parked in front of her parent's house in Bloomfield discussing their relationship.

"Laura, please reconsider, there are any number of fine graduate schools in the metropolitan area, you could get your PHD at one of those, and we could be married. I would support you and you could study full time and not be obligated to teach those recitation sessions required by that assistantship MIT gave you."

She felt horrible, hearing him plead with her to stay and attend a local graduate school. What kind of woman was she, she thought, he is really the only man for whom she ever had any deep feelings. It did not make sense leaving him for some goddamn obligation she had to a world that was determined to destroy itself. However, she was a woman who had a deep sense of duty instilled in her. It was almost impossible for her to renege on that serious obligation, no matter how hopeless the situation in the Fated Reality may be. She would try to make Kurt understand that she had another obligation, without actually telling him her secret.

"Kurt, I have become extremely fond of you and feel I could even love you someday, but I can't let those emotions deter me from my goals. I know it sounds like I am only thinking about me, please try to understand I really want to be with you, but I can't, now. You're making me feel terrible by playing with my emotions, why can't we put our relationship on hold. I want to work in solid-state physics and MIT has the best-equipped laboratory in the country. The graduate schools in this area are simply not equivalent to MIT. I've set this goal for myself and must see it through. Please understand."

"Even if it destroys our relationship?"

"Kurt, it doesn't have to destroy our relationship, we can put our romance on hold until I compete my studies."

Laura could see the disappointment in his eyes, and she felt terrible telling him that. When he walked her to her door, she blurted out.

"Kurt, for chrissake, you're a physicist, you know how I feel about my goals. Come on, don't look so glum, that's no way to say good-by."

"You're right. It is no way to say good-by. But, unfortunately, you don't love me enough to make even the slightest compromise. You're blinded by your ambition and someday, perhaps, you'll see that it is destroying us and everyone else who loves you."

With those closing remarks, he kissed her on the cheek and left her standing on the doorstep. It was tearing her apart not to call out to him and plead with him to come back. She wanted to say, she loved him and would modify her plans to accommodate their relationship. *Damn that mission*, she thought; *it's costing me the only love I've ever known. Still, I can't just abandon my obligation to the other reality; it would be a betrayal of trust I could not live with.*

Chapter 5

It was late August of '85 and Lola was sitting in her small apartment in Las Cruces staring at the letter of acceptance she had received from MIT. As she looked at the letter she began thinking about the things that had happen happened to her during this past year. After the FBI completed its investigation last August, her parents had insisted that she come and stay with them. The problems she would be facing became evident when they drove back to Alamogordo. Her ponderings were becoming so real in her mind that she began reliving the events that occurred.

In her rumination she could, now, see her father weaving through the traffic in Colorado Springs as he concentrated on getting on Route 25, south, to New Mexico. Her mother began questioning her about her sister Carmen. At this point, her parents thought Carmen was her mother. She knew that her real aunt Carmen was probably living in Spain with her husband, but decided it was better not to mention that at this time.

"Aunt María, she had only one child, me. The last I remember, she was in good health and talking about moving to Albuquerque."

"My god, maybe she's there now and we are going to pass near Albuquerque on our way to Alamogordo. Maybe we can find her address in the telephone book," Maria quickly replied, excited by the prospects of finding her sister.

"I'm sorry, Aunt María, for getting your hopes up, but I told the FBI about her plans, and they said she wasn't there. Maybe she changed her mind when I disappeared." Lola's voice was cracking a little because she wanted desperately to call them mother and father, not aunt and uncle.

"María, let's change the subject, we can talk about that later. She's having a hard enough time coping with the disappointment of not finding her mother, without us reminding her about it," her uncle said.

Lola was just as happy to change the subject, because the cover story she was telling was starting to get complicated.

"Aunt María, you mentioned you had a daughter Lupe. How old is she?"

"Guadalupe is twenty years old and looks a lot like you. We have another daughter named Conceptión; she's nineteen. We call her Concha for short and have a son, Francisco; we named him after his uncle Francisco, but we usually him Paco. He's seventeen now," María answered.

Lola was delighted to hear she had so many siblings in this reality and could hardly wait to meet them. She recalled her mother mentioning another child, Dolores, who had died in infancy. Now, she was wondering what caused the child's death.

"Aunt María, you mentioned on the Base that you lost your first daughter. What caused her death?"

"We were at the wedding of a cousin in Zaragoza, Mexico just south of Juárez. Dolores was only a year and a half at the time and was playing in the field behind my cousin's house with the other children. The children wandered down to the river, which was swollen from the spring rains. Apparently, she followed them and somehow fell into the river and was swept away by the strong currents. We found her down stream a half hour later and rushed her to the hospital in Juárez where they pronounced her dead. Later, we buried her in the family plot outside Zaragoza."

"I am deeply sorry to hear that, Aunt María and Uncle Pedro."

"We still have a three-hour ride left before we get to Alamogordo, let's get out of the past and talk about Lola's future," Pedro suggested.

"Uncle Pedro is right, we have invited you to stay with us, but you will need a job to help support yourself. We have to think about that. Maybe Uncle Pedro can get you a job at the Base where he works.

"What Base is that?" Lola asked.

"He works at Holloman Air Force Base, near White Sands. He runs the radar tracking facility there."

"Maria, I can't get her a job there, she doesn't even have a birth certificate or a social security card you heard the FBI. Without those she can't even get a job at a supermarket."

Lola knew he was right and had been thinking herself about how to establish an identity in this reality. She knew if she went to the local authorities and tried to get a birth certificate, they would simply tell her to write to the Bureau of Vital Statistics in New York City. Going that route would lead not lead anywhere because she did not exist in this reality.

"We're going to have to get her papers, Pedro, otherwise she will be forced to take one of those 'wetback' jobs and you know what they're like."

"I don't see how we can get her identification papers without forging them. The FBI can't even find out where she's from. And, I'm not going to get involved with any falsifying of papers. You know how they are around here about that; they'll think we're trying to sneak a wetback into the country. For chrissake, I'll lose my job."

"Pedro, she's our flesh and blood, she has our DNA; you heard the FBI. They can't distinguish her from one of our own children. We have to help her."

Hearing María and Pedro arguing over her made Lola feel her presence was going to be more of a burden than she had first imagined. She really did not want to cause them any more trouble, so she began thinking about leaving Alamogordo a few days after she arrived. She would make her way across country to New Jersey and find Laura. Once there, they could figure out a way to trick the New York City Bureau of Vital Statistics into issuing her a birth certificate. This might affect their timetable a bit, but at least they could work together on their mission objectives.

When they reached Albuquerque, they stopped for lunch at a local restaurant. They were all in deep thought, thinking about Lola's predicament and were happy to take a break. After being seated at a table, Lola excused herself and went to the ladies room. While washing her hands and combing her hair, she began to rehearse how she would tell her parents she would have to leave. Tears began to flow from her eyes as she thought about her situation. Why was she having these damn burst of emotions? Then in the next breath, she answered her own question. In the Fated Reality, she had been hardened to disappointment and continual stress, and never had an emotional outburst or shed tear over anything in her adult life. Here in this Alternate Reality, things were so different and bursting into tears just at the thought of having to leave her parents was an acceptable response. This damn reality was changing her, and she was not sure she liked these emotional fluctuations.

She cursed the problems she was having, and made a big effort to regain her composure. When she finally did, she returned to the table looking as if she was crying. Her aunt and uncle, seeing that she was struggling to hold back her tears, told her they might have a solution to at least some of her problems.

"Lola, we've been thinking hard about your problem and think we might have a solution," Pedro informed her.

"Guys, I really don't want to trouble you anymore. You have been so kind, coming to Colorado Springs for me. I love you very much, but I think it's my problem and I have to solve it. I'll be leaving in a few days for New York."

"Oh, Lola, if the FBI can't find your mother, you won't either and you'll be in that big city with no one to help you. So listen to us, we think we can help," María said, grasping her hands from across the table.

Lola didn't think they could be of much help to her, but listened politely.

"When our daughter Dolores died in Mexico, we buried her there, as we told you a little while ago. In our grief we never filled out a death certificate in Alamogordo, we meant to do it, but one thing or another came up and we forgot about it. When María said you're our flesh and blood; it hit me. We still have Dolores' birth certificate and we could give it to you, and you could claim to be our daughter."

Lola thought for a moment and realized they really had a kernel of an idea. However, it would still be risky for them, and she did not want to get them involved any more than they already were.

"I couldn't let you to do that. It's very risky and would still require an explanation of where I came from. Even your children would have to say I was their sister."

"Lola, no one's more worried about the risks than I am, especially with my job at the Base. But, if push came to shove, we could prove you're our daughter by DNA testing. The FBI even said the DNA test couldn't distinguish you from one of our own children. As for our own kids, they don't know about you. We didn't tell them anything except that the FBI had found some woman who claims to be related to us. We never told them much about their older sister because they weren't even born when we lost her and the subject almost never came up."

"What will you tell them when you arrive with an older sister they never heard of?"

"We will tell them we thought you died in Mexico years ago, but you were found in Colorado Springs, unconscious, and the FBI identified you as ours through DNA tests. We'll show them the birth certificate and say it further proves you're ours."

As Lola thought about what they were saying, she realized their cover story was no less believable than hers was. She agreed with her uncle. They could always use DNA tests as the ultimate verification of any cover story, no matter how questionable the explanation might be.

"Why are you guys doing this for me?" Lola asked, still a little confused about why they were willing to go to this extreme to help a supposed niece.

"Because we know you're ours. We don't know how or why you were in Colorado Springs. Nevertheless, you were there and they called us to identify you. The things you said to us made us believe in our hearts that you belong to us. In addition, I'm a scientific programmer and understand the laws of chance. The DNA tests say there's one chance in a billion that you're not our daughter and with those odds only fools would deny you were theirs."

With her father's words still ringing in her ears, Lola, with tears in her eyes, got up from the table and hugged her parents. She thought: *In a strange way they have identified with me even across bifurcated realities.*

María and Pedro felt they had somehow made a parental bond with Lola, but couldn't explain how or why those feelings were so strong. They did not try to analyze them any further; they just accepted what they felt.

Paco and his two sisters watched, from the living room window, as the family car stopped in front of their home. A strange young woman stepped from the car and joined their mother and father, as they walked toward the house.

"Lupe, she looks a lot like you. I wonder who she is," Concha remarked to her sister.

"That's true, but she's a lot prettier," Paco injected, kidding his sister as he usually did.

"Oh, shut up. Where do you suppose she got those clothes? She's dressed like those gringo college girls from the northeast that are in the movies we see," Lupe observed.

Lola was wearing the jeans, loose shirt, and shoes Laura shared with her from the clothing items Mrs. Claremont had sent to her daughter. She had the fatigues and boots from the other reality in the duffel bag she was carrying. She had told María they issued them to her at the base during the investigation.

When Lola and her parents got into the house, Pedro called the kids to come and meet Lola.

63

"Kids, this is going to come as a shock to you, but there is no time like the present to hit you with this. I would like you to meet your to meet your oldest sister, Lola," their father told them.

The kid's eyes alternated from their father to the strange girl in shocked disbelief, as they stood there dumbfounded by that revelation. Finally, Lupe spoke.

"Where did she come from? You never told us much about our older sister except that she died when she was a baby."

"We thought she had died and wanted to get past that sad period in our lives. You better explain it to them, Pedro," María said.

"All right, let's all go into the kitchen and sit around the table because it's a long story."

Lola wondered what story her father was going to tell her siblings about her sudden appearance. She knew generally, what he was going to say, but they did not discuss the specific details on their trip home. When their father spoke, a hush came over the family as they hung on his every word.

"In the spring of '64 your mother and I attended a wedding of a relative in Zaragoza, Mexico. Your sister was just a toddler and playing with the children behind the house of a relative, with which we were staying. The children wondered down to the river. Apparently, your sister followed them and somehow fell into the river. The strong currents, caused by the spring rains, soon swept her away. We searched and searched for her body but never found it. Eventually the search party gave up. We had to accept the fact that she must have drowned. Then, as you know, the FBI informed us that they found a young woman unconscious in Colorado Springs, who they thought might be related to us. When the FBI came here, they said her name was Lola Gonzalez and showed us her picture. We told them that although she looked a lot like our daughter Lupe, we didn't think she was related to us because Gonzalez is a common name. When they asked us to go to Colorado Springs and speak to her, we refused. We said we would have to have more proof than a last name to make a trip like that. They said they had more compelling information but they couldn't divulge it at that time. They then asked us to consent to DNA testing to clear up the matter. When the DNA test results came back, they showed conclusively Lola was our daughter."

"Why was she in Colorado Springs? Why was she unconscious and where was she all these years?" Paco asked, looking in wonderment at Lola.

"No one knows why she was in Colorado Springs but the FBI said she suffered some kind of trauma and was in a coma for four days. When she came out of the coma, they discovered she had suffered some type of memory loss. She remembers living in New York and even remembers her family there telling her some things about Mexico, but the FBI couldn't locate that family. My guess is that some people saw a toddler in that river in Mexico and pulled her to safety and later took her to New York," their father answered.

"Why would someone do that?" Concha asked.

"Some people will do anything to get a baby," her mother said.

"Why does she have our name if it happened that way?" Paco asked.

"Gonzalez is a common name and maybe it was the name of the family that found her. Who knows?

"Still, what made the FBI look for us in Alamogordo? There must be thousands and thousands of Gonzalez families in this country," Concha said.

Lola could see her father's cover story would come unraveled, if she did not step in with some acceptable explanation. She could see her mother and father were racking their brains for an answer to Concha's question and needed help.

"Dad, she's right, something doesn't hang together," Paco injected.

"Well, I don't know how the FBI found us, but they did," Pedro said, for want of a better explanation.

After a long pause, with the kids looking at each other and their parents, Lola finally spoke up.

"I think I know how the FBI located you guys. They probably searched the birth records in Alamogordo around '64 after I mentioned I thought I had relatives here."

"You have relatives here? Where?" Lupe asked.

"I just mentioned it because the people I called, my parents, said we did."

"You called them your parents? Why didn't the FBI go to them first?" Concha asked.

My god, Lola thought, *this is getting is getting complicated.* Maybe she should have let that answer her father gave, stand. Well, too late now, she thought, she must try somehow to satisfy their curiosity, otherwise things would quickly unravel.

"Kids, kids, when the FBI found her, she had been in a coma for four days. When she regained consciousness, her short-term memory was gone. They think someone wiped her memory with some type of drug," her father quickly injected.

The kids began to feel sorry for their new sister and their line of questioning began to soften.

"Lola, do you remember anything about where you were living before someone did that to you?" Concha asked. Her tone of voice was now a lot more conciliatory.

"I remember living in New York City a few years ago. Still, when the FBI searched my old neighborhood in that City they could not find my parents. The people in my old neighborhood just said they moved, and nothing else. I guess they gave up looking in the New York area and started searching birth records here. They found a child with the same name as mine born to your parents in '64, here in Alamogordo. They thought it might be more than just a coincidence and decided to investigate. The DNA tests, as you already know, eventually, proved that I was their daughter."

"I'll bet the people who took her, way back when, were distant relatives of ours. Probably, they are related to that Gonzalez bunch that lives on the other side of town. I never did like those big mouth payasos, anyway," Paco said, beginning to feel sorry for Lola and filling in some details of the story himself.

Hearing that Maria and Pedro felt relieved, realizing the kids were finally buying into the cover story.

"All right," Maria said, "why don't you kids all give your new sister a big hug and welcome her to our family?"

Finally accepting their parent's revelations, each sibling hugged their new sister and all the children helped their mother get dinner ready. While dinner was being prepared, the kids began firing questions at Lola, again.

"Lola, were you in college back East?" Those clothes you are wearing make you look like one of those gringo college girls," Lupe asked in Spanish. She was trying to find out if Lola even knew how to speak Spanish, and wondering if the story their father had told them was still missing some important details.

Lola responded in an elegant Castilian Spanish dialect that astonished her siblings.

"I do not recall how I acquired these clothes. I suppose I might have been in a school back east, but I don't remember."

As the conversation continued in Spanish, Lola's dialect generated more questions from the kids. The parents already knew, from what Lola had told them, that Maria's sister Carmen married a man from Spain and lived there for a while. They surmised that Lola had probably picked up that accent in Spanish from them, and as a result, they weren't very surprised by the way she spoke.

"Gee, Lola, you sound like one of the Spanish diplomats we sometimes see when we watch a UN debate on TV in school. Are you sure you don't come from Spain?" Paco asked, marveling over his new sister's ability to express herself in such graceful Spanish.

"I do not recall living in Spain; perhaps I did. However, I do remember living in New York City, but my memory of those events, especially over the past year, is completely missing."

After making that remark, Lola realized that her father did not mention anything to her siblings about her mother's twin sister Carmen. He did not mention either that she was her mother and living in New York. Nor did he give them any of the details she had given him in Colorado Springs. She decided at that moment not to say any more about New York. She would stay with her father's version of what happened, leaving out details that could only cause her cover story to become unraveled.

"Let's stop questioning her about her accent," María said, "she speaks better Spanish than you do. Now, let's change the subject."

By the time supper was prepared the kids seemed to be accepting Lola based on what their father told them, even with her Castilian accent. Any more information added to his story would be superfluous and serve only to confuse them. So, Lola kept her answers to their questions centered about her father's explanation.

———————————

Lying on her bed one evening and staring at the ceiling in the room, Lola began to review the things she had accomplished over the past week. Her mother had given Dolores' birth certificate to her, and the match was almost perfect. Her dead sister was only a month younger than she and had the same formal name. Before going to the registry of motor vehicles, she applied for a Social Security Card with her new birth certificate. She then went to the registry of motor vehicles in Alamogordo and obtained a learner's permit using the birth certificate. She had easily passed the written test and they scheduled her to take the road test a week from Monday. Her father soon found out she was an experience driver; a skill, she told him, she had learned in New York.

She had taken the high school equivalency exam at the Alamogordo High School a few days before. Many Mexican immigrants were taking that exam, so they asked very few questions. The only thing they really wanted was proof of citizenship, her birth certificate was all she needed. Although not essential, a high school diploma would help get her a job. However, her real reason for wanting the high school diploma was to take the Scholastic Aptitude tests (SAT) or college boards as they called them in her reality. They were giving them at the high school in two weeks.

Lola was startled out of her thoughts by her sister Concha's yelling that supper was ready. When Lola walked into the kitchen, her mother was smiling and said she had some good news.

"Lola, the man from the high school called and said you passed the high school equivalency exam. Do you know what else he said? He said you had the highest score ever made on that exam. He wondered how you had accomplished that."

"Simple, Mother, I knew all the answers," Lola answered.

"Hey, big sister. Don't you get it? You're not supposed to know all the answers, you're a Hispanic," Paco remarked, caustically.

"What does being Hispanic have to do with it? I knew the answers, that's all that counts," Lola responded.

"Leave her alone, maybe where she comes from they treat people differently," Lupe told her brother.

Those remarks made Lola realize another peculiar difference between this reality and the other. She began to notice over the last few months that racial and ethnic prejudices were more pronounced here than in hers. She could not help observing that the nuclear war had changed the way the people in her reality thought about each other. People in her world had to pull together, because the nation's survival was at stake. They buried old hatreds for the common good. People were concerned about their lives and not the color of their skins. There were still bigots around, to be sure, but they kept a low profile because the people themselves, not just the affected ethnic groups, thought their views were irrational. She thought, nuclear war was certainly a strong medicine for society's ills, but wondered how long it would take this cold war society to cure its ills.

The following week Lola received by mail her Social Security Card. She also took the road test and passed, getting her driver's license. Once she had these credentials, her father suggested that she start looking for a job, and said the Base had a few positions available. Besides cleaning lady positions, one was open in the library. However, her father mentioned, Hispanics somehow never seemed to score higher than the gringos do on the civil service exam they required. He suspected some type of ethic screening was involved but when they filed complaints, the authorities never found any evidence of wrongdoing. He told her to apply, anyway, but he did not have much hope she would get the job.

With her newly acquired credentials in hand, Lola was qualified to take the civil service exam at Holloman Air Force Base. The following week she took the exam, and to the surprise of her family, she got a job in the Base library. Fresh on the heels of that accomplishment, she decided to take the SAT' exams given at the high school. That would complete the preliminary goals she had set for herself when she first came to Alamogordo. On Saturday of that week, she went to the high school and took those exams.

One night while Lola was attending an advanced math class at New Mexico State University's branch in Alamogordo, the Gonzalez family was discussing her.

"Daddy, why did you get our new sister that good job at the Base library and not one of us?" Lupe asked, thinking their father was favoring Lola.

"Kids, I really didn't do much, all I did was to hand in her application, and she did the rest."

"What did she do? You told us once they didn't hire Hispanics in those jobs," Concha said, reminding her father what he had told them last year.

"A friend of mine in the civil service office told me there was no way they could keep from hiring her. She scored better than anyone whoever took that exam did. She's much smarter than any of them and she knows it. My friend said she had their heads spinning at the interview. She knew the computerized reference system that the library uses better than people who have been working there for years."

"My god, where did she learn all those things?" Lupe asked.

"My guess is that she is a lot more than a simple school girl from Spanish Harlem in New York. Maybe in time she'll remember and tell us," her father remarked.

"I was walking with her to the supermarket; she knew the shortcut and seemed to know what was on each street. Are you sure she never lived here before?"

"I don't think she did. Look, why don't you girls try to get a little closer to her, maybe she'll tell you more about herself. Go to the movies or something, introduce her around, she's your sister and you should make her feel like she's one of us, " their mother suggested.

They all agreed they would try to help Lola adjust, but the kids really thought Lola was adjusting very well by herself and did not need much help from them.

The following Saturday Lola's sisters talked her into going with them to a Mexican festival in Las Cruces, which was about seventy miles from Alamogordo. The girls were going with their friend Carmela, who had her own car. They told Lola there were many attractive guys there and many were from New Mexico State University. They also told her NMSU's main campus was in Las Cruces. Lola was not very interested in the festival but was interested in a field generator experiment that one of the university's laboratories was conducting. She had read about that laboratory's research in a journal she found in the Base library, and was anxious to see the high-powered generator they were constructing, first hand.

"Come on, Lola, you might meet a nice guy there," Concha begged.

"Your going to like our friend, Carmela, she's been wanting to meet you," Lupe added.

"Okay, okay, sisters, you've convinced me. Besides, I would like to see NMSU's campus and especially its bookstore."

"Gee, Lola, we're going to have fun not to walk around on that campus and look at books in its bookstore. Come on, when you see the guys that are going to be at the festival you won't want to wander around some old campus."

When the young women from Alamogordo arrived in Las Cruces, they found the festival being held near Messlia Park, which wasn't too far from the New Mexico State University campus.

The smell of Mexican specialties cooking over open fires and the sounds of the guitars playing Mexican music filled the air, as the young women entered the picnic grounds. Brightly dressed men and women dancing on a makeshift dance floor caught Lola's eye. The scene reminded her of stories told by her Aunt Carmen in the other reality. The sight in a strange way was captivating. Moreover, it was drawing Lola into the bygone dreams of another world. She and Carmela found an unoccupied table while her sisters went to buy some food. She was actually beginning to get into the swing of things when the obligations of her mission began to haunt her. With those thoughts breaking the magic of the moment, Lola decided to sample some Mexican cuisine her sisters had brought back. After taking a few bites, she told her sisters that she wanted to walk over to the college bookstore and see what new books were available for the fall semester. The girls thought it was a dumb idea, and said

70

they would meet her at the Concession Stand at six. Then, they would decide what would be next on their agenda.

Arriving on campus, Lola quickly found the laboratory where they were doing the field generator experiment. Walking into the laboratory, the sight of the massive field generator reminded her of a similar component they had used in the construction of the Synthesizer.

The men working on the field generator saw a young woman staring at the field generator from the entrance to the Laboratory. She wore jeans, a colorful red and white shirt, and was wearing white sneakers. Looking at the attractive young woman, with the captivating dark eyes, Henry Vega called out.

"Can I help you?"

"Maybe you can, I was just passing by and saw you working on that field generator. I was wondering how those field coils in that configuration could produce enough energy to trigger the induction field in the cavity resonator."

Her comment shocked Henry Vega and the other men working on the project. They came out from behind the generator and gather around her.

"What configuration do you consider more effective?" Henry asked, amused by the young woman's question.

"You have to change the shape of those coils and move them over here so the field is intense at this location. Then, you'll have enough energy to trigger the induction field," Lola said, as she instructed the men on how to boost the field intensity.

"How do you know that will work?" Henry Vega asked, skeptically.

"It's really quite simple. You solve Maxwell's equations subject to the boundary conditions imposed by the cavity resonator. The coefficients of the resulting wave equations determine the magnitude of the field and where it must be generated," Lola responded.

The men looked at each other in disbelief. This little slip of a girl just walked into the lab and gave them the solution to a problem they had been working on for six months. Henry shook his head, walked over to Lola and extended his hand.

"Hello. I'm Henry Vega, Director of the Electrodynamics Laboratory, and you are?

"Lola Gonzalez, librarian at Holloman Air Force Base. Pleased to meet you," Lola replied, smiling.

The other men introduced themselves and stated their positions on the project.

"Ms. Gonzalez, you really astonished us, we hadn't realized that librarians at the Base had to be experts in electrodynamics."

"They do not. I just do a lot of reading in electromagnetic theory. I'm studying the problem of field generation."

The men went back to their tasks and Dr. Vega showed Lola the equipment he had in the laboratory and engaged her in lengthy discussion about her career goals. She told him she was working in the Base library, temporarily, and was taking night courses at NMSU in Alamogordo. She told him she was going to apply to MIT for admittance in the fall when her SAT scores were available.

"Ms. Gonzalez, why don't you apply at this NMSU campus in Las Cruces? We are doing more work in large-scale field generation than MIT."

"I realized that when people from your laboratory wrote all the papers I was reading on the subject. Nevertheless, as you know, MIT has a first rate reputation in all fields of engineering and I promised myself I would attend that school someday."

Henry was very impressed with this exceptionally attractive young woman whose mind seemed so much more advanced than those of her peers. He decided to ask her, again, to apply to NMSU; he thought that the university needed more students with a strong scientific curiosity like hers.

"Ms. Gonzalez, I strongly urge to apply to NSMU when your SAT scores are available. If you do decide to apply, make sure you take the advance placement exams in the sciences. Because with your knowledge of scientific fundamentals, I could probably get you credit for the elementary courses."

Walking back to the Mexican festival to meet her sisters and their friend, Lola was in deep thought over what Dr. Vega had just told her. She could see NMSU had a laboratory that was developing a field generator that had the potential of functioning as one of the critical component in Laura's Synthesizer. She decided to apply to NMSU in Las Cruces for the winter semester and learn more about the field generator project. However, she would still apply to MIT and meet with Laura in Cambridge. Then they would plan the next step of their mission.

Lola reached the concession stand at six, as planned. The smells of Mexican food hung heavy in the air, and the people were mainly at their tables enjoying the tantalizing feast. Lola's sisters were nowhere in sight. After waiting a few minutes, she decided to walk back to the car and see if they thought they were meeting her there. In the distance, she could see the girls talking to three guys by the car. As she approached, she saw one of them grab the keys out of Carmela's hand and the girls try to get them back. The guys then started pushing the girls into the back seat of the two-door car. The girls were kicking and screaming and one of the men punched her sister Lupe in the face. One of the guys got into the driver's seat while the other two ran around the car to get into the passenger side. He hit Carmela as she tried to get out, knocking her back into the rear seat. The engine was cranking as Lola reached the driver side of the car. She quickly opened the door and hit the driver on the nose with her fist. She then reached in and dragged him out by his shirt and long hair, kicking him in the groin as he tried to straighten up. She then pulled him down by his hair, smashing his face into her knee.

As she turned, the other two came running around the car yelling.

"Where did that spic bitch come from? Come on, we know karate, too. Come on, Jeff, let's give this bitch a karate lesson."

Before the one on the left could raise his hands, Lola kicked him deep in the solar plexus, doubling him up gasping for air. When the other one reached her, he tried to hit her with some kind of karate chop, which she sidestepped and then flipped him over the hood of the car. The three jerks were no match for her; she had learned many lethal defensive techniques in the Fated Reality and executed them with great precision. In the other reality, she was an expert in the martial arts and was very capable in combative situations with skilled adversaries. So, with these punks she quickly got the upper hand.

As the men recovered a bit and tried to get up, Lola kicked them from the front of the car to the back. She kicked them repeatedly in the face, stomach, ribs, and groin until she had knocked them senseless.

"Lola! Lola! Stop! Please stop! You are going to kill them!" Concha cried, while the other girls stood there petrified, their faces swollen from the punches the men had given them.

"Little sister, the first thing you learn in the army is to show 'em no mercy. Because if you turn your back on them, you'll be picking your teeth out of the dirt. Now, give me a hand with this Gringo trash, I want to throw them over there by the curb so we can get this car out of here."

The snarl on Lola's face and her tone of voice sent a chill down the girls' backs. They obediently followed her directions and helped her stack up the "Gringo trash," as she called them, by the curb at the edge of the parking lot.

"Come on, let's get out or here. I'll drive," Lola told the girls.

"Should we call tell police or sheriff and have them arrested?" Lupe asked, thinking they shouldn't just leave them there.

That was the last thing Lola needed; she certainly did not want another run in with the authorities.

"We're not calling anybody. We're getting out of here. Those bastards will have us arrested for assault. Whom do you think they'll believe, the Gringos or the Chicanos?" Lola informed the girls, sternly.

Driving back to Alamogordo, her sisters and Carmela informed Lola that those men told them they were from back east. Nevertheless, one of them let it slip that they were from El Paso and were at the festival to have some fun and raise a little hell. Lola told the girls they got what they came for and asked them to change the subject.

While the girls talked, Lola began thinking about the feelings she had during that altercation. Back in the other reality she would not think in terms of Gringos or Chicanos, as she did when that jerk call her a spic bitch. That ethnic slur made her think those guys were probably from the northeast, it was not a slur that was commonly used around here. In the Fated Reality, she would not have used the "Gringos" or the "Chicanos" terminology because people back there did not think in terms of "us" and "them" anymore. In this reality, thinking in those terms was easy. She thought she would be careful not to let those terms become a permanent part of her thought process.

When the women got back to the Gonzalez home in Alamogordo, Carmela got out of the car and hugged Lola. She thanked her for her help and said she would never forget it. After saying goodbye to Carmela the Gonzalez sisters went into their house, which was dark because their parents and brother were out for the evening. Lola went into the living room to read and her sisters went into the kitchen to put an icepack on the side of Lupe's face. The girls were unusually quiet that evening because Lola told them not to bring up anything about what had happened in Las Cruces, especially, when their parents arrived home. They were still shaking from the fight in Las Cruces; also, they were in awe of their big sister and did not even think of disobeying her. However, when Lola went into her bedroom later that evening, which was a room she was sharing with her sisters, both hugged her. Thanking her profusely for what, she had done for them. Lola thanked them for being brave, and then said, she did not want to waste any more time talking about some Gringo jerks from El Paso.

Sunday morning Lola was out jogging while the family was having a late breakfast before going to church. The girls could not resist telling their parents and brother what happened yesterday in Las Cruces. They described in excruciating detail, how their big sister kicked and smashed the nasty gringos.

"You should have seen her throwing those Gringos around like rag dolls. I tell you I never seen anything like it in my whole life," Concha told her parents.

"Aw, come on, your exaggerating," Paco said, not believing Concha's description of the altercation.

"She's not exaggerating. Lola really busted those guys. She took complete control of the situation, showing no fear, and beat them so badly that we thought she was going to kill them," Lupe said.

"I don't think she's exaggerating, either," Pedro injected, "the paper says three El Paso men were found in the parking lot behind the Mexican Festival, badly beaten. The men said a vicious female attached them. They told police they thought she was some kind of Hispanic witch, because she certainly wasn't human."

"Where do you suppose she learned to fight like that, Pedro?" María asked, puzzled by what she had just heard.

"She told me that the army taught her how to handle such situations. Was she in the army, Daddy?" Concha asked her father.

"I don't know and she doesn't remember. One of the nurses on the Base in Colorado Springs said she was found in military fatigues. My guess is she was in the military and the Air Force didn't want to say what her assignment was. They obviously specially trained her and they're not saying for what. Maybe they wiped her memory on purpose."

Returning home, Lola went directly upstairs and took a shower. While she was dressing her mother, sisters and brother left for church, but her father waited a few minutes for her to come down so he could walk with her.

"Lola, I want to thank you for looking after your sisters yesterday."

"Dad, you don't have to thank me for that. We're family, besides, it was really nothing, I wish my sisters wouldn't make such a big deal out of it."

"Lola, it is a big deal, they could have raped or even killed them. But, tell me were you ever in the Army?"

Lola knew her father was referring to that army remark she made to Concha, yesterday. She told herself she must be more careful about what she said in the future. However, for now she would try to brush off the remark before Pandora's box opened and things came tumbling out.

"Well, Dad, I'm not sure, because I don't remember. Yet when threatened, I seem able to defend myself quite well. It sure seems like they trained me for something, doesn't it?"

"My conjecture is that you were and they had your memory wiped so you couldn't reveal some secret undercover activity. It's odd that you and that other girl can't remember anything, isn't it?"

"It does smell fishy, doesn't it?"

She decided not to dispel her father's secret agent theory. Mainly, because he needed an explanation for the things he saw and heard. In addition, his explanation was as good as anything she could come up with, anyway.

The ringing phone made María fumble with her keys as she tried to open the front door. Juggling the grocery bags she was carrying, she finally opened the door and picked up the phone in the hall.

"Hello, this is Professor Vega at NMSU in Las Cruces, may I speak to Ms. Lola Gonzalez, please?"

"Could you hold for a minute?" María requested, as she ran to the kitchen to deposit the bags she was carrying.

"Lola is not home, may I take a message."

"To whom am I speaking?"

"Her mother."

"Mrs. Gonzalez, I'm calling to inform her that the Electrical Engineering Department at NMSU has accepted her for the '85 spring semester."

"Professor Vega, are you sure you have the right Lola Gonzalez? My Lola in a librarian at Holloman Air Force Base."

"I'm sure, Mrs. Gonzalez, we know she's a librarian at the Base. She had a perfect score on her SATs, and had excellent scores on the advanced placement tests she took. Frankly, she has us puzzled, all her records show are exam scores, has she ever been to school in this country?"

María did not know how to respond to that question, she did not want to tell him about the Colorado Springs business because she wanted to keep that stuff private. Once she said anything about that, one question would lead to another. Then, suddenly the family's business would be public knowledge. No, she would not tell him about that stuff. She would just have to give him another explanation. But, what one would she give him? Finally, an answer occurred to her.

"Not recently, she's been living in Europe with my sister and serving as her companion. My sister had been seeing to her education."

"Well, she certainly has done a fine job educating her. That explains why she did so well even on the French and Spanish advanced placement tests. Tell her we are sending her a conformation letter and have her call me when she gets in."

"Professor Vega, we thought she would be going to the NMSU branch here in Alamogordo in the evenings. She has to work, we can't afford to send her to Las Cruces, we have other children to educate, too."

"Mrs. Gonzalez, your daughter is a gifted person and we won't let financial difficulties prevent her from getting the education she deserves. We are offering her a full scholarship, plus a generous stipend to cover living expenses; we want her at NMSU."

The offer NMSU was making her daughter astonished María. She thanked Professor Vega for giving Lola the full scholarship and said that she would have her daughter call him when she got home.

The late August sun was overhead when a loud street noise startled Lola out of her long rumination. She was still sitting on the sofa and the letter of acceptance she had received from MIT was on the floor in front of her. As she picked up the letter and began rereading it, she recalled Professor Vega was so impressed with her that he gave her a job as his assistant in the Electrodynamics Laboratory. Being in that position, she was able to study the High Energy Field Generator in depth. She verified her initial assessment that this high-energy generator had the potential to duplicate the function of a critical component in the Space-Time Transitional Synthesizer. However, she would have to spend time modifying its design. She decided to call the Team Leader at her home in Bloomfield, NJ and inform her about the possibilities she had uncovered here in Las Cruces.

"Hello, may I speak to Laura Claremont, please?"

"She's very busy. Could I take a message and have her call you back?" Helen said, hurriedly.

Helen was helping her sister pack. Laura was going to attend MIT this fall and leaving before Labor Day to get settled in the apartment she had rented for herself in Cambridge.

"I must talk to her, now, tell her it's Lola Gonzalez."

Helen informed Laura it was Lola Gonzalez; it surprised her when Laura dropped what she was doing and took the call in her room closing the door.

"Laura, I figured we better touch base before we rendezvous in Cambridge and appraise each other of our status."

"Lola, this phone isn't private. Give me your number and I'll call you back in a few minutes from the public phone around the corner."

A few minutes later, the women continued their conversation.

"Lola, I'm scheduled to start graduate work at MIT in a few weeks, and I'm getting ready to leave tomorrow. I was able to step into my counterpart's shoes, although it was a bit awkward, I managed to graduate with her class. Were you able to get accepted to MIT?"

"I got accepted, but I didn't have any one's shoes to step into, so I am supposed to start as an advanced undergraduate."

"That's great, Lola. The level doesn't matter."

"I'm not calling about my level. Something far more interesting has come up. First, let me tell you. My family accepted me as their daughter; it's an interesting story and I'll bring you up to date later, but for now it suffices to know I'm their daughter. My family is not in a position to support me so got a job as a librarian at Holloman Air Force Base near Alamogordo, where my family lives. I used the facilities available in the library to search for businesses or laboratories doing research on high power field generation. I found a research laboratory at New Mexico State University that is working on a project called the High Energy Field Generator experiment or the HEFG project for short."

"Isn't that area near where they tested the first atomic bomb?"

"Yes, but let me go on. In short, I applied to NMSU last fall and was accepted by the Electrical Engineering Department. They gave me a full scholarship and living expenses, and I have been attending classes since last January. I got a summer job working on the HEFG project; I verified that its high-energy generator had the potential to function as that critical component in the Synthesizer. But, it will take time for me to work myself into a position so I can determine how to modify its design."

"Good work, Lola, that information does require that we revise our original plans. I will also need time to ingratiate myself at the MIT solid-state physics lab before I can design and develop the required power chips. They're behind us in this reality and we'll have to invent the components we need."

"I would like to suggest that we work apart a few more years and get the complete educational credentials we need to command the respect of the scientific community. Those credentials should enable us openly to work on the components we require. If we play it right, we could have them formally accepted as legitimate research projects at our respective universities."

"I'm thinking similarly. The components we need to develop have many important applications other than for use in the Synthesizer. Therefore, we won't have to disclose our personal reasons for developing them when we apply for funds. OK, it'll probably take a few years to get our doctorates and establish ourselves as experts in our respective fields. You will work in high-energy field generation, and I will work in the physics of solid-state chip design. In a few years we'll select the site where we'll design and build a Synthesizer that will link the Alternate and Fated Realities."

"Sounds good, Team Leader. However, I suggest that we make contact periodically to brief each other on our progress."

"Also, Lola, make contact if any problems develop."

The conversation ended abruptly, with the women exchanging addresses and phone numbers, because Laura was calling from a pay phone and she was running out of money.

Chapter 6

The Gonzalez family was preparing to go to Las Cruces and attend their daughter's graduation from New Mexico State University. She was graduating with a Doctor of Science degree in Electrical Engineering. María had planned to have a celebration at their home in Alamogordo later that day. They wanted to honor of their daughter for being the first in their family to obtain an advanced degree. Her father had obtained a bachelor's degree in computer science and the other two daughters were studying for bachelors' degrees in education. Still, Lola's achievement amazed everyone; she earned a Doctorate after starting college four years ago and did it while holding a job at the Electrodynamics Laboratory. They were indeed proud parents and had invited family and friends to celebrate this accomplishment. Among the people invited were her professor, Henry Vega, head of the Electrical Engineering Department at NMSU and Director of its Prestigious Electrodynamics Laboratory.

After the graduation ceremonies were over, Lola's parents rode back to Alamogordo with her. While driving home, they told her how proud they were over her accomplishments and asked her about her plans for the future.

"Lola, now that you have your Doctorate, do you plan to teach or work in industry?" her father asked.

"Well, first, I have to finish the project I'm working on at the Electrodynamics Lab. I have to wrap up a few things, do the final report and that will take me at least until Labor Day to complete. After that, I'm not sure what I'll do; I have several offers from industry and a few from universities. However, I'm seriously considering working at Lawrence Livermore National Laboratory in Livermore, California."

"Why would you want to leave this area? I heard that Electrodynamics Lab at the university made you an offer to head a new project they're starting," her mother responded.

"They did, but I think I want to try something else. Who told you they made me an offer?"

"I spoke to Professor Vega a few weeks ago when I called to invite him to your gradation party. He said the University made you a handsome offer to work at the Electrodynamics Laboratory after you got your doctorate and you hadn't responded yet."

"Mother. You spoke to Professor Vega about my career plans. For god sake that is embarrassing."

"Why is that so embarrassing? He's your college advisor isn't he and he seems as interested in your career, as we are."

"Mom, he's also my boss at the Electro Lab and I'm annoyed he would speak to you about my career."

"Oh, Lola, he is very impressed with you, he holds you in the highest esteem. In fact, he told me you're the best doctoral student he has ever had the pleasure of working with. In fact I think he is interested in you."

"Mother! Now, you're going to play matchmaker."

"No, I'm not, but you could do a lot worse than him. He's so handsome and intelligent."

"Oh, Mother, he's not interested in me that way," Lola answered, now beginning to think about what her mother was saying.

"You know, Lola, you may be a brilliant girl, but you sure are slow at detecting when a man is interested in you."

"Are you really saying he's interested in me?"

"Lola, why do you think he is coming to your party? He must get invited to many graduation parties, but he's coming to Alamogordo to yours. I can assure you he's not coming to just sample the Mexican cuisine.

Her mother's remarks had startled Lola. Could her mother be right, could her professor really be interested in her, she wondered? He certainly was a handsome man; he was tall and rather slender and had dark wavy hair. His eyes were a dark shade of blue. He had sideburns and wore a well-trimmed mustache. She had always liked his type but had never shown him any interest because she had a mission to perform and romance was not on the agenda. Anyway, her mother was probably wrong. He was probably coming to her party because he wanted to find out why she did not accept the offer the University had made her.

It was a glorious June night in Alamogordo, the sun had just set and the evening was getting comfortably cool. The graduation party at the Gonzalez home was well underway when Henry Vega walked into the backyard. The sounds of old Mexican tunes played by a group of guitarists filled the air. The tantalizing smells of homemade Mexican Cuisine were everywhere. Henry saw Lola in the middle of a crowd of people, all of who were congratulating her for her achievements. She had changed clothes and was now wearing a beautiful white skirt with red and gold trim. Her blouse was red and white, and matched the skirt. She was like the picture of a beautiful, carefree, Mexican-American, young woman that one sometimes sees in television commercials or in the fashion magazines. She had a unique touch of class that is hard to describe, but easily observed when she is speaking to someone or doing some task. She appeared this evening so different from the brilliant young woman he had hired to be his assistant a few years ago. He loved the air of mystery about her, but he never made an advance toward her while he was her advisor. He felt it would be improper.

When Lola would cast a glance in his direction and smile, he would return the smile and then turn away. Could a young woman like her ever be attracted to a man twelve years her senior, he wondered? At times, he felt she was more mature than he, especially when they had occasion to speak about subjects not of a scientific nature.

Through a crowd of well-wishers, Lola would catch sight of Professor Vega from time to time. Now, he was by the table selecting some samples of Mexican cuisine her mother and her lady friends had helped prepare. He seemed lonesome, so she decided to go over and thank him for coming to her party. Squeezing through the crowd and catching glimpses of the professor as she made her way toward him, she could see could see his face light up when he finally caught sight of her.

"Professor Vega, I want to thank you for coming to my party. I would like to apologize for not responding to the offer you so kindly extended. I didn't respond because…."

The professor stopped her in the middle of her sentence.

"Lola, I didn't come here to talk shop, I came here to congratulate a brilliant young woman on her accomplishments in electrical engineering. Don't worry about the offer. We can talk about it another time. Another thing Lola, would you please call me Henry. You and I are now equal colleagues and no longer in the student-teacher mode."

When professor Vega made those comments, Lola could hardly believe her ears. Their conversations in the past had always been so formal and professional sounding. She thought: *He wants me to call him by his first name, could my mother be right? Maybe he does have an interest in me.*

"Professor, er, I mean Henry. Let's take a little walk; I can hardly hear a word you're saying. The party seems to be reaching a crescendo."

As they walked down Porto Rico Street, they talked about many subjects including her family and where her ancestors came from. She told him she was descendent of Ignacio Zaragoza, a Mexican general, whose bravery incited the Mexicans finally to expel the French from Mexico. She also told him her family came from a town in Mexico that bears the general's name.

"Tell me, Lola, you obviously had a fine education when you applied to NMSU, but what puzzled me was why you only presented us with test scores at that time. Were your records lost?"

Lola did not like this line of questioning and she certainly was not going to reveal anything about the other reality. However, he was a good guy and she liked him; so she decided to follow up on what she recalled her mother had told him when he had asked her a similar question.

"Henry, I had spent several years with my aunt Carmen Zaragoza de Saucedo, as her companion in Europe. She was very rich and employed tutors to educate me. When we were in France, she hired tutors from the Polytechnique to instruct me in math and science because I had such an interest in those subjects. One of them claimed to have been a student of the great physicist, Sommerfeld. The best tutors in the humanities that my aunt could find were also engaged to round out my secondary education."

"It's amazing how much they could teach you, our best students in this country don't know a fraction of what you did when you apply to college."

"I guess I paid better attention to my lessons than they did. But, enough about me, tell me, Henry, about your family and where they came from."

"Well, since you started with your ancestors I will start with mine. I am a descendant of Lope de Vega, the founder of the National Spanish theater. They say that he wrote more than two thousand comedies. Some of his descendants emigrated to California many generations ago and I'm the result of that emigration."

Walking with Henry slowly down the street, the light evening breeze blowing gently on her cheeks had placed Lola in a carefree mood. The sounds of the graduation party were fading in the distance, and the pleasant conversation was creating a special ambiance; she was enjoying the pleasure of his company. It all gave her a feeling of contentment that she had never felt in the other reality.

Walking back to her house, he paused and asked if she liked the works of Cervantes, the famous author of "Don Quijote de la Mancha."

"Of course I like Miguel de Cervantes Saavedra. He is my favorite Spanish author."

"That being the case, would you like to attend a summer stock performance of Don Quijote with me? It's playing at the NMSU Theater for the performing arts, the last Saturday of June."

That offer took Lola by surprise; she could not believe he was asking her for a date. She wondered if she had misunderstood.

"You mean you want to take me to see that performance of Don Quijote?" Lola asked, still not sure of his intentions and still mystified by the request.

"Yes, I cannot think of anyone else with which I would rather go to the theater. Will you go with me?"

Lola thought for a minute: *My god, my mother was right he does want to date me.*

"Yes, I think I would like that."

"Thank you, beautiful lady. I'll pick you up at your apartment in Las Cruces at six that Saturday evening. We'll have dinner first and then go to the theater. The performance starts at eight."

"That sounds like fun, Henry, I'll be delighted to go with you."

They walked a few steps farther and stopped. He turned toward her and gazed deeply into her eyes. In the dim light of the street lamp her beautiful dark eyes shown like sparkling onyxes, they enraptured him. The black top and bottom eyelashes encased her dark eyes, beautifully, giving them a certain unforgettable allure. Her delicately rounded chin, graceful face and light olive skin were reminiscent of the fine Spanish ladies he saw when he was in Spain.

Looking up at him, Lola felt entranced by his dark, blue eyes. That classic look of a Spanish gentleman made her knees feel weak. She thought: *What is the matter with me? I never felt like this before, maybe there is something in the air in this reality that doesn't exist in mine.*

As she looked into his dark, blue eyes she felt herself drawn to him; then suddenly she was in his arms and he was kissing her, passionately. He pulled back, slowly, looking deeply into her eyes. Then, feeling his lips brush softly against her cheek caused her heart to beat more rapidly in anticipation of his next kiss. She could smell his aftershave as it blended with his clean, manly scent. This combined with the pleasant sensation of his kisses, as his lips gently pressed against hers, made her return them, ardently. These were simple joys that she never knew in her world. Finally, these beautiful caresses ended and they began walking slowly, hand in hand, toward her house. Reaching the Gonzalez dwelling, she kissed him again, recapturing, briefly, the feelings she had just experienced.

As the party wound down and guest began to leave, Henry thanked Lola's parents for inviting him to the party and bid them farewell. Lola accompanied him to his car and he held her hand as they walked and chatted. After opening the car door, he kissed her fondly on the cheek, and said he was looking forward to the pleasure of her company in late June. After Henry had driven off, Lola turned and saw her mother standing on the front porch. She had been watching her with a sly smile on her face that seemed to say, I told you so.

"All right, Mom, you were right. He is interested in me."

"Has he asked you out?"

"Yes, he's taking me to see a play in late June."

Before her mother could ask more questions, other guests began coming up to her and thanking her for inviting them to Lola's party. A little later Lola herself decided leave. She wanted to get back to her apartment in Las Cruces because she had to be at the laboratory early the next morning for an important staff meeting. She thanked her parents for the wonderful party they had given her and then kissed them and each of her siblings, goodbye. Seeing her family waving to her from the porch made her feel a little depressed and guilty for leaving them, especially after they had given her that wonderful party. She now knew what it was like to feel the love of a wonderful family. It was a comfort and a reassurance denied her in the Fated Reality.

Driving back to Las Cruces, Lola began to think about the intimate moment she had shared with Henry. She wondered if meeting a man like Henry in the other reality would have ever been possible. She had a few short relationships in that world, but they never amounted to anything. She was so consumed by the defense effort that romance never seemed to be on her agenda. She had reached forty-six years of age in the other world without being romantically intimate with anyone. All she experienced were some quick college affairs that she chalked up to spontaneous lust. Back then; she recalled thinking that she was never going to find anyone working in that hole in the ground where the Chronometry Lab was located. Even if she did, she could not get involved because she was absorbed, completely, with the Time Crease Project. Even now, her sense of duty was preventing her from thinking that anything could develop between her and Henry. Yet, down deep she wished it would.

Picking her up promptly at six, Henry took Lola to dinner at the La Postita, an excellent Mexican restaurant right there in Las Cruces. He told her he knew she had plenty of Mexican food at home but the chef made a few specialties that he wanted her to try. When they arrived at the restaurant, everyone seemed to know Henry, the chef, the management and all the waiters. The chef made them a dinner fit for royalty and the waiters fussed over them. Eating dinner while a guitarist played softly, created a unique ambiance that Lola thoroughly enjoyed. Later Henry confessed that the restaurant had made a special effort because its owners were friends of his family in California.

The summer stock performance of Don Quijote at the NMSU Theater was excellent. Lola enjoyed both the way they did the play and the musical scores that accompanied the performances. During intermission, Lola and Henry somehow got into a discussion on the correct spelling of Mexico.

"As I recall 'Mexico' is and always has been spelled 'México', my little linguistic expert," Henry informed Lola, thinking he finally found something she misunderstood.

"My dear Professor, you are only partially correct."

"Partially?"

"It depends upon where you're from."

She had that sly, but innocent look on her face; he knew she was trying to slip out of the slight misunderstanding she had been embracing. But, damn it, he was right and he was going to make her admit it.

"My dear beautiful lady, I'm afraid you are laboring under a misconception. 'México' is the correct spelling of Mexico no matter where you're from. Now just admit it so we can continue with our discussion of Cervantes' 'novelas ejemplares' and in particular 'La ilustre fregona.'"

Lola thought for a moment before answering: *Maybe I should just stand corrected and gracefully admit to a misconception. But, I love him dearly and taking that out, just to placate him, would be unfair to both of us. He is so very clever in his engineering field but his understanding of Old Spanish spellings leaves something to be desired. I don't want to hurt his feelings, so I better be careful how I phrase my response.*

"I would like nothing better than to discuss that short story, but first, could you indulge me a little further on the spelling of Mexico and perhaps correct my misconception?"

"Sure, I would be happy to," Henry responded to her request. He would correct her very gently since it was obvious she was trying to concede the argument to him.

"When I was studying in Spain they taught me that 'México' is the Old Spanish spelling that is preferred America, but in Spain the correct modern spelling is 'Mejico'. Have I misunderstood that lesson, my dear professor?"

Henry thought for a moment as he looked deeply into her big, beautiful dark eyes that were waiting patiently for his answer. Thinking: *This brilliant little thing has turned what may be, on the surface, an obvious misconception on her part, into my misconception, leaving me in a corner that only an apology could get me out of.*

"Come here, my little linguistic expert, and let me apologize for being so adamant. Now, I realize, it was I who should stand corrected."

Henry kissed her on the forehead, then took her by the arm and escorted her back to their seats to see the rest of the play.

On the way home Lola learned that Henry was a CALTECH graduate, and had completed his education in 1974. He had been at NMSU ever since, and became the head of the Electrical Engineering Department in 1982. As he drove, she looked at him pensively and wondered why this handsome professor wanted to date a twenty-four-year-old woman like her. There must be dozens of attractive women who wanted him. She then thought about how much she was attracted to him, perhaps too much, she was here on a mission and romance was not permitted. She had heard at the lab that Henry had brought a summer stock actress to some faculty parties. He liked that actress, they told her, because she had a level of maturity he valued in women.

During their conversation, she asked him if he felt uncomfortable about their age difference. She knew she should not ask such things on a first date, but the tone of the conversation prompted her to ask that question.

"No, I'm very comfortable with you because you're more mature and intelligent than anyone I know. Why do you ask?"

Well, at least he's not concerned about my age, she thought.

"Oh, some people at the lab remarked that they thought you liked older women, and if that were true, I wondered why me, I'm only twenty-four."

After her brief response he was silent the rest of the way home. He kissed her on the cheek when he dropped her off at her apartment and made no promises about when he would call her again. Lola surmised that he probably thought her question about their age difference was a bit childish. Maybe he would never call her again, especially, after the way she informed him about the different spellings of Mexico. *My god,* she thought, *I'm so inept at dating etiquette that, perhaps, it would be better for both of us if he didn't pursue me.*

Contrary to how she thought he felt after their first date ended, he dated her often that summer. He took her to various summer stock shows, and they dined at popular restaurants in Las Cruces and El Paso. She had never been on such wonderful dates; her head was spinning with him treating her as if she was some kind of important celebrity. The dates she had in the other reality were not anything like the ones with Henry. Even her parents were pleased she was dating Henry. She was not sure whether it was because they liked his ethnic background, or they were pleased that she had found someone that was intellectually compatible. However, their reasons for liking Henry did not concern her, she was just happy to be pleasing them for all the help they had given her.

Their romance took on a more serious nature in mid September, when Henry decided to attend a symposium in Los Angeles at which Lola was giving a paper. This was a prestigious event, and almost everyone she knew, from the Electrical Engineering Department, would be there. When she arrived at the Hilton hotel in Los Angles that Saturday in September, she found her Lab had reserved a block of rooms at the hotel for its attendees. The Lab administrator never consulted her, just took it for granted that she would accept whatever was available at the group rate. For department heads, however, the administrator reserved large separate suites on the first floor that had bars and small conference tables in them. In these rooms, they each could have private meetings, as required, with company and government representatives that were their benefactors. They booked Henry, because of his rank, in such a suite.

The hotel was at an ideal location in LA and in the afternoon, a group from the lab, including Lola, went on a sight seeing tour. Henry begged off going with them. He told Lola his family was from the LA area and he was quite familiar with what the tour had to offer. He said he needed the time to tend to a more pressing matter. Actually, he wanted to shop for a new sport jacket, because his suit jacket ripped when it somehow caught in the elevator door. As a result, he now was stuck trying to match a jacket to his suit pants. Perhaps, he should have brought a spare suit with him but he hated to travel with more things than he needed. He rushed from store to store in downtown LA trying to find an appropriate jacket because later that evening he was attending the symposium banquet with Lola. He certainly did not want to explain this silly dilemma to her or anyone else. He began to wonder if all the silly accidents he was having, lately, were in someway related to Lola. Was he falling in love with her?

It was about eleven in the evening and the crowd at the symposium banquet was beginning to thin out. Lola and Henry walked out of the hotel onto the Boulevard and heard the sounds of a big band coming from a nearby nightclub. Lola had seen the billboard advertisements, while on the tour she had taken that afternoon, touting the big band music. Now, hearing that sound made her want to stop by the nightclub and listen to the band play those old Latin melodies. The music reminded her so much of the other reality that she coaxed Henry into taking her to see the last show.

About halfway through the show the band took a break and its leader came over to their table. He knew Henry and asked if he could buy some stock in the Mexican restaurant chain that his family owned. The remark astonished Lola.

"Oh, Professor Vega has an avocation, isn't that interesting. You never told me that. Now, I understand why we received the royal treatment at the La Postita," Lola remarked, teasing Henry.

"Lola, I didn't tell you because I didn't think a food chain would be of interest to a woman with your scientific bent."

"It's not," Lola replied. She was smiling because, she thought, the food chain was probably a single Mexican restaurant in downtown LA and his people were acquaintances of the La Postita's proprietors."

When they got back to the hotel, Henry asked Lola if she would like to stop by his suite for a nightcap. Lola thought for a few moments and then accepted his offer. She felt that a pleasant conversation over a drink with Henry might be a delightful way to end the evening. Entering his room, Henry offered her a seat on the sofa that was in sitting room area of the suite. He excused himself and then made them each a drink at the bar in the corner of the room. She watched him as he dexterously mixed the drinks and thought: *He certainly knows how to do that, if I didn't know better I might think he was a bartender.* When he finished, he turned and walked to where she was sitting, smiled and handed her a Margarita, which he knew she liked. Then raised his glass and said.

"I would like to drink a toast to the most beautiful and intelligent lady ever to grace the halls of science."

"Winning a beauty contest in the halls of science isn't much of an achievement, but I guess I can drink to that," Lola quickly remarked, facetiously.

"I didn't mean it that way. Perhaps, I should have used 'person' instead of 'lady.'"

Henry amused Lola by the way he clarified his words when he thought she was taking something the wrong way. She wondered why he did that; he was usually very careful in selecting his words when he was using them to describe his scientific findings. Here in this romantic ambience he was clarifying them even when she responded jokingly. Now, she noted that his response even needed more clarification.

As they sat on the sofa sipping their drinks, Henry realized he had offered a rather dull or even insulting toast and was beginning to feel embarrassed. Looking at her sitting next to him fiddling with the drink, he began to realize that he should say something. Otherwise, she would excuse herself and go back to her room. He was usually quite capable with the ladies but this one was having such a disarming effect on him that he was now cringing over his behavior. First, he ripped his jacket and now he was at a loss for words. Was it her intelligence, her clever responses or was he simply falling in love with her and unable to get his thoughts straight?

Seeing he was in deep thought and thinking she had offended him with that "beauty contest" remark, she decided to offer a toast of her own.

"Here's to the man that I'm so impressed with that I become flustered at the sight of him. When I'm in his presence, I sometime act like as a silly college freshman dating the school's heartthrob. Henry, please excuse my silly 'beauty contest' remark. I know you were trying to pay me a compliment and I responded, whimsically.

"No need to apologize, it was I that made that made that rather dull toast and you simply pointed out that it was flawed."

With those sentiments expressed, the tension between them relaxed. They put down their drinks and moved closer together on the sofa. After staring into each other's eyes for a few minutes, he impulsively took her in his arms and kissed her. She was a little startled by the suddenness of his embrace, but it stirred something inside her and she fervently returned his kiss. Her passion rose, steadily, as he began kissing her on her forehead, face and neck. He slowly progressed toward her lips, making her wait for him to kiss her again. Then, when she couldn't wait any longer, he sole-kissed her with such passion that she could feel the sensation down to her toes. Her pulse quickened as he began kissing down her neck, and then reaching behind her, he unzipped her dress in the back. She stood up, twisted a bit and let it fall silently to the floor. Suddenly, in heated desire, she removed his tie, unbuttoned his shirt, and began kissing his neck and chest. Then becoming aware of her actions, she thought: *What the hell has gotten into me? I'm here on a mission not a romantic interlude.* However, she quickly forgot that thought as he pulled her to him and kissed her. He then kicked off his shoes and removed his pants. A few moments later, she eagerly helped him remove his undershirt.

Carrying her to the bed and laying her down, he slipped off her shoes. Then, reached under her and gently pulled off her panty hose, kissing her legs as he removed them. Strange he would do that, she thought, having never experienced anything as exciting in the other reality. However, she soon forgot the other reality and thought only about him as he began to make love to her. He removed her bra, and brushed his lips lightly over her nipples. Then, he stopped to kiss each tenderly as she groaned with delight. This intimate caressing caused a beautiful sensation in her that she had never experienced in the other world. Then, overcome with desire; he rose, quickly, removing his briefs as she watched, wide-eyed.

The appearance of his erected manhood startled her. She sat there feeling still little anxious, wondering if he could really put all that in her. She had never let him go this far before and all sorts of thoughts raced through her mind. She had no practical experience with female contraceptives and it made her very apprehensive, but she did not really want to stop him. He saw the concerned look appear on her face and surmised what was troubling her. He reached into the pocket of his pants that were now lying on the floor, quickly removed a condom, and rolled it on. He could see the relief come over her face. They embraced passionately and quickly took up where they had left off a few moments ago. All she asked was that he be gentle because she had not much experience and was still a little uneasy. Soon, all she could think of was how much she wanted him as he pushed slowly into her. Aching with pleasure as the rhythm of his thrusting reached its peak, she began clutching at his back and kissing his face. Then, she seemed to be floating in space for an indefinite amount of time, enjoying the pleasures this beautiful act of love afforded.

Soon they began to drift slowly back to the real world. Henry lay exhausted, dosing off beside her. Many thoughts were passing through her mind. She had been seduced, and had finally taken by a real man. Moreover, it sure seemed worth it. Then her thoughts came around to her mission and her team leader. Laura was such a taskmaster. She certainly would not approve of this kind of behavior, especially on a mission as serious as theirs. Then, she thought, she was under no obligation to discuss her personal behavior with Laura, if it did not compromise their mission. So, she snuggled closer to Henry and fell asleep.

At breakfast, Lola and Henry were enjoying a pleasant conversation when a suggestion Henry made took Lola completely by surprise.

"Lola, honey, I've been thinking, this may be a good time for you to meet my family. We're in LA and they have a home nearby."

That suggestion concerned Lola, she thought: *He wants to take me to meet his parents, and I'm not prepared for that. Meeting parents is serious business for Hispanic people; I'm not free to take that step. This whole thing is moving too fast and I had better slow it down.*

"Henry, it's not a good time for me, I have to prepare for the paper I'm giving at the symposium tomorrow."

"Nonsense, you know that material cold and don't need any more preparation. Besides, I want them to meet the most beautiful, intelligent woman I had the good fortune to find and fall in love with."

That statement really upset her, she was falling in love with him, too. However, everything was wrong; she was in this reality for a reason. This was a conflict of interest. She had always performed her duty, and never let personal feelings distract her. The team leader would tell her to get rid of him, now, but how could she do that; she loved him.

"Lola, you looked so troubled. Perhaps, I have misjudged your feelings for me. Maybe we should take things a bit slower."

He had given her a polite way out, he is so kind and clever, she thought. The hurt look on his face showed the disappointment he was feeling and she would not disappoint him, mission or no mission.

"Oh, darling, it's not that, I do love you, but I have some very deep concerns. Of course, I do want to meet your family."

"Don't be concerned, I know they will like you. We'll take a ride over there this afternoon."

Lola knew meeting his family was taking their relationship to the next level and further knew that getting this involved when Laura was depending on her was not wise. In spite of that knowledge, she accepted his invitation to meet his family.

Driving west on Santa Monica Boulevard, Lola noticed Henry was turning on the road to Beverly Hills. As he drove, she noticed beautiful homes began to dot the landscape. She wondered if his parents could own one of those homes. The farther they drove the bigger the homes got and soon turned into estates. As Henry turned into a side road, she noticed the street sign said, "Casa de Vega Road." After driving a bit farther, she saw a huge mansion rising in the background just around the bend. Approaching the mansion, Lola thought: *Could that place possibly belong to his parents? Maybe his parents work for the people that own it and live in a caretaker's cottage outback.* When they reached the mansion and stopped, she began to realize that his family must live there and must be extremely rich. The remark the bandleader made last night about his parents owning a chain of restaurants, she now realized, was most likely true. Getting out of the car, Lola stared wide-eyed at the beautiful home. When they rang the bell, the huge Spanish doors opened and a servant greeted them.

"It's don Enriqué," the maid said, as she hugged him and then ran to tell his parents.

When his parents came into the vestibule, they greeted their son warmly, but it surprised them to see the young lady standing beside him. Henry had never brought a woman home before and her presence stirred their curiosity.

"Mother and Father. This is my friend and colleague Dr. Lola Gonzalez. Lola, these are my parents, Maruja and Ramón Vega."

After the introductions, they all went into the large, exquisitely furnished living room. The wide-eyed Lola began taking in the room's elegant décor and the beautiful paintings on the walls. The thick blue rug muffled the sound of their footsteps as his mother guided them to a stylish, off-white sofa near the fireplace. Henry's parents had not seen him for a year and had many things about which they wanted to talk. While Henry and his father went into the library to discuss some urgent family business, his mother remained to speak with Lola.

During their conversation, his mother switched from English to Spanish. Affluent Hispanics sometimes did that to find out from what social class one's family was. Lola surmised this to be the case and spoke with a Castilian accent like her aunt's, who, in the other reality, had lived in Spain. She figured it would re-enforce what she had told Henry about her education in Europe and be least likely to lead to any discrepancies in her cover story. Concluding her conversation with Senora Vega, after Henry and his father returned, Lola was not sure what impression she had made on his mother. Although his mother was cordial, she projected a certain air of coolness during their conversation. Maybe, it was a natural part of the woman's demeanor, she thought.

Senorita Gonzalez's elegant Spanish astonished his mother, and, when Lola had gone to the powder room during dinner, she questioned Henry about it.

"Henry, you say she is from Alamogordo, but her Spanish sounds like she comes from Spain and in fact she sounds like a Spanish aristocrat when she speaks. I fear she hasn't been telling you the truth," his mother said, concerned some kind of ruse was being perpetrated upon her son.

"What your mother is saying is that maybe she found out about our financial status and your inheritance, and is really some kind of gold digger from Spain. You've heard how the Old Spanish aristocracy needs a new infusion of cash."

Those remarks by his parents caused Henry to burst into laughter.

"Mother, of course she speaks that way, the finest tutors in Europe educated her. As a teen, she was a companion to a rich aunt who lived in Spain and had seen to her education. I've known her for years and she's the brightest person I ever met. I've met her family and they're quite down to earth. Mother and father, I'm in love with her and want to marry her, someday. So, please don't accuse her of being a gold digger or anything else."

Henry told his parents how clever she really was, and how she, effortlessly, completed the requirements for her doctorate. He told them that she had no interest in their money and was only interested in science, like he was.

Returning to the dinner table, Lola found that the somber mood of his parents had shifted to one of congeniality. When asked about her ancestry, she told them that she was a descendant of General Zaragoza. They were not too interested in her Mexican history, because they knew she could have easily found that in a book. They wanted to make certain she was what she claimed to be, without antagonizing their son. They questioned her in depth about the time she spent in Europe. In particular, about France and the time she had spent there with her aunt. She responded with vivid descriptions of Paris and her aunt's home there.

His mother still was not satisfied and she asked her to tell them something about the place in Spain where she had lived with her aunt. Even Henry was interested in hearing that, and Lola felt it would be better telling them something in detail than speaking in generalities. Because generalities at this point could even make Henry question the cover story, she had given him. With her unique mind, she could recall perfectly her aunt's descriptions of the events that had occurred in Madrid, Spain; so, she decided to give the Vega's the benefit of the knowledge she had obtained in the other reality.

"Let me see. I was my aunt's companion at the time and living with her in Madrid. An interesting event occurred when I was there. They hold a celebration called a Verbena, which is a festival in honor of a virgin or a saint. We lived in the district of Chamberí on Fuencarral Street. It was the custom for each district in Madrid to hold a Verbena at a different time of the year. My aunt's name is Carmen and we celebrated, enthusiastically, her namesake's Verbena. They held Our Lady of the Carmen Verbena on the sixteenth of July, and the festivities of that day are vividly etched in my mind."

Lola vibrantly described the festivities that she said she recalled. Upon finishing her description of the way they celebrated a saint's day in Spain, Henry's parents thanked her for sharing those memories with them. They later told Henry that they were extremely pleased he had brought home such a fine young woman and told Lola they would like to meet her parents someday.

While driving back to the hotel, Henry discussed his parent's impressions of her.

"You know, Lola. You really amazed them with your description of that festivity. Do you know what they thought when they heard you speak Spanish?"

"That I was being a snob? My mother says, 'Stop speaking like that, you sound like a Hispanic snob, speak our Spanish'."

"No, they thought you were a gold digger from Spain who was after our money."

"See, they caught onto me and you didn't," Lola responded, causing him to burst into laughter.

Examining the job offers on her desk at the Electro Lab in Las Cruces, Lola found the one for which she was searching. Actually, it was an invitation to interview at the Lawrence Livermore National Laboratory, in Livermore California. She had been waiting for that invitation before she went to the symposium in LA, but it was the first part of November before it finally arrived. According to her team leader, this opportunity would allow them to achieve their goal. Laura had been working there since she got her PHD in Physics, a year and a half ago. She claimed that she had found the ideal project under which to accomplish their mission. The time had come for them to combine forces and carry out their plan to save the Fated Reality from self-destruction.

The required technology to accomplish their task was now available and Laura had found the ideal place to do the work. It would soon be 1989 and Laura wanted to get started because it would take a few years to design and build the necessary equipment. Through their phone conversations, they managed to come up with the rudiments of a plan to accomplish their goal, but now needed to be together to carry out their ideas. These thoughts went through Lola's mind as she studied the letter from Lawrence Livermore National Laboratories. She then placed a call to the National Labs' personnel office and arranged to interview with Dr. Claremont on the first Monday in December. As she was completing the call, Henry Vega walked into her office.

"Lola, I could not help overhearing you make a date to interview at

Lawrence Livermore Labs with Laura Claremont. She's the one who has been writing those papers in solid-state physics and microchip technology. What possible interest could you have in working with her? You're working in the generation of huge electromagnetic fields," Henry asked, confused by Lola's interest in working with that woman.

"I have been reading her papers, too. She contacted me when she read that paper I presented at the Electrodynamics Symposium last September. She has a project at her Laboratory that needs my expertise and is willing to pay handsomely for it. She is the leading expert in her field. I felt it wouldn't hurt to go out there and find out what she has in mind before I decide where I want to work next."

"But, I thought you were going to accept our offer and work here with us?" Henry asked, disappointed that she would even consider leaving the Electro Lab. He was also concerned about the impact such a move would have on their relationship.

"Henry, don't worry, I just want to hear what she has to say."

Lola knew she was just stalling, but could not bear to tell him she was already committed to working with Laura and the interview was just a formality.

Chapter 7

Settling back in her seat, as the plane reached its cruising altitude, Laura began to thumb through a magazine left in the forward seat pocket. A picture in the magazine, showing two earths, one in a vivid rosy color and the other in dull gray, caught her attention. Ignoring the captions under the globes, the picture seemed to highlight the contrast between the Alternative and Fated realities. Staring at the rosy red one, for a minute or so, started her thinking about her life in the Alternate reality. It was going to be a boring five-hour flight to the East Coast, and a review of the many tasks still on her agenda seemed like a good way to occupy the time. In spite of her efforts to review and organize her thoughts, her mind kept returning to Kurt Peyser. The remaining tasks and the interview she would conduct with Lola after the Thanksgiving weekend soon receded in her mind. Instead, she began daydreaming about events that had occurred over the past few years. The muffled drone of the plane's engines caused Laura to return in her reverie to a party her family gave her.

After she graduated from MIT with a PHD in Physics, her parents gave her a graduation party she would never forget. They had invited dozens of relatives and friends. They even invited relatives from Trois Rivieres in the Province of Québec, Canada. Relaxing in her seat on the plane, as it cruised at thirty five thousand feet, she began to recall that memorable party. She had just arrived in Bloomfield after the four and a half hour drive from Massachusetts. Her car was pulling a trailer loaded with the things from her apartment in Cambridge. A big sign hung over the front door of her parent's home, which read, "Congratulations, Dr. Laura Claremont."

As she opened the front door, dozens of people in her parent's living and dining rooms were yelling congratulations. They had removed and replaced most of the furniture with folding chairs. People began surrounding her, hugging her, kissing her and shaking her hand. She was quite overwhelmed and tears of joy appeared in her eyes. Never in the other reality had they showed so much affection and adulation. In that drab, crisis-driven world, they expected and almost never applauded her achievements.

Through the crowd that surrounded her, she caught a glimpse of her old professor, Kurt Peyser, the man she left behind. It was a wonderful surprise and gave her an opportunity to apologize for not trying to contact him. Even after three years, she could not forget him and had wished they had never parted. She wondered, how he came to be here, he seemed out of place with the people around him. Then she realized her mother must have called him. Her mother said, he would call from time to time and ask about her progress. Then someone shouted something in French to her, and she responded, but could not take her eyes off Kurt. Greeting guests and exchanging light conversation with people she had not seen in years, she gradually worked her way through the crowd to where Kurt was standing.

"Congratulations, Dr. Claremont, I applaud you for your accomplishments," Kurt said, rather formally.

Laura could see he was cool and formal in congratulating her. She could tell he had not forgiven her for leaving him and going to Massachusetts. The crowd was going into the backyard, where her father had setup a bar. Her mother, with the help of her sisters from Trois Rivieres, made a buffet laden with French Canadian dishes on a table near the bar. Laura grabbed Kurt's arm and tugged on it, suggesting she wanted him to wait until the rest of the people went into the backyard. When the last of the guests left, she looked deeply into his eyes and spoke in low tones.

"Is that anyway to greet your old girlfriend?"

He was a surprise by that remark. But, it wasn't long before he took her into his arms and kissed her.

"That's better. Come on, let's go into the living room and talk a bit," she responded, seeing he had relaxed a little.

He thought: *She's gone for three years and now acts as if we hadn't seen each other for three weeks. She tore my heart out and now wants to sit and have a pleasant chat.* With those thoughts still on his mind, he followed her into the living room and sat on the sofa with her. He wondered whether coming here had been wise, but when her mother called, he had accepted the invitation because he wanted to see her one more time. However, seeing her now, beautiful as ever, made him realize he had not gotten over her.

"Kurt, I want to apologize for cutting off our relationship three years ago. You were absolutely right, I was obsessed with my ambition and it was destroying us. However, you were wrong when you thought I didn't love you enough to make even the slightest compromise. These years apart gave me a lot of time to think about our relationship. I realize now that I loved you back then and still do. I want you to know that and I want to know, if there is a chance for us to get back together?"

He thought: *Laura never changes, she always says exactly what is on her mind; she is a much-focused scientist and, as such, is very blunt. Oh, what the hell. That's what attracted me to her in the first place.*

"Laura, I also loved you back then but that didn't matter to you, what's changed? I'll bet you still have another agenda."

"I have. Nevertheless, I really want us to try again. However, I guess I must tell you the downside. I got myself wrapped up in something and I cannot get out of it."

"There was something always hanging over our heads back then and now you're still not going to tell me what it is, are you? Why can't you tell me what you're involved in? Does it involve another man?"

"No, of course not. I have to work this thing out for myself, you must trust me, if you still love me."

She could see from the look on his face that the "trust me" answers to his questions were not going to fly. She certainly was not going to tell him about the Fated Reality, he would think she had taken leave of her senses. No, he was not ready for the truth at this time. If she still wanted him, and she did, she must come up with something more plausible than the truth. Thinking for a moment, she thought, a partial truth would better serve her purpose and perhaps alleviate his concerns.

"Kurt, I can see that the 'trust me' answers aren't very satisfying. So, I'm going to tell you something that you can't repeat to anyone, not even my parents."

"Are you in some kind of trouble?"

"No, it's not what your thinking, it concerns national security. While doing my research at MIT, I got involved with a highly classified program. The Lawrence Livermore National Laboratory in California sponsored it. In short, they made me an offer and I agreed to start working there in September."

"That story is certainly short, if you expect me to trust you, you must tell me more than just that. I read your papers on microchip technology and they weren't classified. Was that what you were working on?"

"You read the 'white world' portion of my work."

"White world? I don't understand."

"Oh, Kurt, it's like Pandora's box once you start pulling things out you can't stop."

"Laura, if you want me to trust you, you have to explain at least something about what you're dealing with, even if you can't go into details."

"In the federal budget there are line items defining the procurement of weapon systems and associated research. Those programs, whose names appear in the national budget, are considered 'white world' programs because their names are public knowledge, although they may have classified parts. There are programs, however, that are so secret that their names don't appear in the federal budget. They call them 'black world' projects."

"My god that is heavy stuff. Where does the money come from for those projects?"

"It comes from secret funds that are kept out of the public's eye for national security reasons. Now Kurt, please let's get off the subject because I can't tell you any more without breaking the law."

All that Laura told him about the black and white worlds was the truth but she left out many details.

"I think I'm beginning to understand your reason for being so evasive, but I want you to think carefully about what you're doing. You're a brilliant young person, and I can see why the government wants you involved in their clandestine projects. However, remember one thing, most of the scientists that worked on the atomic bomb regretted letting that genie out of the bottle. Maybe you should get out now before you regret it, too. Why don't you just chuck it all in and come teach at Rutgers with me? I'm sure you will enjoy working in the carefree 'white world' as you call it."

"Kurt, if you only knew how much I want to do that. Maybe someday I will."

The thought of how the government was using this brilliant young woman in the so-called "black world" angered him. Somehow, he would get her out of her commitment, he did not know how or when, but he would do it.

Rather than continuing the cover story, Laura decided to change the subject.

"Kurt, we have a lot to catch up on but first let's go out back and join the party; I'm starved and I would like you to sample some French Canadian cuisine my mother and her sisters from Canada have prepared. Let's see if our dishes are similar to your family's."

Laura knew he was of Belgium decent. He had told her once that his family spoke French and had made some traditional French dishes.

When they got in the backyard, she took him to the buffet table.

"Kurt, try some of this Quiche lorraine a la canadienne and some of that Quiche aux poireaux and tell me if your mother made anything like that.

Kurt said his mother made something like the Quiche lorraine a la canadienne but not the Quiche aux poireaux.

After guests had consumed most of the food on the buffet table, and the beer and wine had cleared their throats, music and singing broke out. As the party reached its height of jubilation and the guests made toasts to Laura's achievements, her relatives dragged Kurt in to help sing several choruses of Alouette. The lead singer made up funny little verses, with sexual nuances, about her and him in French.

After many of verses of Alouette and other French merrymaking songs, the party finally ended and Laura walked Kurt to his car. Pausing for a moment along the way, they stopped and gazed into each other's eyes. She suddenly reached up, put her arms around his neck, and kissed him passionately. He thought: *I shouldn't let her do that to me after the way she just cut off our relationship three years ago. But, gee it felt so good and I haven't been kissed like that since she left for MIT. I guess a fool never learns.*

She kissed him again in the dim moonlight, this time he put his arms around her and kissed her back as she pressed against him in an intimate embrace. Oh, she thought: *God help me, I still love him, but I'm afraid to let this go on because my mission will only get in the way. Maybe it doesn't have to get in the way; maybe I can somehow compete the mission and still not lose him.* She did not know how she could achieve such conflicting goals, but thought it was at least possible. However, if she was to succeed, she must start by getting him back right now.

"Kurt, honey, I still love you, and always have. I thought of you often in the last three years. I know I hurt you, but you did come to my doctoral celebration and I know you still care. Now that we found each other, again, I never want to lose you."

"Laura, don't say those things to me if you don't really mean them. I could not take another rejection."

Laura kissed him again, long and lovingly.

"Kurt, I mean everything I say, but I beg of you to bear with me while I finish my research for the government."

"How long will that take? Don't you have to live in Livermore, California to do that?"

"Kurt, I won't lie to you, it might take a few years and, yes, I do have to live in California. Nevertheless, I must fly back to New York for meetings at Brookhaven every month, so we could see each other quite often."

While they walked the rest of the way back to his car, Kurt's resistance was crumbling. He started to warm up to the idea of them getting back together again, even if she was still putting conditions on it. Why did he come here, anyway, if he was not seeking a reconciliation of some kind? Damn it, he still loved her.

"You know that it's only nine o'clock. Would you like to drive to Glen Ridge and see the house I bought, it has a great view over looking a country club?"

"How far is that from here?"

"It's only five miles off Bloomfield Avenue, it will take only ten minutes or so to get there, come on."

"OK, but I'll have to tell my parents I'm going with you."

She ran back to the house, and told her mother she was going for a ride with Kurt and not to wait up for her.

Pulling in Kurt's driveway, Laura thought: *It's a quaint little house, just right for a college professor.* Getting out of the car, she could see, even in the dim moonlight, that the house was actually larger than most in that neighborhood and even bigger than her parents' home. When they got inside Kurt fixed them some drinks. Then, took Laura out back on the deck and showed her the view. She could not see much in the pale moonlight, but imagined that the home did have a pleasing view over looking the abutting golf course. The air was faintly fragrant with the smell of nearby spring flowers, and the dim moonlight was casting its magic spell. Soon, the couple began to embrace each other. However, before they could sit on a glider Kurt had placed on the deck, intruders began invading this cozy setting. It was as if the Jersey mosquitoes wanted this secluded place for themselves.

"Kurt, these pests are going to eat us alive, let's go back in."

"Damn it. Why don't they spray around here? I guess I have to have this deck screened in. Come, let's take our drinks and go inside."

Getting back inside Kurt suggested that Laura wait in the living room while he refreshed their drinks. A few minutes later, he returned and he saw Laura standing by the sofa studying a painting that was hanging on the wall. As he stood there with their drinks watching her, he found himself seduced, again, by her charms. Laura's blond hair, a little wind blown from the breeze on the deck, made her appear like a young woman he once saw in an automobile commercial. Her eyes seemed like deep blue pools of clear water, he felt like the proverbial moth drawn, hopelessly, to a flame. As she turned, she smiled at him and he put the drinks on the end table and took her into his arms. Looking down at her, her eyes closing, and her lips reaching up to his, made any thoughts of further discussion about his wounded pride irrelevant. Soon, they found themselves locked hopelessly in a passionate embrace, hugging and kissing each other. Long repressed feelings of desire stirred deep within her. He now felt certain that she meant what she had said before about still loving him; only a fool could miss the strong feelings that she so clearly transmitted with her kisses.

She thought: *This is moving too fast, I haven't had any sex in three years and I must not appear too anxious. Maybe, I should stop this, right now.* She decided she should act quickly on those thoughts. So, while catching their breath from their impassioned embrace, she asked him to show her his office and the rest of his house. The tour of the house ended in his bedroom; she noticed it had an early American-style, queen-size bed, matching chairs and dressers all in light maple. The wallpaper, drapes, and bedspread were well coordinated in shades of tan. She wondered who had done the interior decorating.

After discussing the print of a seascape that was hanging on the wall, they sat on a deacon's bench that was against the foot of the bed. He kissed her tenderly on her neck, on her cheeks, and then on her mouth. Those old feelings she had for him a few years ago, all came back and her desire mounted. A lustful longing filled her mind; she unbuttoned his shirt, then, kissed his neck and chest. He still had that athletic body, she thought, as she pulled his undershirt off. He finished the job and then took off his pants and shoes.

Laura felt a little guilty for letting things get this far, again. This was not the appropriate behavior of a team leader, she thought. Still, this reality was causing her to have these lapses of judgment and making her primal instincts dominate.

Before Laura realized it, she was sitting on the bed taking off her panty hose. Kurt stood in front of her and excitedly watched as she removed them. She then removed her bra, he knelt down to kiss her breasts and thought they were a little bigger than they were a few years ago, but still girlish looking. Her girlish figure had always excited him and it still did. When he stood up, she pulled down his briefs and helped remove them from his feet.

He pulled back the spread and sheet, and then he and Laura slipped under them, feeling their coolness pleasantly engulf their bodies. Kissing him tenderly as she climbed on top of him and she put her breasts into his face for him to kiss. Her playful teasing was more than he could stand. He slipped out and rolled on top of her in one continuous motion. She noticed he was fumbling excitedly and whispered to him.

"Take it easy, Kurt. I haven't done this in a long time."

"Don't worry, I'm not as inept as I look, just very eager."

When he got between her legs, he pushed in gently, thrusting very slowly at first. As the rhythm of his trusting increased, she felt that wonderful, tingling pleasure begin to mount. As the level of their mutual gratification reached its peak, Laura's hands were all over his back and she was hugging and squeezing him. Soon, her mouth pressed tightly against his in a long, ardent kiss that lasted throughout the period of ultimate pleasure.

Relaxing in each other's arms after they came down from those exalted heights, she realized how much she had missed the last three years. She had deprived herself of conjugal bliss with Kurt because of her dedication to the goals of her mission. Now, she was promising herself, never to let it happen again. Was she crazy? How could she accomplish her mission if she let this continue?

———————————

The plane suddenly hit turbulence over Michigan, jolting Laura out of her rumination. She was going to New York on business, but would stay in the metropolitan area for the Thanksgiving weekend. She would usually stay at Kurt's house when she came east on business; he would stay in her apartment when he went west on vacation or after attending some symposium in San Francisco. This had been going on for a year and a half and Laura thought it was a good holding pattern for their relationship, while she set the stage for accomplishing her mission. Working at Lawrence Livermore for the past year had given her the time to find the appropriate program. The program she had found would allow her to covertly mix mission tasks with program tasks. She was ready to bring Lola to the laboratory.

When the plane landed in New York Laura went directly to Brookhaven for a meeting and then spent the night on Long Island at a motel. The next morning she drove to Kurt's house in Glenn Ridge, New Jersey, after which she and Kurt drove to her parent's house for Thanksgiving dinner.

After dinner, while Laura was helping her mother in the kitchen, Kurt wandered in and her mother started asking questions about their relationship.

"The two of you have been seeing each other for five years. Isn't it about time you started thinking about getting married and settling down?" What kind of relationship is that, with you living on the West Coast and Kurt living here?"

Laura wished her mother had not started on that again. It was hard enough for her to keep Kurt in the holding pattern without her mother aggravating the situation. Kurt smiled, knowing her mother's questions were annoying Laura.

"Mother, we've been through this before, you know we have important business to attend to before we can settle down. Now, stop spoiling this perfect day and talk about something that is more interesting."

"What do you mean, 'we,' Mrs. Claremont? I will marry the lady anytime that she wishes. I don't have any business so important that it would stop me from marrying her," Kurt remarked, knowing his answer was putting Laura on the spot.

Laura was extremely angry; her mother was going to start an argument between her and Kurt, just when things were in a pleasant holding pattern.

"Kurt, would you mind going into the living room and talking to my father, I want to speak to my mother in private, please."

Kurt, went into the living room, smiling. He felt, maybe her mother could make her see that living on opposite coasts was highly undesirable, even on a short-term basis. Over time, it would be disastrous for them. He loved her, but he was caught hopelessly in this long distance romance. He hoped her mother would make her realize how foolish going on this way really was.

"Mother, stop prying into my personal life, I have important business that I can't just drop. I have other commitments that I must keep, and I'm trying to maintain the semblance of a relationship with Kurt, while I honor those

106

commitments. You know we separated once and you got us back together. I am eternally grateful for your help back then, but you are not helping me now. Please, let it be, before I lose him again."

"What is so important that you're willing to risk losing a man you apparently want?"

"Mother, it's a highly classified matter that concerns national defense and I cannot go into details."

"Good God, Laura, what have you gotten yourself into? Are you sure it's worth it?"

"I wonder myself, Mom, I really wonder if it's worth it."

When Laura and Kurt left her mother's house after Thanksgiving dinner, she assured Kurt she still loved him and wanted him. Because of what her mother kept bringing up about their getting married, she felt obligated to tell him that she could finally see a conclusion. She also decided to tell him she would be interviewing a person who is a national expert in an area that she needs to complete her project.

"Laura, would you mind telling me whom you're trying to hire?"

Laura felt to keep dodging his questions, even on scientific experts, would further strain their relationship. After all, he was also a prominent physicist. So, she decided to tell him whom she was going to interview.

"I'm going to be interviewing Dr. Lola Gonzalez, and it's very important that I hire her."

"Lola Gonzalez? Isn't she the one that's been writing those papers on generating huge electromagnetic fields?"

"Yes."

"Why the hell would you need her expertise, you're working in the solid state physics of microchips, aren't you?"

"I am usually, but the project I'm working badly needs her expertise. I can't say any more than that because the program is black."

Kurt let his next question drop because he could see her answers would soon cause her to violate the national security agreement she signed with the federal government. He was annoyed that the government would hide the research of this ingenious scientist and force her to keep silent, under the penalty of treason. He was further annoyed that they got people like her to work on their covert projects, by appealing to their sense of patriotism. However, he supposed, it was better than being forced to work on those type projects by some totalitarian government.

———————

Laura was in her office at the Lawrence Livermore National Laboratory when her secretary buzzed and informed her Dr. Gonzalez was here for her interview. Laura asked that she bring her in, immediately. When the secretary left the office the two women from the other reality embraced each other, warmly.

"Lola, you look so young and radiant, living in the southwest certainly has agreed with you."

"I guess I have to say the same about you, Team Leader. You know, Laura, I still can't get over how youthful we appear, coming to this reality has been like jumping into the fountain of youth. We could really enjoy it if we didn't have that problem still hanging over our heads."

After exchanging some generalities about their professional and private achievements in the Alternate Reality, they got down to business.

"Lola, I am the director of the HAVE-FIELD project, which is the white world code name for a black world program called RAVEN-EMP. We are investigating how to create devices that can generate large electromagnetic pulses of the size generated by nuclear explosions. I have created this project with full knowledge of its potential for our purposes. If designed properly, these devices can neutralize a nuclear missile threat by destroying its computer chips, without seriously damaging the population or any living organisms. The project has gotten the attention of the highest government officials, because it can potentially eliminate the third world nuclear threat without destroying its populations or contaminating its food supplies. Because of the impact the proposed devices would have on the world's balance of power, the government has given me a free hand to develop those devices."

"Laura, that is exciting. Even with the little information you have given me, I can already see avenues of research that may be fruitful in generating huge electromagnetic pulses. With the devices you refer to, we could design a special version of the Space-Time Transitional Synthesizer. With it, it seems possible that we could affect the balance of power in the Fated Reality. Laura, that set of devices could go a long way to help us achieve the goals of our mission."

"You're a quick study, Lola. Since you already see where I'm headed, I guess you can also see why we must start working together as soon as possible. I want to make you the Deputy Director of the HAVE-FIELD project, which, as I mentioned before, is the white world code name for the black world program, RAVEN-EMP."

"I understand, but before you continue, Team Leader, I have something to confess. I have done something that may make you less anxious to bring me on in that capacity. Perhaps even disqualify me from the mission."

"What the hell have you done that would disqualify you? Kill somebody? That's still not enough to disqualify you. Lola we are survivors of a nuclear war and like sisters, because we have the same kink in our DNA's. No matter what you have done I'm sure we can get you out of it."

"Laura, it's nothing like that. A man has come into my life and I'm in love with him. It has been tearing me apart. As you know, that behavior conflicts with our mission oath and is grounds for disqualification."

Laura looked at her second in command and smiled.

"Well, I guess I'll have to take it back. I can't get you out of falling in love. Lola, what have you told him about us?"

"Nothing, he would think I was insane."

"Lola, I'm going to confess something to you that you would eventually find out, anyway, by having to work as closely together as we must. A man has come into my life, also, and I fell in love with him, too."

Lola sat there for a few moments in shock and when she finally regained her composure, she said,

"Laura, you were always my role model in the other reality, with your impeccable discipline and uncompromising sense of duty. I guess this reality has made us weaker, hasn't it?"

"No, just more sensitive to feelings that they heavily repressed in the other reality. I've given this much thought and started figuring out a way to accomplish the mission and keep the wonderful guy I found. How about you, do you want to try it?"

A smile appeared on Lola's face as she realized she was not in this thing alone.

"Of course I do, but as you must know, this new objective further complicates things. And it's certainly not clear how we may accomplish it."

"Let us take it one step at a time and always work toward that goal."

The women shook hands on their new goal of permanently maintaining the relationships they had developed in this reality. At the same time, they resolved that they would accomplish the goals of their mission. Laura invited Lola out to dinner and they exchanged information on the men in their lives. They exchanged the names and addresses of the men so that in case something happened to one of them the other could call her man and offer a proper explanation. This way, they could cover for each other when difficult situations arose.

Henry Vega met Lola at the airport in El Paso when she flew back from California the second week in December of '89. Driving back to Las Cruces, Lola told him she had decided to take Dr. Claremont's job offer and move to Livermore, California.

"Why the hell do you want to work for the Lawrence Livermore National Laboratory?" Henry asked angrily.

"Henry, it is a considerable step up for me. She offered me a six-figure salary on top of it."

"If it's money you want, marry me, I'm a multi millionaire, remember?"

"Henry, it's not money I'm after. It's just something I have to do."

"How about us?"

"What about us? Nothing has changed; we still love each other, don't we? Besides, Laura told me I'll have to visit the Los Alamos National Laboratory every month on business so we can get together then."

"Los Alamos! That's where they do research on atomic weapons and make nuclear bombs, what the hell are you getting yourself into? How the hell did she convince you to take a job that involved that kind of research?"

Lola did not know what to say now and sat silently while Henry fumed over what he thought was a colossal mistake. She was trying to find just the right thing to say while waiting for him to calm down a bit. Finally, a ploy occurred to her that had some truth in it.

"She appealed to my sense of national patriotism and told me it was my chance to serve my country," Lola murmured, in low serious tones.

"Oh, for chrissake, you accepted the job because of your sense of national patriotism?"

He thought: *Those bastards take a brilliant young woman like this and appeal to her sense of patriotism so they could get her to work on weapons of mass destruction. I know she doesn't care about the money. So, it must be her sense of duty that is motivating her. I should be proud of her, not angry with her.*

When he pulled up in front of her apartment, he pulled her over to him and said,

"Come over here my little patriot and let me kiss you. I love you and the sense of national pride you have and respect you for it; I will even keep your job at the Electrodynamics Laboratory open for you until you can return."

"Thank you, Henry, for understanding that I must do this project. I'm not going to the moon, only to California, and besides business trips we can spend holidays and vacations together. There's no rule at the National Laboratories that says a person can't spend their leisure time with someone they love. Remember that I still love you whether I'm working at the Electro Lab or the Lawrence Livermore National Laboratory."

With Henry accepting her patriotism ploy, Lola felt better about going to California and working at the National Laboratory. She was able to establish a safe holding pattern of her own with Henry, as Laura had done with her man. Now, a real chance exists, she felt, of accomplishing their mission goals and staying in this reality with the people they love.

Chapter 8

Working for two years in the black world with Laura at Lawrence Livermore Laboratories, Lola had developed a system that could generate huge electromagnetic pulses. They would be as large as those generated by modern hydrogen bombs. The news of Lola's invention created immense interest in the black world. If the design proved feasible to manufacture as a warhead, it would be extremely valuable for national defense. Such a device would have an enormous impact on the balance of world power. A nation could totally disarm the nuclear arsenal of another nation, without harming that county's population, by simply detonating the warhead in the general area of its arsenal.

The chief of staff at Lawrence Livermore Laboratories called a meeting to present the new RAVEN-EMP technology to General George L. Haig, the commanding general of black world programs. He was a man with enormous influence in the Department of Defense and had the power of life or death over all black programs. With General Haig and his staff in attendance, Laura began the presentation on RAVEN-EMP Technology.

"Gentlemen, I am Laura Claremont, Director of the RAVEN-EMP project office. I know you are all anxious to hear about the Kiloton Nuclear Field Generator, which we now call KILOGEN. The inventor of KILOGEN is Dr. Lola Gonzalez and without any further discussion, I will turn the meeting over to Dr. Gonzalez for a description of its important features. Dr. Gonzalez."

"Thank you, Dr. Claremont. Gentlemen, let me begin with this slide, which depicts the general configuration of the KILOGEN device. Briefly, the energy developed by the one-kiloton nuclear warhead shown here, is used to drive this scaled down version of a field generator that I developed at NMSU. It's that device that generates the huge electromagnetic pulse."

"Question, Dr. Gonzalez. How big a fireball does that Kiloton Nuclear device generate? Will it cause damage to the population?" one staff member asked.

"It has a fireball that has a diameter of about five hundred feet. We have designed the device to have minimal radioactive fall out, so that the damage to the population, wild life, or vegetation will be insignificant. However, if someone should stare at the fire ball for a length of time, damage to the retina could occur."

"How serious would the eye damage be?" another staff member asked.

"The eye damage that could occur would compare with that caused by the sun, if one stared at it for the same length of time."

"Gentleman, please let her continue," General Haig requested.

"Now, let us get back to the diagram in this slide. When the nuclear explosion occurs, this chamber converts 60 percent of the fireball energy into electromagnetic energy. Dr. Claremont designed the chamber's energy converter. The converter has these hardened amplification stages that ramp up the field energy in the coils. They in turn radiate multi spectral energy, equivalent to an immense EM pulse."

"That is impressive, Dr. Gonzalez, now I would like to hear more about the ways we would deploy it," General Haig remarked.

"Sir, for that discussion, Dr. Claremont has prepared a number of slides. Dr. Claremont."

"As Dr. Gonzalez has shown, the device can generate a gigantic EM pulse. Our calculations show that we can package it in a conventional size nuclear warhead, and mount it on a variety of missiles. We can deploy it exo-atmospheric or endo-atmospheric depending upon the neutralization problem we are faced with."

"Neutralization problem?" I'm afraid you're moving a little fast for me. Could you elaborate a bit, Dr. Claremont?" a staff member asked.

"The exo-atmospheric deployment strategy is the one used in the Star

Wars interdiction mode. In this mode, we assume that intercontinental ballistic missiles have been launched. The defender responds by launching a KILOGEN tipped missile. The KILOGEN warhead is boosted above the atmosphere and detonated. Its EM pulse disables the enemy warheads' arming mechanism, rendering the warheads harmless.

"In the endo-atmospheric deployment strategy, we operate KILOGEN in the preemptive mode. In this mode, we mount the KILOGEN on missiles that detonate five hundred feet above the ground. Detonated at that height, the KILOGEN's gigantic electromagnetic pulse disables all electronic devices within a five hundred-mile radius, including the ones in missiles still in their silos."

"Can the EM pulse penetrate specially hardened electronics?" General Haig asked.

"Sir, our design can disable any of our specially hardened electronics, so my guess is that it can disable any other nation's."

A hush comes over the conference room, as the general and his staff contemplated what they just heard. The meeting then resumed with the women fielding many questions about the ingenious invention they had revealed. When these questions finally subsided, Laura's solid-state energy converter produced, yet, another barrage of questions. The women explained how the amplification stages of this device ramp up the field energy in the coils, which in turn radiate the gigantic multi-spectral EM pulse. The questions went on for another hour, addressing different aspects of the women's proposal, before the General finally decided to stop the discussion.

"Thank you for that excellent presentation, Drs. Claremont and Gonzalez. We would like to caucus at this point, could you step outside and take a break. We'll call you back in a few minutes."

When Laura and Lola left the conference room, General Haig addressed the evaluation committee.

"Gentlemen, I am extremely impressed with these women and their KILOGEN device. Besides being brilliant scientists, they seem to know exactly how we think and exactly what we're after. Their presentation has a format like that of senior officers. It's almost like they spent many years in the military. They seem to have the discipline of career officers, but their records show that they only got their doctorates a few years ago. I suppose they're naturally well organized and I like that. I think they're excellent candidates for the next echelon of clearance in the black world. I'm going recommend we send them to the war college in Washington for the next month. The courses given there will prepare them to take command of the prototype stage of the RAVEN-EMP project in Los Alamos."

A few minutes later, they called the women back into the conference room and informed them of the evaluation committee's findings. The general spoke first.

"Drs. Claremont and Gonzalez, we are very pleased with the progress you made in your design of the KILOGEN device. Now, to take the project to the prototype level, we have to do two things. First, you'll have to get the next level of clearance. However, before we can grant you that clearance level you must take a one-month course at the war college in Washington. After that we will give Dr. Claremont command of the RAVEN-EMP project in Los Alamos and Dr. Gonzalez will be her deputy director. We want you to first develop an experimental prototype model of the KILOGEN device. Then we will conduct a test on one of our islands in the South Pacific. If the test proves successful, you will build ten KILOGEN devices in a pilot production run, before we go into production at our plant in Alamogordo. Are there any questions, ladies?"

"Just one question, General Haig. How much funding do we have?"

"Don't worry about that, Dr. Claremont, the project has first national priority and whatever funds are required will be made available."

January of 1992 arrived before the women knew it and their move to Los Alamos, New Mexico was imminent. Preparations for the move had been on going for the entire month of December. They were looking forward to spending a week with their boyfriends before leaving for Los Alamos. The men had met each other often over the past two years. They had gotten along well together, probably because they were both science professors and had many interests in common. Besides having similar professional interests, they soon found they had some common goals. First, they wanted to convince the women to start thinking about their own lives, which meant getting rid of those jobs in the black world. Those jobs were causing them to push themselves at a grueling pace and they felt the women would ruin their health. Second, they wanted to marry them and wanted them to settle down in the less hectic lives of college research professors.

Both men were on semester breaks and were spending a week in California with the women before they moved. They conferred with each other and agreed to take the women to dinner the night before they were ready to leave for Los Alamos. They thought they could jointly persuade the women to leave the National Laboratories and come work at their respective colleges. Henry suggested they go to an upscale Mexican restaurant just outside Livermore that his family owned. At that restaurant, they would serve them in a secluded dining room where they could have a very private conversation.

Arriving at the restaurant, they quickly ushered the Vega party into a private dining room. The room had a graceful Old Spanish décor, with a brightly burning fireplace that had the swords of Spanish nobility carefully positioned on the wall over it. The table was beautifully set with flowers and elegant Spanish dinnerware, and the gleaming candlelight added to the room's ambiance. The whole setting spoke of a bygone era of Spanish elegance.

"Boy, this is very nice. I bet they're priming us for something," Laura remarked, winking at Lola.

"Actually, girls, we have something serious to discuss this evening," Kurt said half smiling, because he did not want to put a damper on the evening before it began.

"Well, Laura, I guess we're in for it."

"Ladies, we're not fooling around. Let me speak plainly, we arranged for the private dining room so we could jointly try to persuade you to leave the National Laboratories and come work at our colleges. We feel you're pushing yourselves too hard and you're going to burnout. No, no Laura, hear us out before you respond. There is more to life than living in a black hole and coming up for air, occasionally, when your boyfriends are in town. Come on girls, how long can you keep this up? How long can you expect us to put up with this arrangement?" Kurt said, his face and Henry's showing, clearly, they were becoming fed up with the understanding they had with the women.

"What Kurt and I are trying to say is that we have known you two for eight years, now, and have loved you for nearly all that time. Isn't it about time we settle down, get married and start living like normal people, instead of just seeing each other on holidays and vacations?" Henry asked, expecting them to stop the excuses and answer positively.

"Of course it is and you deserve an explanation. But, first, excuse us for a moment. Come, Lola, lets go to the powder room."

The men looked at each other wondering why no answer to the simple question they asked. Did they need time to make more excuses? The women just suddenly decided to go to the powder room and it did not look like duty called.

"Do you think we're pushing them too hard, Kurt?"

"Damn it, Henry, you know they've been avoiding this discussion for a long time. We have to bring this thing to a head before these arrangements we have, become permanent. We know they're brilliant women heavily involved in vital military research. Still, they have to decide if they want at least the semblance of an ordinary life or want to go it alone. How long do they expect us just to hang in there?"

As soon as the women were in the lady's room and were sure no one else was in there with them, they began to discuss what the men had said.

"Lola, they are getting frustrated with the arrangement we're imposing upon them. We are going to have to do something if we want to keep them."

"I certainly want to keep Henry. You said yourself, completing the mission and keeping our men was going to be a challenge, but we both agreed to accept that challenge. What do you propose we do, Team Leader?"

"To complete the mission and keep them willing to accept the status quo for a while, we're going to have to level with them and ..."

Lola quickly cut Laura off.

"Oh, Laura, we cannot tell them about the other reality, they'll think we've gone mad."

"I wasn't going to propose we tell them that. I was going to suggest that we tell them about the KILOGEN device and swear them to secrecy."

"Gee, Laura, that would violate the agreement we signed with the government. If it got out, they could put us on trial for divulging information vital to the national interest."

"We can't be loyal to the governments in two realities. We are going to windup committing a crime against the government in this reality, anyway, if we are to complete our mission."

"What are you saying, Laura? Are we going back to the other reality? For chrissake, we'll lose them, anyway, if we do that."

"Lola, listen to me, we haven't had a chance to discuss this yet because you were too busy with KILOGEN. I plan to build, surreptitiously, the Space-Time Transitional Synthesizer along with the KILOGEN devices in Los Alamos. Then use it to synthesize the KILOGEN devices at certain critical locations in the other reality. Seconds after they are synthesized, they will be detonated. The gigantic electromagnetic pulses they produce will wipe out all electronic devices, including the nuclear warhead activation circuits."

"What areas would be targeted?" Lola asked.

"All nuclear missile sites in the Fated Reality, friend and foe alike. We may need to double the KILOGEN pilot run to deactivate them all, but I haven't done the lethality analysis, yet."

"How, do we get out of the facility in Los Alamos after we shove the KILOGEN devices through the Synthesizer's aperture? As you know, they will heavily guard that facility."

"We'll work that out over the next few months, but right now, I'm thinking some kind of diversion will suffice. There's going to be many details to work out, but that is the gist of what I have in mind."

Lola sat on the bench in the lady's room, and thought for a moment, before responding to what she just heard.

"That is beautiful Team Leader, beautiful. It's going to work I can feel it. We're going to disarm that whole Fated Reality, at least temporarily. Wow, we complete our mission and get to stay here with our men. I love it. My faith in your ingenuity has been clearly justified."

"And mine in yours. However, let's not applaud yet. The road to the finish line is still a mine field."

"Come on Laura, we've been in here for fifteen minutes, the guys will think they scared us off or something. I think I know, now, what you were suggesting when you said we'll tell them about the KILOGEN device and swear them to secrecy. Just tell them as much as you think we have to, and I'll pickup the tune and play along."

Returning to the table, the women found their men quite concerned about their absence. It was obvious to the women that they should start talking.

"What happened, you were gone for more than fifteen minutes, did one of you fall in? We were ready to call the rescue squad," Henry asked, joking a bit but really wanting an explanation.

Laura began their explanation.

"We were discussing your concerns about how our relationships might be stuck in holding patterns. So, we decided to tell you everything and seek your advice. What we are about to tell you is top-secret information, and they could try us for treason for divulging it to you. But, we love you guys, and yes, it is about time we settle down, got married and started living like normal people. So, if you guys are willing to be accessories to this act of disloyalty, we will tell you everything and accept any advice you may have to offer."

Both men looked at each other stunned. It was obvious they were wondering what the women had gotten into. Then, after thinking about it for a moment, both realized that the women were willing to compromise themselves out of love for them.

"I realize, now, and I'm sure I speak for Henry, that we have put you in a compromising situation. We want you to know that we release you from any obligation to tell us anything that would further comprise you. We're here for you no matter what, because we love you," Kurt said.

He was trying not to appear as if they were forcing the women to do something they would all regret, but still giving the impression they wanted some kind of explanation.

"Lola and I appreciate that sentiment, but something has to be said, we cannot expect you to continue to indulge us any longer without some explanation. So what I propose is to leave out all reference to project names and classified data, but even doing that entails some risk. Anything we do in these jobs has risks; even allowing these relationships to continue has risks. However, we also run the unbearable risk of losing you if we don't say something, so we decided to tell you about our predicament."

After Laura said that, Henry got up and closed the door to the private dinning room and the men pulled their chairs close to the table. Laura then spoke.

"Guys, as you know, I am the director of a program at Lawrence Livermore that they are transferring to Los Alamos. Under that program, Lola and I have developed a very special type of nuclear warhead. To summarize briefly, the energy developed by the detonated nuclear warhead drives a scaled down version of the field generator that she developed at NMSU. When the nuclear energy is converted to field energy, it generates a huge electromagnetic pulse. It is important to note that the fireball created in this process is small and the damage to the population, wild life, or vegetation is insignificant. However, if someone should stare at the fireball for a length of time, damage to the retina could occur. When the nuclear explosion occurs, most of the fireball energy is converted to electromagnetic energy. We designed the amplification stages so that the field generator coil radiates the multi-spectral energy of a gigantic electromagnetic (EM) pulse."

The men, being accomplished scientists in their own right, appreciated the importance of the accomplishment the women had made and told them so. Lola continued with the description.

"As Laura just said, the device can generate a gigantic EM pulse. The device can be mounted on a variety of missiles, and deployed either in exo-atmospheric or endo-atmospheric modes. Which means, they can deactivate enemy missiles either above the atmosphere, or on the ground."

Silence came over the dining room, while the guys digested what they just heard. Finally Kurt spoke.

"My god, ladies, that's brilliant and it's clear why you're between a rock and a hard place. That device you invented could affect the balance of power in the world today. I can see why there is so much pressure on you to complete its development."

"Pressure is a mild way to put it. We've been ordered to build a prototype and test it. Then, if the test proves successful, we'll have to build several in a pilot production run before they will even contemplate releasing us from the program. It has priority one, nationally, and extricating ourselves from the program is almost impossible. Now that you've heard the essence of the situation we're in, how do you suggest we handle it?" Laura asked the men, putting the ball, so to speak, in their court.

After the meal was served and they finished eating, the men gave them their advice on when to extricate themselves from the program. Kurt spoke first.

"It's obvious that program is in the highest national interest. The government will make every effort to see that you bring it to fruition. It's hard to see how you could get out of seeing it through the pilot production phase."

"There is a downside to the whole thing that is not immediately obvious, Kurt. With the Soviet economy failing, the removal of the girls or their abduction by Soviet agents would go a long way to maintaining parity between the powers. When the news about this defensive weapon leaks out, and it will leak out, the women will be in danger of being abducted or killed. With the Iraqi challenge in the Gulf and war there imminent, it is conceivable they would even be of value to the third world. Given all the danger associated with the alternatives, I suggest the women see their project through the pilot production phase. At least that way, they will be under government surveillance. I'll bet they are watching us right now, because of the girls' importance to that project, and I'm certain they have already investigated us."

After the dinner was over, the women spoke briefly while the men got the car.

"You know, Laura, I'm happy with the way that turned out. We really didn't compromise ourselves, too much, because we gave them no numerical data or any other numerically classified information."

"True, and they really gave us good advice about when to exit the program. I think we can complete the mission, now, without alienating the guys or making ridicules excuses for not being able to be with them."

During the summer of 1992 Laura and Lola completed fabricating the prototype model of the KILOGEN device at Los Alamos. The war in the Gulf was over and the RAVEN-EMP project had its priority rating restored. General Haig selected a site in the Pacific Ocean near the old Eniwetok Atol atomic bomb proving grounds to test the KILOGEN prototype device. The Navy scattered a hundred and fifty vessels over a four hundred square mile area, which also included two abandoned islands. They placed an assortment of electronics equipment at various locations on the ships and islands.

On 1 September 1992, they detonated the KILOGEN device five hundred feet above the test area. Sixty days later, the bomb damage assessment (BDA) team submitted its findings to General Haig and his staff. They called in Laura and Lola for a briefing the following week.

"Drs. Claremont and Gonzalez, we would like to congratulate you on the successful performance of the KILOGEN prototype device. As you predicted, animal life, vegetation, and all structures, natural and manmade, were unharmed. Only the missile control circuitry and other sensitive electronic devices were rendered useless. Also, as you predicted, equipment in vessels submerged a few hundred feet under water survived unscathed. We'll have to leave missiles launched from the submarine fleet to the Star Wars version of KILOGEN," General Haig informed the women.

"Were any of the animals blinded by the KILOGEN fireball," Laura asked.

"As far as the BDA team could tell, no animals suffered eye damage. In some ways they're smarter than humans, they won't stare at the sun or a nuclear fireball. OK, now that the prototype has been proven successful; I want you ladies to proceed, post haste, with the pilot production run, only increase it to thirty KILOGEN units. I want to have extra spares, for reliability testing. Oh yes, I'll need an estimate of how long it will take to set up the line?"

"We can give you that right now. We estimate it will take about six months to set up for the run and about two months to build the thirty units, barring any unforeseen difficulties. I would say the units should be ready by midsummer 1993, Sir," Laura responded.

The meeting ended on that note and the women directly went back to their laboratory in Los Alamos.

One afternoon while Laura and Lola were walking back to their laboratory from lunch, Lola made an interesting observation.

"You know, Laura, those tests verified that the EM pulse dissipates rapidly in the ocean water. But, I don't think that will be a problem in our reality because the defense establishment there never had time to develop an underwater threat, and nether did Soviets. Instead, they each prepared for immanent attack, right after the 1962 nuclear confrontation. Both sides developed mobile and silo based ballistic missiles. Trucks, trains, and surface ships were the most available mobile launch platforms in our reality. With that being the case, they fully developed those launch capabilities and never had time to developed submarine launched missiles."

"That's why our plan to use the Synthesizer to synthesize the KILOGENs in the other reality is going to work. They deploy all weapon systems there on the surface, where the KILOGENs are effective. Although we could synthesize the KILOGENs in the exo-atmospheric mode against submarine missile launches, if they had the capability, we could never get the timing right. Not being in that reality, we would never know when they launched them," Laura responded.

By the end of July of 1993, Lola finally got the KILOGEN pilot production line ready to run. They blamed several glitches on the failure of critical components and procurement errors. But, they were just diversions for Laura's maneuvering, as she procured the necessary parts for the Space-Time Transitional Synthesizer. She had originally planed to build a dual mode version that would permit two-way space-time travel between the bifurcated realities. However, the required technology was proving to be quite elusive. Rethinking the principle upon which the Synthesizer rested, Laura realized her efforts were futile, again because of causality.

"Lola, we can't do it, and we should have known better than to think that constructing a dual mode Synthesizer was possible. Because going back and forth in space-time, as the dual mode version of the Synthesizer implies, violates the time laws of the aperture it would create. Reversing the direction of the aperture apparently changes the direction of time in one of the realities, which is of course impossible. I should have realized that right from the start."

"Team Leader, don't be so hard on yourself, I didn't question it either. I guess this really means that in order to get back to this reality, one has to have a synthesizer already built in the other reality. As a result going back and forth in space-time between the realities really requires that a Synthesizer exist in both realities. Since we are not planning to leave this one, only send the KILOGENs to the Fated Reality we shouldn't waste any more time on this subject. Instead, we should concentrate on modifying the one-way version of the Synthesizer. We need to expand its effective range, and adapt it so that it could rapidly accept a sequential set of space-time parameters."

"I agree, Lola. We should also develop a software patch that would allow us to type in the desired space-time coordinates for the KILOGEN warheads. Doing that would let us shove them, sequentially, through the aperture created by the Synthesizer. We would detonate the warheads within a few seconds after we synthesize them in the Fated Reality. This approach would require us to place a manual switch on each of the pilot run warheads. Turning on that switch, as we shove each warhead through the aperture, would arm the warheads for the timed detonations."

As their strategy for staying in Alternate Reality evolved, pushing the KILOGEN warheads into Synthesizer's aperture remained as its centerpiece. The proximity forces of the aperture would suck the warheads in, so, the women would not have to get very close to accomplish their task. However, they still would have to get close enough to the high-energy aperture to perform their work, especially if something went wrong. So, they decided to fabricate suits similar to the space-time travel suits fabricated for them in the other reality. The suits they designed were a bit of an over-kill. Nevertheless, they did not want to take the chance of being injured when they got near that high-energy aperture. Their eyes would be especially at risk so they designed helmets with visor shields' having a sufficient margin of safety. They were not worried about the KILOGEN warheads suffering any damage in going through the aperture, because they already hardened them for high temperature passage through the atmosphere.

The women decided, after some deliberation, to carry the laser pen weapons that they issued them in the other reality. These weapons could knock out an elephant at a hundred yards. The women thought they might be useful, if something went wrong, when they exited the Los Alamos facility, after sending the warheads through the Synthesizer's aperture.

The last items modified, were the women's microchip communicators that were surgically implanted behind their left ears. They designed advanced versions of the ones built in the other reality and added a number of useful new features. The old ones were still operational, but Laura felt they had a shortcoming. People could hear them talk if they happened to tune to their frequency. Security was very tight at this facility, and a monitor had picked up someone talking on a hand-held two-way radio. They heard at a staff meeting that the persons involved were dismissed because they were security risks. After hearing of this incident, Laura felt their microchip communicators could still be quite useful. However, she decided to fabricate new ones that encoded the voice vibrations before they were transmitted and then decoded them upon reception.

The new chips were about the same size as the old ones and Laura, who had some surgical training in the other reality, decided she would replace the old ones. She had set up a few mirrors in her apartment's kitchen and had Lola watch her as she replaced Lola's chip.

"Lola, all you have to do is to make a small incision here behind the left ear like this. Then with the tweezers remove the old chip and replace it with the new one. Then stitch it like this. See there's nothing to it, now, do mine the same way."

After wiping the blood with a cotton pad, Laura placed a little antiseptic on a band-aid and put it on the tiny incision.

Lola was a quick study and performed the procedure quite efficiently for a novice.

"Laura couldn't they record our conversation, decipher the code and tie the transmission to us?"

"Not likely, for two reasons. First, the communication is digital, not analog, so they never transmit our voices directly; they're represented by a binary code. Second, I used one of those none repeating codes developed in the other reality and it's unbreakable without our microchip units to give them the reference points."

"Well, Laura, I guess that covers all the hardware we'll need. Now all that remains is to work out the timing and the exit routes for the plan."

"True, and we'll have two months to work those details out."

Over the next few months, the women worked out the timing and the plans required to accomplish their mission goals at the Los Alamos facility. First, they needed a practical way to send the KILOGEN warheads though the aperture created by the Synthesizer. To accomplish this, they ordered a skid with rollers on it so they could roll the warheads into the range of the aperture's proximity forces.

Next, their plan to escape from the facility, after they jettisoned the warheads, involved using a small plastic explosive device. They would use it to destroy the surveillance system's recorders and create a diversion as they exited the facility. The device would be placed in the vent of the utility room where the recording equipment is housed. They would detonate device with a remote control unit carried by Laura, destroying the recording system and any record of their entrance or exit from the building. The explosion would also serve to draw away any security guards that happened to be by their Laboratory entrance.

Once outside the laboratory, they would simply leave the building through the side entrance nearest their lab. The explosive device would have already set off the alarms and exiting through the side entrance would not be detected. Even if someone discovered them, they would say they were going to their Laboratory to check on some data their computers were processing. They did this frequently during the last few months and would not be suspected of wrongdoing. Coming to the Lab late in the evening, they would usually use the entrance nearest their laboratory. They would enter the building by keying in the security code on the touch pad by the door. There would be only two security guards on duty then, and one of them would be in the front office. The other would be on his rounds somewhere in the building. This gave them confidence their plan would work.

One final detail had to be taken care of before the plan for accomplishing their mission was complete. The women felt that destroying the Synthesizer's hardware was absolutely necessary before they exited the laboratory. They did not want that thing remaining there intact and have to explain to the authorities what it was. It would be difficult enough to explain their whereabouts when the KILOGEN warheads were reported missing. They decided to handle the problem by placing an explosive device in the Synthesizer's equipment bay. A timer set to go off several minutes after they left the building would trigger the device. The explosion would not explain what happened to the thirty KILOGEN devices because no fragments of the nuclear warheads would be found in the debris. However, it would send the authorities off chasing foreign agents for stealing the KILOGEN warheads and take the spotlight off them.

As Lola rethought this strategy, she realized she would be leaving her aunt to fend for herself in the Fated Reality. How could she leave aunt Carmen in that godforsaken place? Laura had no immediate relatives there, but she did. *My god*, she thought, *I could have Laura send me back there right after we send the KILOGENS, but I can't bear to leave my loved ones here. I can stay here, but I can't bear to leave to my aunt there. Oh, this is terrible, what am I going to do?*

Laura could see something was bothering Lola because she suddenly looked like she had seen a ghost.

"All right, what's wrong? I thought you agreed with the plan."

"I did, but it suddenly occurred to me that I would be leaving my aunt in that godforsaken reality. She was like a mother to me, Laura. I just can't leave her there. Damn it, if that dual mode Synthesizer idea worked we could have simply opened an aperture near her in that reality and bring her here, first?"

Laura could see Lola was starting to panic, but what she said about opening an aperture there might still be made to work.

"I wouldn't want to leave my mother in that place, either. Maybe, we can still simply open an aperture, as you put it, and bring her here, if we do it right."

"I'm all ears, Team Leader, please explain."

"Well, suppose we open an aperture in some secluded place in the other reality and sent you there with an extra space-time suit. You could then find your aunt and bring her back to some pre-designated place and time, at which I would then open an aperture. If reciprocity of the aperture boundary conditions held, both of you could simply step into the aperture and you would be back here a moment later. We could do all that before we send the KILOGEN warheads to the Fated Reality. Do you think it would work?"

"Boy, that's a very big if, isn't it. Assuming reciprocity holds, and it probably would for me, but it might not for my aunt Carmen. She might still exist in this reality, and the aperture might kill her counterpart coming from the other reality to this one."

"That's only one problem. But, the more I think about it, Lola, my equations seem to indicate it won't work because the proximity forces push on the other side, not pull. Maybe, I have a sign error in those equations, but you or I couldn't find it when we were working on the dual mode concept. Who knows what will happen if you try going through the aperture when it opens in the other reality. It's probably not worth the risk."

"I think your right, but maybe we should try it, anyway."

"No, Lola, the risk is too high. What I'm proposing, now, is that we go with the plan as is because it postpones a nuclear holocaust in the other reality, indefinitely. This also increases you aunt's chances of survival until we can think of something."

"I guess, I'll just have to hang my hat on the 'something' we'll dream up later."

"Actually, it's not that hopeless. You know they'll eventually make us rebuild the KILOGEN warheads and then we can order enough parts to build two synthesizers. Once we have one built, we can send the subassemblies of the other to somewhere in the other reality. Then you and I can go back, reassemble them, and then bring your aunt here."

"Thanks, Laura, that makes me a lot feel better. At least there is hope of me seeing my aunt again."

The women studied the details of their proposed plan over the next few days. They finally concluded that, while they could possibly devise a better plan, better plans are always late in coming. They also knew that there is never enough time to devise the perfect plan. However, the plan they had now was adequate, and they were going with it, because the window of opportunity would soon close and the next one may never appear.

Chapter 9

It was the Labor Day weekend and the women had completed the KILOGEN pilot production run. They planned to complete their obligation to the Fated Reality on the following Friday. Their men were in Los Alamos to spend the holiday weekend with them and were taking them to the Capistrano restaurant that evening. The restaurant was near the Laboratory where the women worked, and owned by Henry's family. The women chose to go there because the restaurant was to be part of their cover story for next Friday evening. They had eaten at the restaurant every weekend for the past two months, both with their men and by themselves. The management was very much aware that Lola was Henry's fiancée and gave them special attention every time they dined at the restaurant. Their plan for the following Friday evening was to eat a late dinner at the restaurant. Then, cross over to their Lab from the rear of the restaurant's parking lot. They would get on the Laboratory's grounds, through a loose section of Cyclone fence that separated the two properties. After they completed their mission objectives at the Lab, which should take thirty minutes to three quarters of an hour, they would return to the restaurant lobby. Once there they would noticeably use the ladies' room and then walk back to their apartment.

Right on schedule, the men arrived at the women's apartment in Los Alamos. The women were patiently awaiting their arrival and were planning to enjoy the holiday weekend with the guys, before completing their mission obligation on Friday. Reservations at the Capistrano restaurant were for seven thirty and the two couples left for the restaurant when the men arrived.

After being settled at a private table in the restaurant, the women began telling the men what they had accomplished at the Laboratory.

"Well, guys, Lola and I just completed the pilot production run at the Lab."

"Does that mean you can leave the Laboratory, now, and come join us at our universities?" Kurt asked.

"Just about, we've requested permission to leave the Laboratory 1 October," Lola responded.

"You requested permission? Why can't you just simply resign?" Henry asked.

"We can't do that, the program has national priority and we have to request to leave. The paper work is in the mill and they understand we want to return to university research. They've been training people to set up the production line for the devices in the Alamogordo plant," Laura told the men.

"That is wonderful. We have been looking forward to that day for a long time. When I get back to Rutgers, Henry, I'm going to draft a formal letter offering Laura a research position. How about you?"

"I won't have to do that. Lola has been on leave from the Electro Lab for the past few years, and all I have to do is to place her on active status."

The women told the men they were very excited about returning to university life and that for once in their lives, they were truly happy. They wondered how they managed for so many years to put up with that drab "martial law" existence in the other reality.

"Well, ladies, Kurt and I have a surprise for you, too. We are planning to celebrate your leaving Los Alamos National Laboratory by giving a dinner in your honor. We plan the dinner for the first weekend in October. At that time, Kurt and I will have another surprise for you, but we can't tell you now."

"Aw, come on. No secrets," Laura said, winking at Lola.

"Should we tell them, Henry?"

"Well, maybe we can give them a little hint. The surprises come in something the size of ring boxes."

"Gee, that is a hard one, give us another hint," Lola requested.

"No more hints. If the most brilliant women in the nation can't figure it out by now, another hint won't help."

Although the hint the men gave them was about as subtle as the intentions of a bear in heat, the women kept asking the men for more hints. This silly game went on until the Labor Day weekend had nearly ended. However, before it did end, both women finally consented to think about setting a date for their future marriages.

Returning to the apartment Friday after work, the women started dressing for the long evening that was ahead. They were very apprehensive about the tasks they must do and started talking about the clothes they would wear for the evening.

"Lola, we should probably dress as if we were going out for the evening, we want to give the impression that we're going somewhere after dinner."

"Right, but no dresses, because they will only get in the way when we start shoving those KILOGEN devices around. We had better wear those casual pantsuits we have. They look dressy enough and we can easily pull those heat resistant suits over them."

"Sounds good, but we better wear our low heeled walking shoes, because we have to walk or maybe even run through that field behind the restaurant."

After dressing, the women left the apartment and walked a half-mile to the Capistrano restaurant. As they walked, they went over each stage of the plan they were about to carry out. At dinner they continued reviewing each part of the over all strategy, finally, focusing on the endgame.

Finishing dinner at the restaurant, the women paid their bill. They told the manager, with whom they were quite friendly, they would be waiting in the lobby until someone they were going to meet picked them up. It was to be part of their cover story. After they completed their mission objectives for the Fated Reality at the Lab, they would return to the restaurant lobby. They would stay there for a few minutes, thereby, firmly establishing their alibi.

The lobby was now crowded and no one would notice if they were gone, the manager would probably think they were waiting outside or in the ladies' room. Walking rapidly in the dim moonlight across the parking lot behind the restaurant, they noticed the pavement still had the smell of wet concrete; the smell told them that it must have showered while they were in the restaurant.

"Laura, we should be careful crossing the field it may be slippery and we don't want to slip and sprain an ankle."

As they reached the security fence, they found it was dripping. Damn it, Laura thought, they didn't need another stupid thing to slow them down, especially coming back. Pulling the loose section of the fence away from its post and squeezing through the small opening wet their pantsuits, causing them both to curse in low tones. The women crossed the grassy wet field, silently, and arrived at the entrance to the building nearest their Lab, stamping their wet shoes. Punching the access code into the number pad, they gained entry to the building unnoticed by the security guards. The retina identification unit at the door to the pilot production Lab scanned the women's eyes. This Lab was where they kept KILOGEN devices. Behind the KILOGEN room, was a supply room where Laura had secretly assembled the Space-Time Transitional Synthesizer.

The pulses of the women now beat rapidly; as they began pulling their safety suits over their clothes, their damp pants made the task more difficult. Finally, after cursing and wiggling a bit, they got them on. With that task complete, they donned their helmets and lowered their visors. After the Synthesizer had completed its ramp-up cycle, Laura imputed the space-time location list. This set of numbers specified to the Synthesizer, when and where to synthesize the KILOGEN warheads in the Fated Reality. With the list loaded in the memory of the Synthesizer's computer, Laura and Lola started moving the KILOGEN warheads. They placed them on dollies and brought them to the aperture created by the Synthesizer. It was taking longer than they had thought, and their anxiety level rose. They then placed the KILOGEN warheads on the skid with rollers and set the detonation timer on each of them. As the warheads rolled down the skid and came into the range of the proximity forces, they were sucked into the aperture. The whole thing had taken longer than they anticipated, but besides that, and the wet pantsuits resisting their dressing effort, everything seemed to be going well.

They had planted, a small plastic explosive device in the vent of the utility room, a few days ago. The device, when exploded, would destroy the surveillance system's recorders and create a diversion, as they exited the facility. Laura had the hand-held control unit in her pocket, which she would use to set off the plastic explosives in the vent. They striped off their suits and helmets, and Laura, nervously, punched the activation code into the hand-held unit. One more button remained to be pushed and the TV recording system and any record of their entrance to or from the building would be destroyed. The resulting explosion would also serve to draw away any security guards that happened to be by their Laboratory entrance. However, before pushing that button, one final thing had to be done. The Synthesizer's hardware had to be destroyed after they exited the laboratory. To accomplish this they had placed an explosive device in the Synthesizer's equipment bay, triggered by a timer set to go off several minutes after they left the building. Setting the timer, Laura pressed the final button on the hand-held unit. The explosion rocked the building and the women went quickly to the laboratory exit.

"Laura, this goddamned door won't open," Lola shouted, starting to panic.

"The bastards must have put some kind of failsafe circuitry in this damned building that we didn't know about. The explosion activated something in that circuitry, causing it automatically to lock the laboratory doors. Son-of-a-bitch, why didn't I think of that!" Laura said, smacking her palms hard against her head, repeatedly.

"Laura, that explosive in the Synthesizer's equipment bay is going to blow in a few minutes. It will take too long to try to deactivate it, now. How the hell are we going to get out of here? The Lab door is four inches thick and made of steel."

The women began to panic, their hearts were pumping rapidly and many thoughts raced through their minds. Finally, Laura blurted out.

"Hit that Synthesizer switch and let's get these suits on."

Lola immediately knew what she was thinking, because the same thought crossed her mind a moment ago. She knew now that Laura wanted them to escape by synthesizing themselves in the Fated Reality.

"Laura, I know what you're thinking. God almighty, I don't want to go back there, we have made good lives here for ourselves and we're going to lose everything."

"Don't worry about that now, just get that goddamn suit on."

"Mother of God, I can't get this thing on, my damn wet pants keep riding up and my shoes are catching on something. This fucking thing won't come up far enough to get my arms through. Maybe, I should just take off these damn pants and shoes."

"Don't do that, Lola, we may have to walk some place when we synthesize in the other reality. You had that suit on before and you can get it on again. It's a little damp inside from having it on before. I didn't get as wet when we slipped through that fence, so mine went on easier. Calm down and let me try to hold the pant legs out while you pull."

After some more struggling, with Laura pulling and pushing, Lola finally got the suit on.

"Lola, I don't want to go back either, but if we stay we'll lose those lives anyway. If we go back there is always a chance, we can return. So, let's not procrastinate, do you remember the exact coordinates of the Chron Lab? You worked with that data before we left."

"I remember the spatial coordinates of the Synthesizer in the other reality."

"OK, Lola, set in an offset to those coordinates, somewhere in that space in front of it, we don't want to synthesize in or near that Synthesizer." Lola then entered the offset spatial coordinates.

"Now, how about the time coordinate. We already know that the space-time laws will not allow us to synthesize in the other reality, earlier than the time at which we left. That's true because, before that time, we already existed in that reality. If we synthesize too long after that time, they may have moved things in that chamber and we might synthesize in something solid, and die," Lola responded.

"Input the time coordinate for twenty minutes after we left the Fated Reality in year 2010. We don't want to synthesize when the old Synthesizer is still on. Because, we can't tell what will happen if two apertures are open simultaneously and in proximity of each other."

"Why twenty minutes?"

"Because that old Synthesizer unit can only run for twenty-five minutes before it melts down. So they must have shut it down a few minutes after we left and can't turn it on again for a half hour."

"Team Leader, it's a good thing you remembered that. I'll input plus twenty-five to be sure."

"OK, do that and let's get our asses out of here before they become dead asses."

The aperture glowed in a brilliant colored light, with blinding intensity, but the special visors on their helmets protected their eyes. The women hesitated for a moment and then stepped sequentially into the aperture of the Synthesizer. A minute after they disappeared into its fiery eye, a second explosion rocked the Los Alamos facility.

Almost Immediately after the explosions, police and firefighters were on the scene. They notified General Haig a few hours later that explosions had occurred at the Los Alamos facility. When he received the news in Washington that the Laboratory housing the KILOGEN pilot production run had been demolished, he was on the next plane to Albuquerque, New Mexico. By the time he arrived in Los Alamos he received even more baffling news. They told him no remnants of the KILOGEN warheads were found in the wreckage of the Laboratory.

By the next day, it was obvious that the scientists who designed and developed the KILOGEN devices had also disappeared. This was a serious breach of security and a threat to the nation's vital interests. Every law enforcement unit in the nation was on alert. The FBI launched a national investigation and set a national manhunt into motion to find the women. General Haig suspected a foreign plot had been put into effect to steal the KILOGEN warheads and abduct the scientists who built them.

The FBI interviewed all persons that had any contact with the women including family, friends and their fiancés. They investigated every step the women had taken that day. Apparently, the manager of the restaurant had seen them last. A small army of agents converged on the restaurant and questioned all help on duty, including the manager who appeared to have the most information.

"They were in here Friday evening, dressed in nice looking pant suits, and looked like they were going to a show or something. They're very pretty ladies, you know. Oh, yes, we chatted for a moment before they left. We're quite friendly, you know, they come in here every week to eat. They told me they were going to wait in the lobby, someone was supposed to be picking them up," the manager told the agents.

The agents went to the apartment the women were sharing in Los Alamos and did a thorough search. They uncovered nothing except a crumpled scrap of paper in Lola's wastebasket. It was a note from Laura reminding Lola, about their meeting with G. H. about paperwork Friday. When the Agents uncovered this information, they called for a meeting with General Haig.

Pacing the floor in the conference room of another National Laboratory facility in Los Alamos, the General awaited the arrival of the FBI agents. When the agents finally arrived, they began briefing the General immediately.

"General, as you read in our report, the manager of the Capistrano restaurant said the women were waiting in the lobby of the restaurant for someone to pick them up. The note Dr. Claremont wrote to Dr. Gonzalez reminding her of a meeting, said they were having a meeting with G. H. about some kind of paperwork. Assuming you are the G. H. they were referring to, do you know anything about the paperwork mentioned in the note."

"I do, the paperwork is about their request to leave the program they were working on and resume their university research. I was going to discuss it with them Friday, but I had pressing business in Washington and had to cancel."

The General's itinerary on Friday was easily verified and showed the women did not meet with the General.

"Something doesn't sound right here. A highly classified research facility is blown up and thirty nuclear warheads are missing. Then, the research scientists that worked on the nuclear warheads vanish without a trace," an agent said.

"Were the warheads a new or special type? another agent asked.

"They were, and Drs. Claremont and Gonzalez were also special. I suspect Soviet agents abducted the women. Someone on the inside gave them a message to meet me after dinner on Friday. They abducted them and stole the warheads. In addition, the explosions demolished the TV monitoring system and the new pilot production line."

"But, Sir, the old Soviet Union has fallen apart. How could some warheads change that?"

"They're important enough to change the balance of world power if they were in their hands and not ours. That technology might even save their crumbling empire."

"If those warheads are so important why not just bring in some other people and make more of them," an agent asked.

"Unfortunately, without those scientists we probably can't duplicate them, at least not for a long while. That's because all of the critical design memos were in file cabinets that were destroyed in the explosion and resulting fire."

The agents now understood why this thing had such a high national priority.

"How about their boyfriends, have you interviewed them yet?" the General asked.

"Our agents in Las Cruces and Newark interviewed them after we talked with their families. I can tell you, sir. They're pretty damn angry. They're blaming the government for putting the women's lives in jeopardy. The women have been missing a month and they are demanding an explanation. They have bombarded the head of the Bureau and the Attorney General, with questions about the whereabouts of those women. The senators from New Jersey and New Mexico have requested that FBI give the families some answers. The Bureau Chief suggested that you have a private meeting with them, and inform them about the status of the investigation."

"I suppose we have to tell them something. I guess I'm the right person to do it, because I am familiar with the classified nature of their work. I know how much we can reveal without compromising the nation's vital interests. OK, set up a meeting in Washington and have the families brought there," the General ordered.

"And if they want to bring the boyfriends?" An agent asked.

"I suppose they're almost family, so if the families make that request, let them come along."

After the meeting concluded, they arranged to bring the families, Henry Vega, and Kurt Peyser to Washington. They scheduled the first week of November 1993 for a private meeting with General Haig.

Arriving in Washington Monday, the families of Laura and Lola met in the General's waiting room for the first time. Henry and Kurt introduced the families to each other and soon everyone was deeply engrossed in conversations.

"You know, Mrs. Claremont, when the girls were found ten years ago in Colorado, I suspected they knew each other. That was long before they started working together," María Gonzalez said.

"I think they probably met in Europe before Laura disappeared behind the iron curtain. A girl that was with her said they met another girl in France. They were kidding around, and someone dared them to cross into East Germany. Laura, and the girl they met in France, decided to accept the challenge. But, as you remember, neither of them could recall what happened to them," Joan Claremont responded.

Henry had not heard that about the women and started asking questions.

"I knew that Lola had spent time in Europe with her mother's sister but she never told me she met Laura there. I wonder why she didn't tell me that?"

"Probably because she didn't remember and neither did Laura. I believe they were both missing for about a year," Joan informed Henry.

"Disappeared behind the Iron Curtain and don't remember? How could they forget something like that?" Henry asked, more puzzled than before about what he was hearing.

"Yes, Henry, they were found unconscious by the police in Colorado back in '84 and couldn't recall what happened to them. The Claremont's and we had to go there and identify them. Joan may be right, because Lola was in Europe traveling with my sister at the time," María informed him.

María was not certain where Lola was then, but picked up on Joan's explanation. She did this, because she recalled telling Henry, years ago, why her daughter did not have a school transcript. She did not want to open Pandora's box and have to explain all that stuff about her sister, her husband's brother and Lola.

"You people were called to identify them nine years ago? Something is wrong here. Lola never told me anything about that. She is my fiancée. I should know more about what happened to her back then, so, why don't you people tell me."

"Henry, I knew Laura was missing for about a year, back then, because it was in all the New Jersey papers. I also knew something about the problem because I was her advisor at Rutgers University and had reinstated her in college when she returned. Joan is right, they probably met in Europe ten years ago, but let's not cloud the current issue with that stuff. Let's let the General tell us what happened. They're just looking for something irrelevant to hide behind. I'll fill you in on what I know, later."

"I agree with Kurt, let's not bring up that stuff in front of the General. Still, something bothers me about this meeting. Do you people think the government might be covering up something about the girls? Maybe, they didn't just disappear, maybe, they were hurt in those explosions," María asked.

"That seems unlikely, because if that were the case, someone would have leaked it to the press, already," Mr. Gonzalez answered, trying to allay his wife's suspicions.

"Well, I agree with María, the government is hiding something about the girls," Joan said, with a troubled look now clearly showing on her face.

"Come on Joan, let's not panic, let's just listen to what they have to say. We can ask them about that later, if we're dissatisfied with their explanation," Mr. Claremont said.

A few minutes later, the group was called into the General's conference room.

Entering the conference room, the group could see several other people were sitting at the conference table. The General introduced the members of his staff that were present and the FBI agents that were in attendance. After the introductions, the General spoke.

"I called you here today to bring you up to date on the investigation we have been conducting into the whereabouts of Drs. Claremont and Gonzalez. The women have been working for the past two years on a top secret project and security regulations prevent me from disclosing any information about the nature of their work. The FBI and my people have pursued every conceivable lead in this case and have been unable to find the women. Frankly, because of the classified nature of our investigation we can't give you any more details at this time. We called you in, to let you know that the government is continuing to work on finding your daughters. At this time my staff and I would like to ask you some questions that may lead…."

Seeing where this meeting was headed, Henry interrupted the General.

"Come on, General Haig, you have to do better than that. Your talking about two brilliant women working on a very secret project for you and you can't reveal anything. What were they working on? Either you tell us what happened or we'll go on national television and tell what we know. You're talking about our loved ones and we have a right to know," Henry demanded.

"People, I can't reveal the nature of their work because it affects the nation's vital interests."

"You black world guys are always hiding behind the flag to cover up big mistakes you've made. Do you know what I think? I think one of the jerks working for you leaked something, and now two of the nation's brightest people are missing and their lives have been put in jeopardy. Now, come on, tell us what happened," Kurt responded, tiring of the General's evasive maneuvering.

"You can't expect the General to divulge classified information," a staff member injected.

"If he can't divulge anything, we'll divulge it for him. It doesn't take a rocket scientist, and the people before you are at or above that classification, to deduce the nature of what the women were working on. The Los Alamos National Laboratory does research on nuclear devices, such as warheads, and knowing how bright those women are; they must have made a significant break through. Otherwise, their project would not have a national priority and you wouldn't be turning over every rock trying to find them," Henry remarked, starting to hit close to home.

"Go on Dr. Vega, let's hear your theory," the General remarked, speaking in a patronizing voice to the college professor.

"All that I'm telling you is a matter of public record. I know you think you'll just patronize us and get this meeting over with. All right, I will tell you what I think. With the Soviet Union falling apart, the abduction of the girls by Russian agents would go a long way to maintaining parity between the powers. When the news about the women's work leaked out, and it did leak out, they targeted the women for abduction. Even though the Iraqi threat has been removed, it's conceivable that a third world power would find their work valuable and try to abduct them. Given all the danger associated with these possibilities, why haven't you guys been more vigilant? Now, we want you to level with us and tell us what is going on. Your not dealing with some sophomore high school class, your dealing with informed people," Henry said.

The general could see these were intelligent people and were not going to buy a superficial explanation of what had occurred. Those young women had impressed the General, and he wanted desperately to find them. Because of both personal and official feelings, he decided, a spirit of full cooperation would best serve all those involved. It might even help to determine what happened to those valuable scientists.

"All right people, I'm going to tell you as much as national security permits. I hope that a spirit of cooperation will be beneficial to both the government and all those involved. Remember, in the best interest of Drs. Claremont and Gonzalez, it would be best to keep what we say here today, private."

A hush came over both the family groups and the government officials in the room, as the General began to speak.

"Let me start with a summary of what we uncovered to date. Within hours after the explosions at the Los Alamos National Laboratory, government agents interviewed the manager of the Capistrano restaurant. This restaurant is on the street behind the facility where the explosions took place. The manager said he knew the women very well, because they frequently ate at the restaurant. That evening after they finished dinner, they told him they were going to wait in the lobby because someone was going to pick them up. Soon afterwards, the agents searched the women's apartment and found a note Dr. Claremont wrote to Dr. Gonzalez. It reminded her of a meeting they were to have Friday with me about some paperwork. The paperwork was about their request to leave the program they were working on and resume their university research. I was going to discuss it with them Friday, but I had pressing business in Washington and had to cancel."

"General, on that information alone you must have suspected foul play of some kind? Kurt remarked.

"I did, but let me go on. Something didn't sound right, a highly classified research facility is blown up and several nuclear devices were missing. Then, two key people working on the project vanish without a trace."

"Were the devices you spoke of nuclear warheads?" Henry asked, he surmised that from what the women had told him and Kurt a few months ago.

"I can't go into that because it's classified. However, I can tell you the devices were very valuable and so are Drs. Claremont and Gonzalez. I suspect Soviet agents abducted the women and someone on the inside gave them a message to meet me after dinner Friday."

"General, do you really think Soviet agents are involved? Even after the Soviet Union fell apart," someone asked.

"We know all about the chaos in the Soviet Union and also know there is some kind of covert activity going on there, but I can't speak about it. The devices are important enough to change the balance of world power if they fell into their hands. With the technology that those devices represent, the 'old guard' might even be able to resurrect the old Soviet Union."

"Why do those people want Laura and Lola, they're just two nice young women? They can't be that important, can they?" Mrs. Gonzalez asked, trying to fathom what she was hearing.

"General, I agree with María, exactly why would the Russians want our girls, they have their own scientists. You hear every day how great they are," Mrs. Claremont injected, feeling perhaps the General was making up this story because he was covering up something.

The General didn't quite know how to respond to the ladies' questions, but finally responded.

"I know they may seem like just ordinary young women to their mothers, but I can tell you ladies, they're not. They're brilliant scientists and unfortunately without those scientists we, or especially the people who have abducted them, can't duplicate the devices they invented."

"I think Joan and I do have an understanding of our daughters' capabilities. But, there is something else troubling us. You talk of someone abducting them. Is it possible they were blown up in the explosion and revealing that to us at this point would be inconvenient for the government?"

"Ladies, I think I see now what you're getting at. No, I'm not trying to avoid government responsibility for your missing daughters. And, I'm not trying to cover up the fate of your daughters at the Laboratory. We carefully examined the contents of the area after the explosion and we made two observations. First, no bodies or body parts were found in the debris and second, no devices or parts thereof were found. Clearly that suggests that they removed the devices before the explosion and the women were either abducted or went willingly with the perpetrators. I am disinclined to believe the women went willingly, because I know, personally, they felt very deeply about their work and were very loyal to their country."

On that note, the meeting ended, with the General asking for the families' cooperation and the family members thanking him for his candor. They asked that they be informed about any progress in the case, and said that they would report anything they might discover about the women's whereabouts, immediately to the FBI.

Chapter 10

All the members of the Chronometry Laboratory had left the laboratory several minutes after the Claremont team passed through the aperture and were, supposedly, in the Alternate Reality. They had just taken the Synthesizer off line to prevent meltdown when an announcement came over the loudspeaker system. The announcement requested all personnel to report immediately to the main conference room for an emergency meeting.

Soon after the people assembled in the main conference room, the Director of the prestigious Laboratory, Harold G. Farnsworth, addressed the assemblage. The people had been expecting nuclear war to break out for the past two years. In fact they were expecting war, on and off, for the past thirty-one years.

"The United States has been attacked by a number of low-yield nuclear devices that give off disproportional amounts of electromagnetic radiation. Huge electromagnetic pulses disabled electronics equipment all over the country. Apparently, they detonated the devices five hundred feet above each of our missile control centers. These devices deactivated or destroyed the command centers' electronics equipment. They even destroyed the electronics in the ballistic missile guidance and control computers."

"Was our entire missile capability disabled?" a worried staff member asked.

"There was such an intensity of electromagnetic radiation caused by those devices that just about all of our capability has been immobilized," the Lab Chief responded.

"Does that mean that we're at the mercy of the Soviet Bloc?" a frightened staff member asked.

"Oddly enough, the attack seems to have been centered on all nations having a nuclear arsenal. Washington and Moscow are trying to sort this thing out, as we speak. When I have more information I will get back to you, I suggest you return to work until we find out just what is going on. We also request that you remain in the laboratory until we decide if there is any danger from radiation at the surface."

Returning to the chamber in the Laboratory where they housed the Synthesizer, technicians made an astonishing discovery. There about fifteen feet in front of the Synthesizer, lying motionless, were two figures dressed in some kind of metallic suits with their heads covered by strange looking helmets. The suits looked something like the ones that they designed for the space-time mission of Dr. Claremont. The technicians decided not to touch anything and called Dr. Farnsworth. The Time Crease staff kept the other Lab members out of the Synthesizer Chamber until Farnsworth arrived. Rumors had spread rapidly about strange figures being discovered in the Synthesizer Chamber.

When Farnsworth arrived a few minutes later, the entire laboratory staff was milling about in the outer laboratory. He quickly went into the Synthesizer Chamber and closed the door.

"They look something like the suits Drs. Claremont and Gonzalez were wearing when they went through the aperture an hour or so ago, don't they? Pull off those helmets and let's see who they are," the Lab Chief directed.

Removing the helmets, the Time Crease staff was further astounded by who was in the suits.

"Sir, it's them. It's really Claremont and Gonzalez!" an astonished staff member said.

"Are they alive?" someone else asked.

"They're alive all right, but in some kind of coma!" Another staff member shouted.

"All right, someone call for an ambulance, we don't want to lose them," Farnsworth shouted.

After the medics came and took Laura and Lola to the Base hospital, the Time Crease Team met with the Laboratory Director in his office. The group immediately started to speculate about what happened.

"Harold, do you think Claremont and Gonzalez are responsible for those nuclear devices you mentioned at the briefing?" a staff member asked.

"It couldn't be just a coincidence that they return in different suits within thirty minutes of their departure and the whole world is disarmed. Those clothes they had on under those suits didn't come from anywhere around here. Their hair is several inches longer than when they left and they are wearing some kind of make up," the Director responded.

"But, Sir, how could they possibly have delivered and detonated all those nuclear devices to all parts of the world, almost simultaneously?" another staff member asked.

"I'm just as mystified as you, but remember they went back to 1984 in the Alternate Reality and had many years to accomplish their mission. During that time, they may have figured out a way to do it. Remember, they're among the smartest people we have and besides who knows what technology was available in that reality."

"I hope they regain consciousness, so, we and the world can thank them. They rescued this godforsaken place from certain destruction," the chief of staff remarked.

"I'm afraid we can't say a thing about what happened here today and certainly not until we find out from them exactly what occurred. You don't know how the authorities in this country will react to unsolicited and non-sanctioned acts affecting our national defense. The women and even us may be tried for treason. So, let's keep a lid on this until we learn more about their journey in the Alternate Reality."

The room was spinning more slowly, now, and the objects in the room were finally coming into focus. As Laura regained consciousness, she smelled antiseptic of some kind and could make out the sanitized decor of a hospital room. Her head ached a bit, but nowhere near as much as it did when they synthesized her in the Alternate Reality. She could tell from the symptoms of the headache that it was highly likely she had synthesized in the Fated Reality. As she started to move, the door opened and a nurse, in a uniform that clearly indicated she was in the Fated Reality, appeared. She knew now that she had escaped the explosion that must have taken place in the Alternate Reality, but the thought of their unplanned departure began to depress her. *Damn it,* she thought, *how the hell did I manage to screw things up so badly back there? I should have suspected they had a failsafe lock-down in that security system.*

"Well, Dr. Claremont, you're finally awake, how do you feel?" the nurse asked.

"I have a little headache, but it's starting to subside."

"Funny, Dr. Gonzalez said the same thing, it looks like both of you had the same kind of trauma," the nurse commented.

"Oh, then she's awake, too. How long have we been unconscious?"

"Nearly thirty-four hours. But, tell me something, where were you ladies? The clothes you had on were very damp and we had a hard time getting them off," the nurse remarked.

"It was a classified mission and I can't reveal where we've been or why we were wet."

"Well, wherever it was, the women there sure wear strange clothes. They beautifully tailored those pants and matching jackets that you and Dr. Gonzalez had on, and those stockings with pants attached to them are so shear. What are those things called?"

Laura realized she should be careful what she said to the nurses, because they were not privy to any information about their mission. However, she felt she should say something to end the speculation that was probably circulating among the nurses as they spoke. Leading them down the wrong path was better than letting them piece together things from the rumor mill.

"They call the stockings with pants 'pantyhose'. The pants with matching jackets are called pantsuits. They are in style now in the country that I was in."

"Is the make-up in style there, too? I had to scrub your face to get it off, but I must say it sure made you look pretty. Do all women there wear make-up like you had on?"

"The women there are more concerned about their appearance than the ones here. Even the uniforms women wear during their military service are more stylish than ones we have."

"How about the men, are they nice, too? Dr. Gonzalez said she thought they were very handsome and the women here would like them."

After that question and remark by Lola, Laura felt she should end this girl talk with the nurse and get in touch with Lola over their microchip link.

"They are attractive. But, could you get the needles out of me, there're getting a little uncomfortable. I'm feeling fine now and I think they should be removed."

"I have to get permission to do that. I'll be right back."

"Thank you."

When the nurse left the room, Laura pressed in the coded sequence behind left her ear to activate Lola's microchip receiver.

"ART2 this is ART1, please acknowledge."

"ART1, I guess you have finally regained consciousness. I'm fine, but depressed over our unplanned exit from the other reality. ART2 out."

"I am, too. Be careful what you tell the staff here or for that matter anyone else in this reality. Remember, you and I vowed to return and, as far as I'm concerned, when we stepped into that fiery aperture, the mission went into its second phase. Mission protocol is still in effect, agreed? ART1 out."

"Agreed. However, we still need to think about a plan that gets us back to the other reality, and I don't think we should do it over this micro communication link. I know you updated the microchips and they can't decipher our binary coded words. They can and will, however, locate the sources of transmission; it's just a matter of time. So, I suggest we use the microchip link only for emergencies. ART2 out."

"That's a valid assessment of the situation. This reality gets paranoid over any unauthorized transmissions. However, we must agree upon something quickly. We must not give them any reason to suspect that we want to return to the Alternate Reality, because they will surely want to stop us. Once our story gets out, they will probably put us on special assignment and have us build KILOGEN devices. If they think we want to return, they will have us under continuous surveillance and never let us near that Synthesizer. ART1 out."

"Do you really think Farnsworth would divulge anything about the mission, he seemed to be very interested in keeping our work and the mission under wraps? ART2 out."

"Look, Farnsworth wanted to keep a lid on everything just in case the whole thing didn't work. He was afraid they would accuse him of spending government funds on some ridiculous time machine ideas. You remember what they did to the lab head that sponsored the anti-gravity machines; they drummed him out of military research. We will have to tell them eventually about those KILOGEN devices because our Lab team has already guessed that we're responsible for the world wide nuclear explosions. Top-level officials will descend upon us like locus after a cotton crop. I'm quite sure Farnsworth or somebody else, who knows about the mission, will either leak or divulge the story openly."

"Do you really think someone would divulge information about our mission?"

"Why in the hell not, there are going to be big rewards for the people involved in the project. Lola, our best strategy will be just to play along with them until we find an opportunity to get close enough to that Synthesizer and get out of here. But, there will be many details to work out before we are in that position. ART1 out."

"I read you loud and clear, ART1. But, for now let's see if we can get the nurses to let us visit, so we can stop using the micro communication link. ART2 out."

When the nurse returned, Lola asked her for permission to move about, and in an hour, they granted it. The officials made the women spend another day in the hospital to make sure they had recovered completely from the coma-like stupor they were in.

After they released them the following morning, they asked the women to go immediately to Harold Farnsworth's office for a debriefing. The women would have liked to have gone directly back to their apartments, showered and changed clothes, but the request sounded urgent. Walking to Farnsworth's office, they felt anxious and uneasy about their situation. Lola express her uneasiness in terms she had not used since she left this reality.

"You know, Laura, I don't trust that sleazy bastard, he always has another agenda."

"I don't either. But, we still have to be debriefed, so, just play along and follow my lead. I'm sure we'll soon find out what spin he wants to put on our sudden appearance."

Opening the door to Farnsworth's office, the women were startled by the round of applause that greeted them. The entire Time Crease Team was there, which was six people including themselves. The entire team rose to shake their hands. When the initial applause and greetings subsided, Dr. Farnsworth welcomed them.

"Drs. Claremont and Gonzalez, let me formally welcome you back from your journey to the Alternate reality. When we first realized it was you in the Synthesizer Chamber, we immediately guessed you were the ones responsible for those nuclear explosions. I guess the big question we all had on our minds, while you were recovering from your space-time travels, is this. How could you possibly have delivered all those nuclear devices to all parts of the world and detonate them in nearly a simultaneous fashion? We are totally mystified and are waiting eagerly to here how you managed to accomplish such an amazing feat."

147

The women had already decided to tell the Laboratory Director and the Time Crease Team most of what occurred in the Alternate Reality. They decided to leave out any mention of the men with whom they had become romantically involved. They felt that mentioning those affairs would lead the Lab Head to surmise they wanted to return to the Alternate Reality. They knew, eventually, they would ask them to duplicate the KILOGEN devices. Unfortunately, that could mean staying in the Fated Reality for an indefinite period, even forever. Even the slightest hint of a desire to leave would cause the authorities to place them under twenty-four-hour surveillance. Under those circumstances, they would never have the freedom required to carry out an escape plan of any type. So, they agreed, reluctantly, to tell the group a reasonably accurate version of their experiences in the Alternate Reality and judicially leave out any of the romantic details. Laura started describing their saga.

"I guess you're all mystified by what we accomplished, but remember we went back to 1984 on the bifurcated timeline. Many problems arose when we entered the Alternate Reality and it had taken us nearly ten years before we were ready to accomplish our mission.

"You mean you left that reality in 1993," the chief of staff asked, astonished by what she had just heard.

"Yes, but it's a long story. We had better start with a summary so you can get a general feel for how we accomplished our mission. After that, we can answer any detailed questions you may have. Will that be acceptable, Dr. Farnsworth?" Laura asked, knowing that in the Fated Reality getting the Lab Head's permission to proceed was the proper protocol.

"That will be fine, Dr. Claremont, but let me make a few remarks before you go on. We don't know how the authorities will react to this unsolicited space-time mission. They could conceivably put you, and the rest of us, on trial for treason, if they somehow misunderstand our intentions. They will misinterpret them, if this story leaks out before we can properly apprize the government leaders of the Time Crease Mission. So, let's keep a lid on all that we say or hear today until we have had time to think about the consequences of whatever action we elect to take. All right with that being said, Dr. Claremont, you may continue."

"When we first synthesized in the Garden of the Gods, in the Alternate Reality in '84, we were in a space-time coma that lasted four days. It was unanticipated in our mission planning and we were discovered lying behind some red rocks by the park custodians."

"Why do you suppose you were in a coma for such a long time?" a Time Crease Team member asked.

"Dr. Claremont and I believe it has something to do with the reverse aging process that our body cells must pass through. It must take time for the cells to reverse or increase age, depending on whether one is going back or forward in time. Only on our return, the time in coma was about a day and a half because the return space-time journey had just a seventeen-year time differential in it."

"Why didn't you return sooner, to save time in the coma?" another team member asked.

"We couldn't. The aperture boundary conditions for going forward in time, work similarly to the way they work going back in time. They don't permit going forward in time to a point in the other reality, if you already exist in that reality at that time. As a result, the earliest we could return to this reality is sometime after we left. We wanted to return as soon as possible to find out if we accomplished our mission, so we selected twenty-five minutes later than when we left. Otherwise, we couldn't be sure where it would be safe to return. Twenty-five minutes was also selected for a number of other reasons, too, which we can get into after we finish the overview of our mission," Lola answered.

"I know you're all very interested in details of their journey, but please, no more questions, let Dr. Claremont finish the mission summary. Please, go on Dr. Claremont," Farnsworth told the group.

"OK. After they discovered us, they took us to the Cheyenne Mountain Base Hospital. You can imagine the stir it caused being found in those suits and with those dog tags around our necks. We were so young looking that they couldn't believe we were military officers and soon found out there were no records of us in any of their military databases. You already know, my counterpart no longer existed in that reality. As it turned out, she probability died behind the iron curtain. It's a very long story and we can get into that later. However, it suffices to say, my family in that reality was found and they identified me as their lost daughter.

Dr. Gonzalez, on the other hand, never existed in that reality and establishing who she was and getting identification documents proved far more difficult in her case than in mine. The FBI found her parents in that reality and she cleverly convinced them she was their niece, even when DNA testing showed she was their daughter. You can imagine the obstacles she had to surmount in order to prove she was a citizen of the United States. The consequences of not proving that would have resulted in her deportation and would have placed the timely completion of our mission in jeopardy.

The process of getting the proper credentials to complete the mission required that each of us return to college. We decided, early on, going our separate ways would be wise, while getting reeducated and establishing careers. That decision proved to be a wise one and helped, considerably, in accomplishing our mission."

"One quick question, Dr. Claremont, did you really have to get reeducated to accomplish the mission? I thought your brain cells and your memories were unaffected by going back in time in that reality," a Time Crease team member asked.

"You have to remember that we physically looked like twenty-year-old women when we arrived there. As such, we could not gain access to the material required to accomplish the mission. Yes, we had the scientific knowledge to work the project, but we had to gain credibility in their scientific community to get anywhere near the materials required. After four years in their universities, we got our doctorates. Eventually they offered us positions in their National Laboratories, which enabled us to work in fields that gave us the necessary background. At that point we convinced them to let us develop a device that would neutralize the nuclear threats to their society."

"Dr. Claremont, what was the nuclear threat in that reality that required neutralization?"

"I see we are going to have to digress a bit and tell you more about the situation in the other reality. Dr. Gonzalez, perhaps this is a good time for me to take a break and let you tell the group something about the other reality."

"As Dr. Claremont mentioned, there was a nuclear threat in that reality. However, for you to understand the difference between their threat and ours, I must take you back to the time of the bifurcation. In their reality, they exchanged no nuclear warheads and their society lived in quasi-stable peace while enduring a thing called the 'Cold War'. That state of affairs lasted until the early nineties when the Soviet Bloc collapsed."

"Dr. Gonzalez, what do you mean by the term 'quasi-stable peace' and what is a 'Cold War'? And what do you mean the Soviet Bloc collapsed?"

The Time Crease Team became intensely interested and began firing those types of questions at the women. The women knew they had to explain those terms. Otherwise, the group would not understand what life in the other reality was like. So, Lola started explaining.

"Cold War was a term they used in the other reality to describe a state in which two potential combatants continuously build their weapons arsenals and maintain large standing armies. But, never actually enter into combat with each other. They used the same term in our reality before the bifurcation. The two combatants in their reality, as in ours, were NATO and the Soviet Bloc. The environment caused by the Cold War gave rise to a period of uneasy peace that was punctuated by small-scale wars. I referred to this general world condition as quasi-stable peace. The Cold War, over a nearly fifty-year period, economically drained to the Soviet Bloc nations. The problem lied in the inefficiencies of the communistic economic system. The Soviet Union and its satellite nations economically fell apart and nearly all, including Russia, seem to be converting to some form of capitalism. That didn't happen in our reality because the Soviet Bloc and NATO did have a nuclear war. The strong threat of that dire situation occurring again, forced the populations in both camps to endure unimaginable hardships just to survive. This tense state of affairs would continue in this reality, until we destroyed ourselves or until one side or both completely burned out economically. We all know that the former in this world was more likely to occur than the latter."

The group took a coffee break before Laura began discussing how they developed the KILOGEN devices, and the way they conceived to deploy them in the Fated Reality.

Returning from the coffee break, Laura continued.

"Having established our credentials in the Alternate Reality, Dr. Gonzalez and I eventually found the right place to accomplish our mission. Working with me in the Lawrence Livermore Laboratory, Dr. Gonzalez developed a system that could generate an electromagnetic pulse as large as those generated by the modern hydrogen bombs. It was an ingenious device that used the energy developed by a one-kiloton nuclear warhead to drive a scaled-down version of a field generator. I had designed the device's solid-state amplification stages. Those stages ramp up the field energy in the coils, which in turn radiates a multi-spectral, gigantic, electromagnetic pulse. That pulse, as you have learned, can destroy electronic devices in a huge area about which the nuclear device is detonated.

The nuclear device we invented impressed the authorities in the other reality and they instructed us to develop a pilot run at their Los Alamos National Laboratory. They called the new device the KILOGEN warhead.

The plan to complete the mission was then put into place. We planned to build, surreptitiously, the Space-Time Transitional Synthesizer along with the KILOGEN devices in Los Alamos. Then use it to synthesize KILOGEN devices at certain critical locations in this reality. Seconds after we synthesized them, we planned to detonate them. We knew that the gigantic electromagnetic pulses would wipe out all electronic devices, including the computers that control missile launches and the nuclear warhead activation circuits."

"What areas did you target, Dr. Claremont?" Dr. Farnsworth asked.

"All nuclear missile sites in this reality, ours and the Soviet Bloc alike. When we finished synthesizing all the devices, we set the timer of an explosive that we placed in the Synthesizer, which we had built specifically for the mission. Then we punched in these coordinates and stepped into the aperture just before the Synthesizer blew up. We made sure we destroyed the Synthesizer because we didn't want to give their military the keys to our reality."

"I think I see your point Dr. Claremont. However, do you really think they would be able to figure out the principle of time travel that underlies the Synthesizer and come after you?

"Dr. Farnsworth, we shoved thirty of their KILOGEN devices through the Synthesizer's aperture in a heavily guarded facility. I'm sure they would be able to figure it out in time, if the Synthesizer was left for them to study. I don't think you realize how advanced they are. They sent men to the moon by 1970, while we were still recovering from a nuclear war."

"Are we hearing you correctly? They sent a man to the moon?" Dr. Farnsworth interrupted.

"Yes, you are. Their knowledge of digital technology and weaponry is more advanced than ours in certain areas. They have developed a smart bomb technology that enables pilots to put bombs though bunker doors from aircraft miles away."

"Why would they develop weapons like that when nuclear warheads don't need that kind of accuracy?"

"That's just it, they don't want to use nuclear weapons, the nuclear powers have signed a treaty that banned the use of nuclear weapons in that reality."

"Dr. Claremont, what kind of war can they carry out with 'smart bombs', as you call them?"

"I know it's hard for you to understand, but they have waged conventional type warfare. A year before we left, they got into a war in the Persian Gulf, with a dictator in that region. The war lasted a little over a month and they crushed the dictator's army. He lost tens of thousands of his so call elite troops and they lost none in combat. That tells you something about the effectiveness of smart bomb warfare."

The questions went on for another hour before Farnsworth finally ended the debriefing session. Farnsworth told them they were national heroes and the women received another round of applause. But, he said, they would have to wait for recognition by the government until he thought of a way to inform the authorities of their deeds. He further said that their mission would have to be put in the proper context; otherwise, they would interpret it as a violation of the national command structure.

After the debriefing, the women walked back the Chron Lab carrying duffel bags. The hospital staff had placed the clothes they were wearing in those bags; so, the women had something to carry them in when they discharged them. The hospital staff had given them military issue to wear. Entering the outer office of the lab, they decided to go to the room where their lockers were located and change their clothes. They soon discovered the same dingy room with gray painted walls that they had left ten years before. Opening their lockers, the faint smell of disinfectant greeted them. They looked at each other and said, "Someone must have just cleaned them." Then they realized they did themselves, last week in this reality. Looking inside, they found another surprise; their spare space-time suits and helmets were still there. These things surprised them because they hadn't looked in the lockers for nearly ten years. Their bodies were now seventeen years older than when they left the other reality, but their time travel experience did not modify the neural cells in their brains. In fact, their brains had the knowledge of forty-seven years spent in this reality plus the ten years spent in the other reality. The clothes in their locker had been out of their sight for only a few days here and not the ten years that it seemed since they last saw them. Resolving this puzzling anomaly, the women quickly removed the fatigues the hospital had given them and changed into the street clothes they had in their lockers. Then, they emptied their duffel bags and hung up the pantsuits with other personal items, taking only the laser pens with them.

Entering the anteroom of the Synthesizer Chamber they noticed armed guards at the door. When the women tried to enter the Chamber, an armed guard informed them no one was to be admitted.

"But, we work in there," Lola responded.

"I don't care where you work, you have to get permission from Dr. Farnsworth," the guard informed them.

"Come on, Lola, let's get the hell out of here, it's late anyway, we'll get permission from Farnsworth tomorrow."

When they were in the parking lot, Laura suggested that Lola meet her at her at her apartment that evening. From there they would go somewhere to dinner. At that time, they would begin to address the problem.

After freshening up a bit in her apartment, Laura was in deep thought as she waited for Lola. The ringing bell brought her out of her contemplative mood and seeing it was Lola, through the peephole, she opened the door. After a brief conversation, the women realized they were both famished and immediately left for the local restaurant down the street. After being seated at a table in the restaurant and ordering their dinners, they began assessing their current situation.

"You know, Lola, Farnsworth originally wanted to keep a lid on everything just in case our mission failed. He was afraid of being accused of spending government funds on some ridiculous time travel idea. However, since we told him all that stuff about the other reality and those KILOGEN devices. I'm sure he's thinking about how he can cash in on what we did. I'm also quite sure Farnsworth will tell the government officials about what his lab has accomplished. He's just waiting until he figures out the strategy that will maximize his gain. Not, as he put it, because our mission would have to be put in proper context so the authorities won't interpret our deeds as a violation of the command structure. You saw those armed guards at the door to the Synthesizer's Chamber, and I suspect security is going to get much tighter when he decides to speak to the government officials."

"I know, your implying that we're going to have a difficult time getting out of here. I also feel they will eventually force us to duplicate the KILOGEN devices, so they can change the balance of power in their favor. The way they think in this reality depresses me. I wish we had never completed the mission the way we did and I regret very much coming back here."

"I certainly share your sentiments, but I still think our best strategy will be to play along with them until we can find a way to get close enough to that synthesizer. Leaving this war obsessed reality is the only thing I think about. However, even if we manage to get out of here, we're going to need a real tall story for the authorities in the Alternate Reality."

"They probably think we were involved with the theft of those KILOGEN devices or, maybe, they think we were abducted, with the devices, by some foreign agents."

"My guess is that they probably think we were abducted. But, we'll worry about that later. For now, let's just play along with Farnsworth and wait for our chance to get into that Synthesizer Chamber."

Chapter 11

The women had been in the Fated Reality for several weeks when Dr. Farnsworth asked them to attend a private meeting in his office. Arriving at Farnsworth's office, the women found that he invited no other members of the Time Crease Team to the meeting. Farnsworth was sitting at his desk studying several documents. Seeing the two women standing in front of him, he invited them to sit at his conference table, then, got up, and closed the door.

"Ladies, I called for this private meeting to inform you that I spoke to the Joint Chiefs about our Lab's accomplishments and specifically about your contributions."

Laura wondered why he so carefully worded that statement. He specifically did not mention their mission. The statement he made and the look on his face prompted her to ask, "Dr. Farnsworth, did you describe the details of our mission to them?"

"No, not exactly. I decided it would be best if we just kept the briefing limited to your fabrication of the KILOGEN devices and your method of delivering them."

That statement left the women very confused.

"Dr. Farnsworth, did we miss something. How can you separate the method of delivery from our mission?" Lola asked.

"I know this sounds confusing, but let me let me explain. After thinking about your mission for the past two weeks, I concluded that it would serve no purpose to complicate your accomplishments with a description of the Alternate Reality. This would just lead to endless discussions of the plausibility of time travel, and in the end, they would seriously doubt our sanity. They would dismiss our coming forward at this time as a group trying to take advantage of a serious worldwide event. They would conclude we were just trying to get money for some ridiculous time travel project. This, at a time of national emergence would go over like a lead balloon."

They had to admit he had a point and could see he was trying to get at least some credit for what they had accomplished. They also realized he was walking a fine line between credibility and lunacy.

"You said you spoke to the Joint Chiefs about our Lab's accomplishments and specifically about our contributions. How did you get around telling them about our journey to the Alternate Reality?" Laura asked.

"Let me explain what happened over the last two weeks, so you can understand why I told them what I did. Rumors began to circulate that our Lab had something to do with deactivating the world's nuclear capability. The government was furiously trying to find out what or who caused the nuclear explosions. They were even cooperating with the Soviet Union. In desperation both sides decided to resurrect the United Nations."

"The United Nations? That organization hasn't existed in this reality for forty-five years. It fell apart a few years after the nuclear exchange," Lola quickly remarked.

"Well, they resurrected it under a different name. They're calling it the Coalition of Nations, with NATO and the Soviet Bloc having most of the say. We can get into that later if you like, but for now let me return to the matter at hand. Realizing that I would eventually have to refute or explain those rumors, I felt it would be better if we give our own interpretation of them. Someone, in or associated with our group, had already leaked a large part of your story. As a result, I needed a plausible explanation for the top brass before they order an investigation. Ordinarily, they would summarily dismiss stories about time machines as pure nonsense and would soon forget those rumors. However, the authorities are desperately grasping at straws for an explanation and someone on the Time Crease staff would eventually cave in, and repeat the explanation you gave of your achievements. So, I concocted an explanation that would refute their stories and, still leave the integrity of Lab intact. In addition, your achievements would be unmarred by the rumors or their explanations."

His explanation of what was happening shocked the women. They could see he had a lot more incisive and intuitive grasp of the situation than they imagined he would. He certainly was not the run of the mill Lab Head they had encountered throughout their careers.

"All right, now that I gave you some background, let me tell you exactly what I told the Joint Chiefs. I told them, what they were hearing about our Lab was just a cover story for what we have actually accomplished. I told the members of the Time Crease staff, except for you two, that we were working on a special type of time travel machine. I also told the Time Crease staff that I sent the two of you on a special mission to another reality. However, in actuality you had been working for years on devices that might save us from ultimate destruction. I told them you had invented two devices; first, a nuclear warhead called KILOGEN and second, a weapon delivery system called the Space-Time Transitional Synthesizer. The KILOGEN device uses a low yield nuclear warhead that doesn't harm the biosphere to generate a huge electromagnetic pulse. The Synthesizer device can synthesize the KILOGEN warhead at any spatial location on Earth."

"Wait a minute, Dr. Farnsworth, it can't synthesize directly from one point to another in our reality," Lola quickly injected.

"Ladies, please, I had to give them a plausible explanation not some time travel fantasy they wouldn't believe. Besides, by the time you get to rebuild the Synthesizer you'll have thought of a way around that problem."

"Rebuild the Synthesizer?" the women asked simultaneously.

"Yes, I told them the Synthesizer had burned out in the process and we have to rebuild it. To cover us, I went into the Synthesizer Chamber, when I returned from Washington, and turned the power on for a half hour to let it melt down a little. This will lend credence to our story by showing clear evidence of the burn out, if they check," Dr. Farnsworth said, smiling.

The women's hearts stopped when they heard him say that. The son-of-a-bitch had destroyed any chance of a quick return to the Alternate Reality and they now realized they would have to play along with the bastard's shaky ruse. The funny thing about it was, he had forced them to join him in his stratagem but really did not know he had inadvertently covered their tracks.

"My god, Dr. Farnsworth, it will take me six weeks or more to repair the damage," Laura exclaimed, her face showing displeasure with his action.

"Dr. Claremont, don't worry about it, you're going to have the highest priority in the nation to complete the new project.

"New project?" Laura responded, thinking this guy was a barrel of surprises.

"I have scheduled you and Dr. Gonzalez to explain your research, your plans to build more KILOGENs, and the new Synthesizer to the Joint Chiefs tomorrow at 9:00 A.M. and...."

Laura interrupted him quickly.

"Dr. Farnsworth you hadn't even told us if we were off the hook for detonating those nuclear warheads, never mind explaining our plan to build more devices."

"I guess I have jumped the gun a bit, but I was anxious to cut to the chase. Let me tell you how we got 'off the hook,' as you put it. They informed me that I must have been insane to authorize such a mission. I could be court marshaled for such foolish actions. I told them that I had an executive order to pursue all research that might lead to defusing the impending and dire crisis between the superpowers. The Time Crease Team's ideas were worth pursuing, even if they were far out. When the more conventional strategies appeared to have failed, I decided to act. The two scientists responsible for the project were extraordinarily capable, and the weapons and the delivery system were ready for demonstration. However, when the world situation took a turn for the worst, the missile bases the superpowers had place on the Pacific Rim, were put on ready alert. I told the women I could easily see that the situation was escalating rapidly into a confrontation that would dwarf the Cuban Missile Crisis by comparison. With the situation so volatile, no one in Washington was responding to a request to observe a demonstration by some laboratory in the Cheyenne Mountain research facility. So, I told them, I'd rather opt for a possible court marshal than die in a nuclear confrontation."

"What did they say when you told them that?" the astounded women asked.

"Nothing, but told me to stand by and wait for their decision. Yesterday, they sent me orders to have you give them a presentation on your research and explain your plan to build more KILOGENs and the new Synthesizer. The Joint Chiefs will be here tomorrow and are expecting us, as I already told you, at 9:00 AM."

The implications infuriated the women at first, because of what Dr. Farnsworth had committed them to do. However, they soon realized his stratagem was quite clever and that he was a cut above all the Laboratory managers they had known over the years. His destruction of the Synthesizer, for whatever purposes, forced them to play their roles in the great deception he had created. There was no other option left for them, so, they went to Laura's apartment that night to plan the presentation they were to give the Joint Chiefs the next morning. Three heads of the military services were flying in from Washington for the presentation and to see the Synthesizer hardware.

The following morning they quickly ushered the women into the Chron Lab's conference room and introduced them to the generals of the armed forces. The women were taken back a bit to see an older, more tired looking General Haig presiding over the meeting. They knew, immediately, he was the counterpart of the one in charge of their project in the other reality. They knew his personality, knew what he wanted to hear, and how best to present their material to him. So, they decided essentially to repeat the presentation they gave to him in the other reality.

"Gentlemen, I am Laura Claremont, Director of the Time Crease Program office. I know you're all anxious to hear about the KILOGEN device we invented in our laboratory. So, let me cut right to the chase. The device is a one-kiloton nuclear electromagnetic field generator and is the brainchild of Dr. Lola Gonzalez, who will now describe its main characteristics. Dr. Gonzalez."

"Thank you, Dr. Claremont. Gentleman, let me begin with this chart, which depicts the general configuration of the KILOGEN device. Briefly, the energy developed by the one-kiloton nuclear warhead, shown here, is used to drive this scaled-down field generator, which generates the huge electromagnetic pulse. The nuclear warhead has a five hundred-foot fireball, which yields minimal radioactive fall out and as a result, the damage to the population will be insignificant. "

Someone tried to ask a question.

"Gentleman, please let her continue," General Haig requested.

"OK, now let us get back to the diagram in this chart. When the nuclear explosion occurs, this chamber converts 60 percent of the fireball energy into electromagnetic energy. Dr. Claremont designed the chamber's energy converter. The converter has...," Lola continued, describing the other features of the energy converter in detail and finally the immense electromagnetic pulse it produced.

"That's sounds very interesting, Dr. Gonzalez, now I would like to hear more about the deployment device," General Haig requested.

"Sir, for that discussion, Dr. Claremont has prepared a number of charts. Dr. Claremont."

Laura could see they had General Haig's undivided attention. So, she had decided he was going to be receptive to the modified Synthesizer discussion and took the opportunity to embellish its usefulness as a deployment device.

"As Dr. Gonzalez has shown, the device we have built can generate a gigantic electromagnetic pulse. Now, I will describe, and show you later, the device that we designed to deliver the KILOGEN warheads. We call it the Space-Time Transitional Synthesizer and its function is to synthesize a warhead at any place on Earth. Its field energy when it ramps up creates a fissure in space-time with an aperture that glows in brilliant colored light. The aperture is a portal to any point in the space-time continuum. We originally devised two deployment strategies."

At this point Laura described the exo-atmospheric deployment strategy used in the interdiction mode. Then she described the endo-atmospheric deployment strategy used for preemptive strikes. She went on to tell them how the KILOGEN warhead in this mode disables all electronic devices within a five hundred-mile radius. This included the ones in missiles that are still in their silos. Finally, she told them that they used this strategy to neutralize the nuclear threats.

"How did you manage to have the Synthesizer deploy so many of the KILOGEN devices simultaneously?" General Haig asked, not sure he believed what he was hearing, but knew the nuclear explosions did occur.

"Sir, they weren't all deployed simultaneously, it only seemed that way. We developed a timed/spatial location list, which specified to the Synthesizer when and where to synthesize the KILOGEN warheads. Once, we loaded the list in the memory of the Synthesizer's computer, we moved the KILOGEN warheads from the secure storeroom, provided by Dr. Farnsworth, to the Synthesizer Chamber. We placed them on dollies and brought them to the aperture created by the Synthesizer. Then, we placed the thirty KILOGEN warheads on skids with rollers and set the detonation timer on each of them. As the warheads rolled down the skid and came into the range of the proximity forces, they were sucked into the aperture. And, as you know, the experiment worked," Laura said, concluding her presentation.

A hush came over the conference room, as the General and the other Chiefs contemplated what they just heard. The women were not sure, then, the Chiefs believed the story they were forced to contrive. Farnsworth, who had maneuvered them into going along with his stratagem, looked worried, too. Finally the General spoke.

"Thank you, ladies. That was an eye opening presentation; you have done excellent work and will be acknowledged for it in the future. Now, we would like to meet with Dr. Farnsworth and discuss future plans for the Time Crease Project."

When the women left the conference room and went back to their offices, General Haig addressed the Joint Chiefs and Dr. Farnsworth.

"Gentlemen, I am extremely impressed with those scientists and their revolutionary weapon and its delivery system. Farnsworth, you should have made their talents known to the weapon system planners long before this. If we had known about their ideas when they first approached you, we could have neutralized the nuclear threat years ago. One thing still bothers me, however, about the reason you gave for neutralizing our nuclear capability along with theirs. Tell me again why you did that."

Farnsworth had been asking himself that, too, and was trying to come up with a plausible reason for the last few days. He had hoped the explanation he had for them would be acceptable, because it was the only one he could think of that had any credibility at all. However, it was the weakest link in the stratagem he had put together.

"Well, General Haig, things were moving fast. I needed a list of the Soviet Block's nuclear missile installations and their spatial coordinates to give to the women. I found a suitable list in the database the Department of Defense had sent to us. The list was for the war games that we were continuously conducting on the simulation bay's computer. Apparently, the targets on the back of the list I gave to the women were the coordinates of the NATO nuclear assets and the women neutralized those, too."

The general did not believe a word of that bullshit and was certain Farnsworth was covering up for some kind of screwy belief in bilateral disarmament. The general knew his kind and was certain he did not come forward, when the women made their discoveries, because he wanted to present the world with a fait accompli. *We desperately need that KILOGEN weapon and its delivery system, now,* the general thought. *But, for the time being I'll his accept his stupid explanation and get the truth out of that bastard later.*

"You know, Farnsworth, you were nearly court marshaled and if it wasn't for the revolutionary devices those women developed, you would have been. Now, let's get started building the KILOGEN devices in a pilot production run, say fifty devices to start. You'll have to get the Alamogordo people on board, as soon as possible, so, we can start producing the warheads in quantity. Next, I want that Synthesizer repaired, as soon as possible, too. Also, see if Dr. Claremont can modify its design so it can synthesize large numbers of warheads without melting down. After she makes those modifications, I want her to have ten of those units built. I want a twenty-four-hour guard put on the Laboratories where this work is being done. Also, I want those women guarded twenty-four hours a day. With something this big, there may be an attempt to abduct them."

Working steadily for a month, Laura managed to get the Synthesizer back on line, but informed no one at the Laboratory. Meanwhile Lola had been busy with KILOGEN fabrication problems. After Laura completed her preliminary task, she decided to meet with Lola privately and discuss the situation. With security so tight on this project, they surmised that the Lab, their apartments and possibly their cars were bugged. Consequently, they decided the simplest thing to do was to talk while walking around the grounds of the Cheyenne Mountain Base. Once they were out of range of any listening devices they began to converse in low tones because, several yards behind, two government agents were shadowing them.

"Lola, you've been looking very depressed, lately. Not that this whole situation isn't very depressing. Is there something wrong with the KILOGEN fabrication project?"

"No, I've ordered all the parts, including the kiloton warheads, and have been given priority on anything that the project needs. I'll start preliminary assembly next week," Lola answered in dispirited tones.

"All right, what's wrong? I miss my fiancé, too."

"It's not that."

"Well, what is it then?"

"Laura, I have been visiting my Aunt Carmen. As you know, she's been like a mother to me in this reality and I can't bear leaving her here when we go back to the Alternate Reality. And, I can't stay here because I miss my family and Henry back there. I'm being ever more torn apart as we near our departure time."

Laura knew about that problem because she and Lola discussed it at some length in the other reality.

"Won't she be all right here? Remember that we have defused the immediate threat of nuclear disaster."

"Oh, Laura, you know as well as I do that they will interrogate her until she either tells them what they want to know or collapses. This project has first priority and they will plague her until they are convinced she knows nothing. Even if she survives all that, the Soviets might grab her and see if they could get something more out of her. I really fear leaving her here. If we were in the other reality, the authorities here wouldn't know about us and she'd be safe. Nevertheless, they do now and she's vulnerable if I leave."

Laura knew that in this military state the police could go to any extreme to get the information they wanted. Lola's aunt would probably die during any interrogation process and Laura knew that the authorities would certainly interrogate the aunt when she and Lola disappeared.

"Lola, get me a slide of her blood. I have the Synthesizer back on line. But, no one knows, because I always reinsert a faulty multilayer board before I leave. If Farnsworth or anyone else should turn it on, it won't enter its ramp up cycle. Remember, we told him it would take six weeks or more to repair, so he hasn't been bugging me about the progress I'm making. If you give me a sample of her blood, I'll run it through the Bifurcation Locator. It will tell us if her DNA is compatible with any period on the bifurcated timeline. If it is, we'll modify our plans and take her along."

"My god, Laura, you would do that for me? You know it will complicate things tremendously."

"Look. I'm not leaving you here to be at their mercy when I leave. I'm still the Team Leader on this mission and I say we try it. For chrissake, Lola, aside from that, you have become like a sister to me over these last ten years. And, sisters like us are joined at the hip."

Lola always considered Laura her mentor and friend, besides being her superior officer. However, the gesture Laura just made sealed their relationship, whether or not what she suggested could be pulled off.

A few days later Lola gave Laura a slide of her aunt's blood. Laura passed it under the Bifurcation Locator's sensors and found that her aunt's DNA was compatible on the bifurcated timeline, from 1991 forward. It meant that in the Alternate Reality, Aunt Carmen's counterpart had ceased to exist sometime in '91. This implied, the space-time laws of the aperture permitted her to enter the other reality after that time. With that information available, the women began developing a revised plan to exit the Fated Reality that included Aunt Carmen.

To bring Aunt Carmen with them, they somehow had to get her into the Chron Lab when they were ready to leave. Making that happen was almost impossible, because of tight security around the Lab and the Synthesizer Chamber. Then, one day Lola over heard a cleaning woman say she was leaving her job and they were looking for a second shift replacement. Lola went, immediately, to Personnel and inquired about that position for her aunt. Lola had already many long conversations with her aunt about leaving this country and going to a safer place. She told her aunt that it was now going to be possible, but she had to be on the Base when the opportunity arose. She told her she had found a job for her that would allow her to remain on hand for a quick departure. She did not tell her anything about the Alternate Reality, but let her believe they would be flying out from the Base. There would be time enough to explain things to her later, but for now she preferred to keep things simple in case something went wrong. Meanwhile, Lola had her aunt move in with her at her apartment in Colorado Springs. She warned her not to say anything about leaving the country, while in the apartment, because it was possible that the authorities had bugged it.

In spite of the complications caused by taking her aunt, Lola was able to get the first few KILOGEN warheads assembled. They were ready to be tested at the White Sands proving grounds in Alamogordo, New Mexico. Meanwhile, Laura felt she could not hide the fact that she had restored the Synthesizer, much longer. They would have to make their move in the next few weeks, if they were going to make it at all. This was doubly true now, because she could see clearly that she could not make the Synthesizer open an aperture on its own timeline. The physical laws governing space-time travel only permitted the Synthesizer to open an aperture on the bifurcated timeline and vice versa. When that fact became known, Farnsworth's stratagem was going to blow up in their faces and she wanted to have her team safely in the Alternate Reality before then.

In spite of all the complications, the planning for their departure was progressing very well at this point. Lola had her aunt working at the Base and able to make a move when the time was right. They planned to make their move in the evening because the aunt was working on the second shift and was cleaning the Chron Lab at around ten each evening. Lola and Laura were often working late at the Lab so their presence at that time would not be suspect. They would simply go into the Chamber and power up the Synthesizer. When the aperture was ready, they would come out and immobilize the guards with their laser pens. Then put on their space-time travel suits and put the spare they had in their locker on aunt Carmen and step through the fiery aperture. The Synthesizer would melt down before the guards' regained consciousness, leaving the authorities to suppose that they were abducted while working on the Synthesizer. They had not decided where or when they would synthesize in the Alternate Reality. They left that detail to be worked out in the next week or so. For now, however, they would have to go to White Sands for a few days to witness those tests on the two warheads Lola had managed to build.

The small convoy of military vehicles carrying the KILOGEN warheads drove slowly down route 54 toward the White Sands proving grounds. Laura and Lola were in the lead vehicle, which was an armored personnel carrier driven by a soldier from the Base. The warheads were in the truck behind them. As they drove along the dusty stretch of road, the women in their boredom began studying the desolate landscape through the windshield and partially opened side windows. In the distance they began to make out what might be a trailer truck blocking the road ahead. The convoy stopped and the driver of their vehicle and the one behind them got out to find out what the problem was. Suddenly, there was a burst of gunfire and the two drivers fell to the ground. The rear doors of the truck blocking the road flew open, and what appeared to be assault troops of some type jumped out of the truck. They ran quickly to the third vehicle in the convoy. That vehicle was carrying the military personnel assigned as security for the convoy. The assault troops fired some kind of explosive round into that personnel carrier and it blew up.

Laura, with her heart now racing, shouted to a thunderstruck Lola.

"Get on that radio while I try to get this vehicle the hell out of here."

The women then jumped into the front seat of the vehicle. Fumbling with the stick shift and grinding the gears until she finally pushed the clutch in farther, Laura shifted the idling vehicle into gear. Uncomfortable with the seat so far back, she cursed the goddamn seat as she slid forward to reach the pedals better. Two assault troops ran toward the vehicle shouting something as Laura drove off the road onto the scrub desert. Driving the vehicle around the truck, she noticed that two more vehicles hidden in front and veered back onto the desert. Lola was on the radio broadcasting an emergency distress call.

"Mayday, Mayday, this is Gonzalez and Claremont, our convoy has been attacked on route 54, many dead, we are trying to escape, two assault vehicles are in hot pursuit."

Just as Lola got that message off, a man in an assault vehicle shot out their tires. As the vehicle thumped along on two flat tires, both pursuing vehicles caught up to them rapidly. Knowing they were about to be captured Laura shouted to Lola.

"Lola, shove your laser pen down your bra, like I'm doing. They won't be much use against those guys, now. These pens only carry enough energy for a few zaps. There're too many of them and if they see them they'll just take them from us."

One of the men ordered the women to step out of the vehicle. The men handcuffed them and placed them into one of the assault vehicles. The women heard one of the men tell the others that they were valuable merchandise and no harm was to come to them. They watched as the other assault vehicle drove back to the convoy. The driver of the vehicle they were in drove back to route 54 and proceeded toward Tularosa. Just before Tularosa, they turned on route 70 and headed for the Mescalero Apache Indian Reservation. The Reservation was now largely abandoned in the Fated Reality because they had effectively integrated the Indians into society following the nuclear war in 1962. The Indians were considered a valuable asset in a society ravaged by war and enticed by the government to leave the reservations. They offered them responsible positions in the on going defense and reconstruction efforts. Most Indians had responded to the offers and joined in rebuilding the nation.

The assault vehicle took a dirt road off route 70 after they passed though Mescalero. They drove for thirty minutes along the dirt road, and finally reached some abandoned shacks on the edge a dirt runway. When the vehicle stopped, they took the women into one of the shacks. Judging by some things strewn around the shack, the building appeared to be a relic from World War II days. An old calendar on the wall had a 1943 date on it, which bore mute testimony to the building's World War II vintage.

Sensing that time was running out for them in more ways than one. Laura quickly took the opportunity to engage one of their captors in a conversation.

"Where are you taking us?"

"Shut your fucking mouth, before I shut it for you," one of the men replied.

"Sarg, don't be so nasty, she's just a little frightened and wants to know what's going to happen to her. They're sure cute little soldiers in those fatigues, aren't they."

"Listen, you jackass, don't get any ideas, you heard the Colonel they're not to be touched, or harmed in any way, and he means it. He said, they're valuable merchandise and he will shoot anyone who screws with them. So keep your hands off them until that plane gets here, understand?"

"Yeah, yeah, OK, but I wonder why they're so valuable. There're plenty of good looking whores down there, what makes these so special, they're not even that young."

"For chrissake, your so goddamn stupid. They do not want them for that, it has something to do with those bombs they are supposed to be taking off that truck in the convoy. The Colonel should be getting here in a few minutes. We will put the bombs and these women on that plane their sending up from Nicaragua. You can have all the whores you want when we get down there."

The women didn't have to guess anymore, they knew their fate would soon be sealed. So, Laura initiated a ploy to get outside.

"Sarg, I have to go to the bathroom," Laura said, wanting to get alone for a moment so she could talk to Lola over their micro communications link.

"Don't call me Sarg and you can piss in you pants, you're not going anywhere."

"Come on guys, let her go out behind the shack. I have to go, too," Lola injected, quickly picking up on what Laura was trying to do.

"All right, all right, but one at a time, you first Blondie. I'll go with her, you watch this other one," the sergeant told the other soldier.

"I'd rather watch her pee."

"Shut up and watch that one, while I take this one out back!"

Laura picked up a scrap of paper and went with the sergeant.

"What do you want with that paper?" the sergeant asked.

"What do you think it's for? Laura asked, pretending to be annoyed over his stupidity.

"All right, take it with you."

"Could you take these cuffs off? I have to get my pants down," Laura asked gruffly, when they got behind the shack.

"No, if you can't manage with those on, piss in you pants."

Laura thought, this bastard is sure making things tough. As she started walking over the bare ground away from the shack, the sergeant followed her.

"For chrissake, give me some privacy, will you?" Laura snarled.

The sergeant stayed by the corner of the shack and watched as Laura walked out about seventy feet. She turned her backside to him and wiggled her pants and underpants down with cuffed hands. As she squatted, she pretended to swat an insect off her hair on the left side of her head. In doing so, she pressed in the code behind her left ear to activate the micro communication link.

"Art2, you don't have to speak, I'll do the talking. We can't let them take us on that plane. They'll probably take us to that Base the Soviets have in Nicaragua, and then somewhere behind the Iron Curtain. They must know we're the ones responsible for those unique warheads and the new weapon delivery system. We'll be forced to develop the new technology for them and then they'll kill us. I'm going to blast the shit head out here with the laser pen as soon as I have the chance. Then come into that shack and blast the one guarding you. When you see me come through the door get your pen out because mine might not have enough power to zap him. Then we'll grab that assault vehicle and get our asses out here. Art1 out."

"Come on what's taking you so long?" the sergeant shouted.

Laura pulled up her underpants and her pants, on one side then the other, with handcuffed hands while her back was still toward him. When she finally got them up, she carefully removed the laser pen from between her breasts and armed it by lifting the clip. She placed it in the palm of her handcuffed hand and covered the pen hand with the other. She turned and walked slowly toward the sergeant holding her handcuffed hands waste high.

"Come on move your ass. Let's get inside."

As Laura came close to him, she snarled at him.

"Did you get a good look?"

The sergeant smiled and started to turn. Laura quickly pointed the pen at his head and hit him with its coded blast of light, on the side of his face. The sergeant turned and went for his weapon.

"You little bitch, I'm going...."

She had hit him with a blast large enough to drop an elephant, and was happy, now, that she had modified the weapon before leaving the other reality. With the modifications she made, there was almost no delayed response to the blast of laser energy and in addition, she had the weapon set on high. The sergeant crumpled to the ground. The blast from the laser weapon put him abruptly into a deep lethal sleep that would eventually cause his heart to stop and as a result, kill him. She quickly reached into the breast pocket in his shirt and took his keys. Then removed the handcuffs and grabbed his sidearm. She was not going to take a chance and use the laser weapon again without recharging it. She had the sergeant's weapon now and intended to use it. Opening the door to the shack, she stumbled in as if being pushed.

"All right, all right. I'll get in, stop pushing!" Laura shouted, pretending the sergeant was behind her.

When the door swung open, the guy inside could see she had a gun and went for his sidearm. Two rounds from the sergeant's gun tore though the bastard's heart before his weapon cleared its holster. He staggered forward trying to grab Laura; his eyes wide open in disbelief. Then with a groan that seemed to catch in his throat he crumpled to the floor. Lola quickly bent over and with handcuffed hands felt for his pulse in his neck; then shouted, "he's dead."

"Lola, the keys to the cuffs are in my handcuffs outside."

Lola ran outside and opened the cuffs. Then took the sergeant's ammo and his rifle. Laura got the other guy's guns and ammo, and the women ran to the assault vehicle.

"Laura, let me drive I know these roads."

The keys were in the ignition, so the women quickly jumped in. Starting the vehicle, Lola quickly shoved it in gear and burnt rubber as she sped down the dirt road. She drove as fast as she could, because she knew the rest of the Colonel's men would soon arrive.

The women were just about to get off the dirt road and onto Route 70, when the other assault vehicle and the convoy truck turned onto the dirt road. The other assault vehicle stopped, the Colonel jumped out and gave the guys in the truck some orders. Laura could see the Colonel jump back into the assault vehicle, then, the vehicle turn and start after them.

"Lola, I don't know where the hell we are going, but wherever it is, put the pedal to metal because they're gaining on us."

"I'm heading for Holloman Air Force Base. It's our only chance. If we try to stop at the police station in Tularosa they'll get us because these guys won't hesitate to kill all the cops there."

Lola, with her heart pounding, tried to keep about a quarter mile ahead the pursuing vehicle. Nevertheless, she lost some ground as she turned onto the four-lane portion of Route 70 in Tularosa. A police car took up the chase after they left Tularosa and caught up with the Colonel's vehicle. As the police car pulled along side of his vehicle, one of the men inside opened fire. Laura's heart skipped a beat when she saw the police car go out of control and crash into an overpass support structure.

"Lola, they just opened fire on the police car and it crashed. That's all the break we're going to get. I hope the Air Force base is still there."

"I think it is, but I can't be sure. I know it was in the other reality, because

I lived near the base and worked there one summer. It's going to take another ten minutes to find out."

The women sped down Route 70 for another ten minutes with the other vehicle in hot pursuit. Finally, the sign for the Holloman Base loomed before them. In this reality, they heavily guarded the gate to the base, and Lola did not stop for permission to enter. They crashed the gate and when they came to a halt the vehicle was surrounded with armed airmen.

"I'm Colonel Claremont. I want you to send an armed cadre after that car."

"What car?"

"For chrissake, the assault vehicle that was just chasing us! Stop them, they're getting away, you idiot!" Laura shouted.

Since he was not responding and noticing the KGB car disappear down the road, she decided it was hopeless and gave him other orders.

"Damn it, you let them get away! Just call the Base Commander, now and have him call General Haig, immediately!"

"Wait right here, I don't know who the hell you are!" the gate sentry said as he motioned to the others to guard them."

Laura and Lola sat in the vehicle, fuming, while the sentry checked with the officer of the guard. A few minutes later, he came running out of the guardhouse and yelled at the military police to escort them to the General's office.

As soon as the women were in the Office of the Chief of Staff, they frantically informed him of the plane that was going to land on the Mescalero Apache Reservation. They also informed him of the two stolen KILOGEN devices, and that the plane would take them to Nicaragua and from there to the Soviet Union. The Chief of Staff let them calm down a bit, before he told them they had notified General Haig and he was on his way. He further said that Haig had ordered a massive search for them when they received Lt. Col. Gonzalez' distress call. But, the abduction had been well planned and, if it was not for their quick thinking, the KGB might have gotten both the warheads and the scientists that invented them.

About an hour later, General Haig arrived with his staff and Dr. Farnsworth to debrief the women. The General greeted them warmly and congratulated them on their heroism.

"You know, ladies, you acted magnificently under stress. You are a credit to the Special Forces Reserve Unit to which you belong. Your record shows that you were superior officers when you were in the Army and I'm going to recommend you both for a promotion in the Special Forces Reserve. However, more important, by saving yourselves, you got us out of a very grim situation, because by having you, the balance of power would have shifted to them."

"General Haig, were the KILOGEN warheads recovered?" Lola asked.

"No, unfortunately the convoy truck and those two KGB guys you killed, were the only things they left on that makeshift runway. We could tell from the tire marks that a plane had landed there, but it was long gone by the time we arrived.

"But, General, couldn't you intercept them before they left our airspace?" Laura asked, thinking they should have shot down that plane.

"They had a two-hour lead if they landed and took off right after you left. They probably flew in from Mexico in a small light plane under our radar net and weren't detected, then left the same way with the warheads. In any case, let's not cry over spilled milk, we have you back and we got the best of a bad situation. I have taken measures to see that it's never going to happen again. I have ordered Dr. Farnsworth to move his entire facility to Alamogordo. Only heavily armed convoys will carry the KILOGENs and Synthesizers out of the Alamogordo facility. We will house Claremont and Gonzalez here at Holloman, in the officer's quarters, and take them to the Alamogordo facility each day under an armed escort. This arrangement will be in effect until the end of the Time Crease Program. It's the only way we can ensure the safety of these critically important scientists," the General said, looking sternly at Dr. Farnsworth.

They concluded the debriefing on that note and the women knew they were really up against it, now. They would have to execute their plan to leave the Fated Reality, quickly. They would dismantle the Synthesizer in a few days and their departure would be delayed for another six weeks or more, if they did not act soon. Taking Aunt Carmen most certainly would be ruled out, if they moved their lab to Alamogordo, because they would never allow her to transfer to that facility. The women left the Holloman Base cursing the dilemma they were in, but more determined than ever to leave this godforsaken reality, and to take Aunt Carmen with them.

Chapter 12

Arriving in Colorado Springs, the women went directly to the Chronometry Laboratory for a staff meeting called by Dr. Farnsworth. As it turned out the only staff at the meeting were Laura and Lola. Farnsworth started by complimenting them; again, on their having the courage to escape from the KGB assault troops. Then, he immediately lost no time in ordering them to dismantle all of their hardware.

"But, Dr. Farnsworth, I was just about to test the timed/spatial location software, which specifies to the Synthesizer when and where to synthesize the KILOGEN warheads. It will take only a few days more and we will have some significant data with which to check the Synthesizer's integrated operation when we reassemble it. Otherwise, it will be like we're starting again with no test data to verify it is operating correctly," Laura informed Farnsworth, trying to buy more time.

"How much time would a few more days save, now?"

"About two weeks."

"That's not worth violating Haig's orders. Besides, a few days may lead to more and so on. No, just finish whatever you're doing tomorrow and start dismantling it Friday."

Laura did not want to protest any more than she had for fear he would suspect something and have her start the dismantling right after the meeting. Instead, she told him she understood his concern and would finish her work on the Synthesizer tomorrow.

After the meeting with Farnsworth, the women went to the cafeteria for coffee. They sat at a table in the back to discuss the latest development.

"Lola, we're going to have to make our move tomorrow evening. You have to get your aunt prepared to leave today. We have to move your space-time suit and our spare one, which she will wear, out of the locker room and into the Synthesizer chamber. Mine's already there, because I put it on to work on the hardware when I start the Synthesizer."

"I think we should wear our work clothes tomorrow, Laura. Oh, yes, we still have those pantsuits in our lockers, so we should probably change into them before we leave. Remember that we have to blend in a bit when we get to the Alternate reality. No, let's not do that, we won't have time. Just bring an extra blouse with you when you come to work, and I will throw the pantsuits into our duffel bags tomorrow with the other things."

"That brings up a number of things we've been putting off and we're going to have to resolve them right now. First, where the hell are we going synthesize in the Alternate reality. Lola, you said you had been thinking about it, but I guess that abduction episode took your mind off it."

"As you know, were going to be unconscious for a day an a half and my aunt maybe out a little longer. We have to pick a desolate place, so we aren't discovered like we were in the Garden of the Gods. That abduction ordeal did start me thinking, however. The Mescalero Apache Indian Reservation where they held us captive might be a good place to synthesize for a number of reasons. First, they have not developed that part of the Reservation, even in the Alternate Reality."

"How do you know that?"

"I joined a mountain climbing group when I was at college in Las Cruces in the other reality. There was an Indian woman in our group who took us on the reservation to climb the twelve thousand feet, Sierra Blanca Peak. We hiked up there from route 70 and I remember seeing those shacks. The woman told us they built them there during World War II and my guess is that they're still there. The more I think about it, the better it sounds. I can get the coordinates of the area accurately from the maps kept in the library computer here on Base. We can stay in one of those shacks until we recover sufficiently, then simply walk out to route 70 and get a bus at Mescalero to Tularosa. From there, we can call Henry and have him pick us up.

"That idea sounds interesting, and it might just work, but we better bring with us those military survival kits that contained enough food and other things to last a few days. We have some extra kits in our lockers stored there from our last space-time journey. They also contain a hand-held laser weapon and we might need extra ones in that area. That reminds me, I should recharge mine when I get back in the lab. The charge is low because I zapped that sergeant with it."

"We better take our foul weather coats with us, too, it gets very cold there at night. I assume we would go back around 1 December '93, which is more than two months after we left. It is unlikely that anybody would be in that area at that time."

"Gee, Lola, if we do that, we must explain where we were for two months. God, this is going to get complicated."

"If we go back immediately after we left that area will have many people in it. We're going run the risk of them finding us in our space-time suits. And, we're still going to have to explain how we got there. Besides having to do that, we'll have a hard time explaining where Aunt Carmen came from. That'll mean we'll have to coach her on every detail, which may be impossible."

"Lola, I guess we're going to have to do that anyway, whether or not we synthesize in December."

"Maybe not, I was just thinking, we could just put her on a bus in Tularosa and send her directly to my mother's house in Alamogordo. We'll have her them tell them I found her in New York and had her take a bus trip to Alamogordo. It will still take coaching but nowhere near as much if we are all found together."

"I guess that story is somewhat believable and you're right, it will be very difficult to explain, if your aunt is found with us. She can't be involved in any abduction scenario that we might devise for the General Haig in that reality. It just occurred to me, we could probably use some abduction details that occurred in this reality, in the other. With those details, we could make a good cover story about what happened to us there for the past two months."

"Good point, Laura. Remember, we told the manager of the Capistrano restaurant in Los Alamos that we were going to be waiting for someone in the lobby. We could say some third world agents abducted us in front of the restaurant and took us somewhere on the Mescalero Apache Indian Reservation. Then say, they held us captive there for two months, until we escaped. We could say we heard them mention the KILOGEN warheads were being taken out of the country through Mexico."

"Well, Lola, I think we have the rudiments of an escape plan, now. It allows us at least to have a chance of establishing a plausible explanation for our sudden disappearance and reappearance. I guess we're going to have to fill in the missing details as we go along. A more comprehensive plan would take months to work out and even then, it still might unravel because we forgot some small detail. So, let's go with the one you just outlined, but for now, we still have to get out of here. How much have you told your aunt about the space-time journey she is about to take?"

"Nothing about the Alternate Reality, she thinks we are planning to fly out of the Cheyenne Air Base to some South American country. I've been waiting until we at least had the semblance of an escape plan in place."

"Well, it's about as in place as it's going to get for now. You had better explain things to her tonight. We're leaving tomorrow evening."

"Laura, I don't think it's going to be easy. Would you mind being there when I explain things to her? We can't talk in our apartment because it might be bugged so I'm taking her to dinner tonight, why don't you come along?"

"OK, I guess between the two of us we can make her understand what's going to happen."

When they left the cafeteria that morning, they agreed that Laura would concentrate only on the task of making the Synthesizer ready for time travel. The rest of the time travel details she would leave for Lola to accomplish.

Arriving at the Antlers restaurant in downtown Colorado Springs, Laura saw Lola and her aunt already seated at a secluded table in its rustic dining room. The table was out of earshot from where the men assigned to guard them sat. The military heavily guarded the women after that failed abduction and, now, they had to contend with this damn intrusion, along with everything else.

After initial greetings and some small talk, the women ordered their meals and Lola got right down to the main reason for being there.

"Aunt Carmen, the reason we are meeting tonight is to tell you we plan to leave this place tomorrow evening. As I told you before, Laura and I are making the final arrangements."

"Where are we going?" Carmen asked.

"We are going to a place we call the Alternate Reality. It's a world similar to ours but not as violent. The people in that reality have a great deal of public control over the military and there is no significant threat of nuclear war. Laura and I have been involved with a secret program known as the Time Crease Project. You know something about it already because you do custodial duties in the lab where we work. But, until now you didn't know what we were really involved in on that project. Laura and I have built a machine called the Space-Time Transitional Synthesizer and it's located in that room called the Synthesizer Chamber, the one that they so heavily guard. Its field energy, when it is fully energized, creates a fissure in space-time with an aperture that glows in colored light. The aperture it creates is a portal to the Alternate Reality and its function is to synthesize a person in that reality."

"Lola, I don't understand a thing you're saying, I'm just an ordinary person, not a scientist. I thought we were flying out of here on a plane from the Base. How does that machine get us out of here?"

"Mrs. Saucedo, what Lola is trying to say is that we are going to walk through the aperture the Synthesizer creates to the place we call the Alternate Reality."

"Laura, what kind of people are in this Alternate Reality and where exactly is it?"

"Aunt Carmen, the people there are just like us in fact my mother and father are alive and well there. When you get there, you're going to see people, who have died here in this reality a long time ago, alive and well. And, you're going to be much younger there and...."

Carmen's face went white as she interrupted Lola.

"Mother of God, what are you saying? We're going to heaven. What are you girls involved in? Are you saying, we're going to commit suicide when we walk into that machine and we're going meet God and our dead relatives? What did you do, join one of those religious suicide cults?" Carmen said, shocked and frightened by what she thought the girls were contemplating.

The women looked at each other and burst out laughing and laughing until their sides hurt. Aunt Carmen looked at the two hysterical women and now, appeared even more puzzled. When they finally recovered their composure, they had to admit what they were saying did sound like that. After they dried their tears, Lola asked Laura if she could take a turn at explaining things to Aunt Carmen.

"Mrs. Saucedo, I can see that you need a more detailed explanation of what we are going to do, so, let me give you some background information.

After I finished college and my tour of duty with the army, I became disenchanted with constantly being involved with military projects and their associated weapon systems. I never had time for a love life or anything else, and I longed for the idyllic times that I read about in books. Lola had similar desires. That's why we joined the Chronometry Laboratory. It gave us a break from the war mentality that we were disenchanted with. It was there, I discovered the principal upon which the Space-Time Transitional Synthesizer rested. The project I was involved in, and still am, was called 'Time Crease' and it was dedicated to the study of the nature of time and its peculiarities. A few years later, your niece joined me and has worked with me ever since. She was also tired of constantly preparing for war and wanted desperately to work on something that would save humanity rather than destroy it."

"I know, Laura, she told that many times, but go on this is starting to make sense to me."

"As I studied the work of the other scientists working on the project, I realized they were seriously trying to determine if traveling back in time was possible. Being a physicist, I initially thought their ideas were absurd, but started thinking about the time travel problem, anyway. The alternative would have been to go back and work on weapon systems. I soon realized their efforts were futile because they were violating the principle of causality. That is, going back in time and changing even the slightest thing, changes ones own future and to my way of thinking that was impossible. I know this sounds confusing, but let me give you a simplified definition of time. One can view time as the measurable aspect of duration. The thing called duration has a past, present and future. And, time flows from the past to the future and can't be reversed. These thoughts led me to formulate a theory of time travel that did not violate any of the basic tenets. In addition, they helped me formulate the principle upon which the Synthesizer is based."

Aunt Carmen still looked confused, but very interested, so Lola picked up the thread of Laura's discussion.

"When Laura discovered the principle of the Synthesizer, the theory also led to an associated device, the Bifurcation Locator. Bifurcation means something splits into two parts. The Bifurcation Locator led to yet another the discovery. It showed that the timeline, on which events of the world are recorded, split into two timelines just before the nuclear war in '62. This was the only split we detected, maybe, there were others but our instrumentation was not sensitive enough to detect them. In any case, two timelines developed since then; the reality we live in and the other one. We call ours the Fated Reality. And, the other we call the Alternate Reality. We soon realized that the only way to save this reality from nuclear disaster was to send some people back in time to the other one. Once there, they could try to do something that would save this world. However, it wasn't that simple, the aperture that one must pass through imposes certain conditions on the one that passes through it. In order for a space-time traveler to be synthesized on the bifurcated timeline they must have a cellular DNA compatible with events on that timeline."

"What does that mean?" Carmen asked, now intrigued by what the women were telling her, even though she only vaguely understood what they said.

"Mrs. Saucedo, there are many implications to this discovery. However, specifically, it means that if we have a genetically identical counterpart in the Alternate Reality, we cannot pass through the aperture. If we try to go through the aperture, when our DNA is incompatible, it could fatally injure us."

"With such limitations how do you know if I can go through the aperture?" Carmen asked.

"Aunt Carmen, a test program in the Synthesizer's computer takes readings from a sample of a person's DNA placed near the aperture and determines compatibility. Remember, I took that sample of blood from you several weeks ago, well, Laura tested it and found out your counterpart in the other reality didn't exist after 1992. Since we're going back to '93 this time, you can come with us."

It seemed the more the women told Carmen about the Alternate Reality, the more she wanted to know.

"When did you girls go there the first time? I'm beginning to understand what you're talking about, but I have many questions."

"We went originally went to the Alternate Reality in '84 because my counterpart no longer existed in that reality from '83 on. Lola could have gone there anytime since the bifurcation because she was conceived here after it occurred and never existed in that reality."

"Why didn't you girls go back before the bifurcation and try to stop the war before it happened? You could have nipped it in the bud, if you did that, couldn't you?"

Lola and Laura smiled at each other because Carmen had asked a good question. They could see she was really thinking carefully about what they were saying and trying to find holes in their explanation.

"That's a good question, Aunt Carmen. Why didn't we simply go back before the war started, and try to 'nip it in the bud', as you put it? That certainly would have been a much simpler approach, but, unfortunately, it would violate the laws of space-time travel, as we understand them. Going back to any point on the timeline before the bifurcation would mean going back in time on our own timeline. We couldn't do that because it would violate the causality principle that Laura told you about. The laws of physics don't allow traveling from one's own timeline to one's on time line, directly. Consequently, we couldn't go back and nip it in the bud. In fact, because we already exist on the Alternate Reality's timeline we can't go back to any point before the time we left and redo anything. If we don't like the way something we did there had affected the future, it's too bad, because the causality principle says we're stuck with it. However, we can go back to the Alternate timeline anytime after we left and that's just what we are doing. The only problem we have is that we have to explain our absence to anyone we were involved with when we left."

Carmen was enthralled by what the girls were telling her, and started firing questions at them.

"Lola, how did you ever convince your mother that you were her daughter, without telling her about the Fated Reality? I'm sure she didn't think she gave birth to you."

"Aunt Carmen, it's very complicated and there's a myriad of cover stories that I told the people in that reality. I better give you the gist of what I said so you can play along."

Lola told her aunt about how they were found in the Garden of the Gods and about the de-aging coma they were in. She told her about the DNA tests that the FBI had done. And that the tests showed that Carmen's twin sister could be her mother and her sister's husband could be her father. She further told Carmen that she claimed her father was Francisco, Pedro's brother.

"But, Lola, your father's brother died before I left and it was the reason I left. How did you explain that to my sister?"

"I made it all hang together by telling them you were pregnant when you left. They believed it because they knew of the affair you had with my father's brother. I told them I lived in New York with you and your husband, a man by the name of Saucedo. They didn't know what happened to you but had heard you were living in Spain. Somewhere along the way, they lost track of you. I suppose your counterpart died in Spain in '92, because our tests showed that she no longer existed in the Fated Reality after that time."

"Mother of God that is certainly a twisted tale, but I suppose it was necessary for you to explain your appearance in that reality. You said they accepted you as their daughter, is that what they think?"

"They think, I am your daughter but to all other people, including my siblings, I'm their daughter."

Lola told her aunt about her parent's dead daughter in the other reality and how she used her birth certificate to get important identification papers. She also told her aunt what her mother told her college adviser about her living in Europe with her Aunt Carmen. Maria did this to explain why she had no high school transcript.

"Oh, Aunt Carmen, I used my mother's cover story for my own purposes many times. And that college advisor, I mentioned, is now the man in my life and I love him dearly. I used what my mother said about me living in Europe with you to explain the Castilian accent I have in Spanish, when he introduced me to his parents. However, we don't have time to go into that, now. Sometime after we get to the other reality, I'll explain everything to you. For now, however, it suffices for you to know just the above summary of what happened in the Alternate Reality."

"OK, girls, I think I understand all that you told me. But, instead of going into all the subterfuge and cover stories, why didn't you simply tell them you were from the Fated Reality."

"Let me take that question, Lola. Mrs. Saucedo...?"

"Laura, please stop calling me Mrs. Saucedo. Let's not be so formal, just call me Carmen."

"OK, Carmen, I will. We didn't tell them we were from the Fated Reality because we didn't think they would believe some story about time travel. We felt telling that story would prevent us from ever accomplishing the mission they sent us on. You yourself thought we had gone insane or we belonged to some suicide cult, when we first began to tell you about our time travel mission."

All the women at the table now broke into laughter about aunt Carmen's earlier conclusion that the girls appeared to have joined some kind of lunatic cult. When the laughter subsided, Laura continued the conversation.

"I don't know if Lola ever told you that we were responsible for all those explosions that deactivated nuclear arsenals in this reality. We were, and it took us ten years in the Alternate reality just to get into a position to construct the necessary devices. After we constructed those devices, we used the

Synthesizer we developed there to deliver them."

"If you girls did such a great thing why are we sneaking out of here?" Carmen asked, still a little puzzled but smiling.

"That's another good question, Carmen, and the answer is a long one, but let me give you a brief answer. When we returned to this reality, Dr. Farnsworth didn't want to tell the government we went to a place called the Alternate Reality and accomplished what we did. He thought they would think he came up with a preposterous time travel story just to capitalize on a serious world event and get funds for his obscure laboratory. So, he concocted a stratagem of his own to gain credit for our work and did not reveal anything about the Alternate Reality. He told them we found a way to deliver those weapons using the Synthesizer but never told them what its real purpose was. He melted down the Synthesizer to buy us time to build one that could do what he said it did. When he melted down the Synthesizer, he destroyed our chances of getting out of here quickly and forced us to go along with his stratagem."

"What's the big rush now, you said he bought you time," Carmen said.

"Aunt Carmen, we found out very quickly that designing a Synthesizer that did what Dr. Farnsworth wanted was impossible, because it violated the causality principle. However, we didn't tell him that because we wanted to use the time to develop a new Synthesizer that would get us back to the Alternate Reality."

"So, Farnsworth knows about the Alternate Reality, what's the problem?"

"Carmen, we're not worried too much about him. But, we've been working on the Synthesizer for nearly two months and the ruse he has been perpetrating will unravel. Because, it will soon be obvious that the Synthesizer we built can't do what he said it could. You can never tell what they'll do when they discover that it won't do the job he promised. When that happens, we want to be out of here, otherwise the opportunity may never arise again."

The women chose not to reveal anything to Carmen about the abduction they had suffered at the hands of the KGB. They did this because they felt that those frightening details would unnerve her and cause her to go into a panic mode. And that, in all probably, would ultimately cause the risky plan they had devised to fail.

By the time the women left the restaurant, they convinced Carmen the plan was as good as they could make it, given the circumstances that had occurred. Although she did not quite understand all she was told, she decided to trust the girls and leave the Fated Reality with them.

The KGB Colonel tried several times in the last few days to recapture the women, but failed because they were continuously guarded whenever they went off Base. An informant on the Base said they were spending the day completing a critical experiment with the Synthesizer, before they dismantled and shipped it to Los Alamos. The Colonel knew that once they were working in Los Alamos and staying at Holloman AFB, their capture would be nearly impossible. However, on the Base where their lab was, they allowed them to move about mostly unguarded because the Base was considered secure. As a result, the Colonel devised a bold plan to capture them right in the lions' den. He dressed himself as an Air Force Colonel and his men as military attachés. Then, in the early evening, with forged orders, drove onto the Cheyenne Base and up to the entrance to the Chronometry Laboratory.

The women were in the lobby area of the Synthesizer Chamber, seated at the small table in the corner discussing quietly the last minute details before their departure. Aunt Carmen was in the lobby dusting and cleaning. The scene seemed quite normal to the security guards seated by the desk in front of the door to the Synthesizer Chamber.

A minor problem had come up with obtaining the coordinates required to synthesize in the Alternate Reality on the Mescalero Apache Reservation.

"Laura, I couldn't get the spatial coordinates of the desired point on the Reservation because the computer in the library was down. They called me a few minutes ago and told me it's back up, so I'm going to run over there now and get them."

"OK, I'm going in and ramp up the Synthesizer so it will be ready when you return. I see you got the suits and the heat retardant duffel bags with our things in them in the Chamber. Let's hustle, because we only have a half hour window before it melts down."

Leaving the laboratory through the long hallway a few minutes later, Lola saw an Air force Colonel and his aid approaching her. As they approached, Lola recognized the Colonel. He was the one that had them abducted a few days ago. Thoughts began racing through her mind: *how the hell did he get in here? I had better get back to the lab.* As she turned, she saw two more men coming up behind her. She immediately pressed in the activation code to her microchip communications link.

"ART1, I have an emergency, I'm in the hallway near the entrance to the lab. The KGB Colonel that abducted us somehow got on the Base and is trying to capture me, they have surrounded me."

"ART2, hang on, I'm coming."

Laura burst out of the Chamber with her laser weapon in hand, yelling to the guards.

"The KGB is trying to abduct Dr. Gonzalez in the hall. Let's go."

The guards drew their guns, as Laura armed her laser weapon. As she left, she told Carmen to wait there, she would be back with Lola.

Coming around the corner in the hallway, the guards and Laura could see Lola struggling furiously with two of the men. A third was trying to put handcuffs on her. They were huge guys and one of them punched her so hard in the face that she dropped like a limp rag to the ground. Laura and the guards opened fire hitting the three men with gun and laser fire. The Colonel and the guy with him shot the guards and Laura dropped to the floor to get out of the line of fire. As she fell, the laser pen was jarred out of her hand. The Colonel and his aid stepped over Lola and the other three men, who lied crumpled on the floor in front of them. Laura grabbed one of the guards' guns and put few rounds into the colonel and his aid. The aid and the Colonel stumbled out the door to a waiting car as she tried to put another round in them, but the guard's gun was empty. She tossed the gun aside and ran to Lola, thinking she must get her out of there because that Colonel may have more men hidden somewhere. She dragged Lola back to the Chron Lab. Carmen was at the door waiting for them.

"Carmen, give me a hand with her. We have to get into that Chamber."

"What happened, Laura, I heard gun shots? Is my Lola all right?"

"I think so, but I have no time to explain. Quick help me get her into the Chamber, we have to get through the aperture before the Synthesizer melts down."

The two women dragged Lola into the Synthesizer Chamber. The door had been left open when Laura left with the guards, so, they did not need the entrance code the guards had to enter. When they got inside Laura addressed the immediate problem.

"Carmen, we have to get that suit on her."

As the women struggled to put Lola's suit on her, the handcuff on one hand kept getting in the way.

"Carmen, hand me those cutters in that tool box. We have to cut this damn chain and the other cuff off, before we can pull this sleeve on and get the glove over her hand."

After some effort, Laura managed to cut the chain with the large cutters, and the women finished dressing Lola and themselves. They grabbed the duffel bags Lola had prepared for them and stepped up to the glowing aperture.

"Carmen, we are going to enter the Alternate Reality, December 3, 1993. But, it won't be on the Apache Indian Reservation, because Lola obviously could not get the coordinates."

"My god, what are we going to do?"

"We're going to the default spatial coordinates. That is, the Garden of the Gods in Colorado Springs. You just follow my lead when we get there. Now, help me stand Lola in front to the aperture. She'll be sucked in by the proximity forces, just let her go."

After Lola passed through the aperture, Laura gave Carmen a duffel bag and pushed her into the aperture. Then she grabbed the other two duffel bags and stepped into the aperture herself. A few minutes later the Synthesizer began to melt down and within fifteen minutes the power transformers on the Cheyenne Base blew and the Base was in total darkness.

The next day when they restored power, an army of military investigators with General Haig descended upon the crime scene. They were turning the Base inside and out, as they tried to find the missing scientists. Finally, the General initiated a nation wide search for the women. Then, in frustration he called an emergency meeting in the Chron Lab's Conference room.

"We have a major problem, here; as you already know, they have abducted the scientists most critical to the balance of power, again, right from under our noses. Men were killed and the perpetrators' bodies are lying all over the hall and Drs. Claremont and Gonzalez are gone. How the hell did they abduct them from a secure military base? I demand some answers!" the General shouted at his staff.

Just then, a messenger from the Base hospital rushed into the conference room and informed the General that the military policeman that wasn't killed, had finally regained consciousness. The General and Dr. Farnsworth quickly went to the hospital to interview the soldier. When they arrived at the hospital, they were quickly escorted to the military policeman's room.

"Soldier, tell me exactly what happened," General Haig ordered.

"Well, Sir, about ten PM, Dr. Gonzalez left the lab to get something she forgot. Then, Dr. Claremont went back into that Synthesizer Chamber to finish an experiment she was working on. Suddenly, she rushed out to the Chamber and said the KGB is trying to abduct Dr. Gonzalez."

"How the hell did she know they were abducting Gonzalez?" the General asked.

Farnsworth knew and answered his question.

"Sir, I had one of those microchip communication devices implanted behind their ears when the program began in case an emergency arose and I guess it really did last night."

"That was good thinking, Farnsworth, at least it gave them a heads up. Go on soldier."

"The three of us rushed out into the hall and when we rounded the corner, we saw Dr. Gonzalez struggling furiously with three men. One of the men was trying to put handcuffs on her. Then she almost freed herself but one of them punched her very hard in the face and she fell to the ground unconscious. The next thing I knew we fired our weapons at the three men, us using guns and Dr. Claremont using one of those laser pens. When the abductors fell, two men behind them opened fire on us and we all went down. One had on a Colonel's uniform and the other looked like his aid. The last thing I remember Dr. Claremont had grabbed my gun and tried to fire it at them."

"How bad were the women hurt?" the General asked.

"I don't know, Sir, but they were both on the ground."

The General thanked the soldier for the information, and informed him that they would decorate him for his bravery.

Walking back to the Lab, Farnsworth commented to the General.

"Sir, we couldn't protect them from the KGB, even on a secure Base. They've got them now, dead or alive, and that leaves us in a precarious position. What are we going to do, now? They're the only ones that can build the Synthesizer we need for weapon delivery."

"Well, at least we got the one they built back in that Chamber. Can't your people copy its design?"

"Sir, it was completely destroyed in the melt down. I inspected it this morning and there's nothing left."

"Son-of-a-bitch, the President is going to have my ass for losing all that technology. Can we still build the KILOGEN devices?"

"Oh, yes. They had the pilot production line running and they have fully trained the people from Alamogordo."

"Well, if push comes to shove, we can use conventional means to deliver those warheads," the General said. Then, he got into his car and headed for a plane waiting on a nearby runway.

Walking the rest of the way back to the Chron Lab, Farnsworth was in deep thought. He did not mention, to the General, another possible explanation for where the missing women went. It was just possible they had recovered enough from their injuries to escape to the other reality, before the Synthesizer melted down. He could not blame them if they did go back there, after all, this goddamn place couldn't even protect them from KGB. In any case, he did not share these thoughts with the General. Because he had decided, long ago, not to mention the Alternate Reality to him. Any revelations about that, now, would surely lead to his removal as laboratory manager. They would never believe any explanation that involved the principles of time travel. His original story was simply to well entrenched to be undone.

Chapter 13

Turning her head slowly, Laura began to regain consciousness as her eyes gradually focused on the horizon. She now had the familiar fuzzy headache associated with coming out of a time travel coma. She noticed things were very dark, then realized she was still in her space-time travel suit and was looking through the visor on the helmet. She unsnapped the clips and took off the helmet, and noticed the formations of red rocks around the landscape; they were in the Garden of the Gods and no one had discovered them. Looking around she could see Lola and her aunt were still unconscious. The day was cold and cloudy and it had rained, which was probably why no park custodians had come upon them. They had lied there for a day and a half in early December and but did not freeze because the suits they wore were well insulated. She decided their luck would not hold out much longer and removed her space-time suit. As she started putting on the foul weather coat that she had in her duffel bag, she noticed Lola begin to stir. Taking off Lola and her aunt's helmets and she saw how swollen Lola's jaw was.

"Where am I? I can hardly move my mouth, it hurts so much, and that throbbing in my head is killing me," Lola murmured in almost a whisper.

Laura realized she was not only coming out of the time travel coma, but also recovering from the effects of the punch she had received in the Fated

Reality. As a result, she started to examine Lola more carefully.

"Lola, do you remember what was happening in the Chron Lab hallway."

"I was struggling to get away from those KGB guys when one of them hit me. I don't remember anything else. Where are we? Did they capture us?" Lola said in a whisper.

"No, they didn't capture us. The guards and I shot it out with them. We probably killed three or four of the sons-of-bitches, but the Colonel and his aid made it to their car and drove off. I pulled you out of there and dragged you back to the Lab. Carmen and I got you into that suit and now we're all in the Garden of the Gods in the Alternate Reality."

"The Garden of the Gods?"

"You never got the spatial coordinates of the site on the Apache Reservation. I had to use the default coordinates, which are still those of the Garden of the Gods. However, the date is still the same one we chose. It's 3 December 1993."

"Where's my aunt?"

"Over there."

"Is she all right?"

"Yes, but still unconscious, I think, because of her age. She's going to take a little longer to come out of the coma. Wait a second; I think she's coming around now. Oh, I nearly forgot, we have to put on our pantsuits and shoes. And let's get your aunt out of her uniform top and into that extra blouse you have in your duffel bag. We want to blend in as much as possible and we don't want having to explain where the other clothes came from when we turn ourselves in."

Laura helped both women out of their space-time suits and gave them their changes of clothes. After the women finished changing and put on their foul weather coats, Laura put their discarded clothes, space suits and helmets in large plastic bags. They looked around for anything they might have, inadvertently, left lying about. There was nothing, however, the cold, damp, morning air, made Lola cough and she let out a painful yelp. Laura and Carmen turned, quickly, but Lola waved them off pointing to her jaw.

"Girls, we are really here, look at those red rocks," Carmen remarked, as she stood there gazing at the landscape.

"Laura, thank you for getting us out of that doomed reality and sorry for not being much help," Lola whispered, feeling her swollen jaw.

"What are you talking about? If it wasn't for your distress call, they would have surprised me, too and we would all be still in the Fated Reality, probably in the hands of the KGB. Now, forget about the apologies. How are you feeling, your face is still very swollen, do you think you can walk out of here?"

"Laura, I think my jaw is broken, but I can walk," Lola whispered, hardly moving her jaw.

"OK, let's get Carmen on a bus to Alamogordo, we'll brief her on the way to the bus station. Once we get her on her way, I'm going to take you to the hospital. Then, call General Haig in this reality and tell him a story that closely follows our abduction in the other reality. I'm going to modify the story to follow a scenario that is compatible with the things that occurred here. Let's get out of here; with any luck we can still complete the final phase of our mission."

"What phase is that, Laura?" Carmen asked.

"It's a phase Lola and I added to the original mission. It's to get back to this reality and reestablish our lives here, free of any obligation to the Fated Reality. We have accomplished the first part of that objective, now what remains is to fit back into this society smoothly."

The women walked out of the Garden of the Gods carrying the bags with the suits and their duffel bags. Reaching the parking lot they realized the site was not open for viewing because it very early in the morning. They now understood why they were not discovered. They saw several large trash containers in the parking lot and tossed all the bags they were carrying into them. They kept money and personal things they had in the pockets of their foul weather coats. Only Carmen carried her duffel bag with valuables from the other reality in it.

Reaching the road, they flagged down a farm truck going to market and hitched a ride to downtown Colorado Springs. From there, they went directly to the bus terminal to get Carmen a ticket to Alamogordo. Arriving at the terminal they soon found out she would have to change buses in Albuquerque and take another bus to Alamogordo. That information caused the women to change their plans.

"Laura, I've been thinking, maybe we shouldn't stay in Colorado Springs. If they find those bags and we show up at the hospital, they might somehow correlate that with the women found in the Garden of the Gods ten years ago, wearing similar suits. If the FBI checks their records, they will see those women are we. They might not find out right away, but eventually they would make a correlation. And, they would question us again. I don't think we would want to go through life waiting for that shoe to drop," Lola said, her voice now a little louder than a whisper.

"Lola, we have to get you to a hospital to have that jaw examined. We'll just have to take the chance."

"It feels a little better than it did an hour ago. It's probably not as bad as it looks. Let's go to Albuquerque with aunt Carmen. Then, we'll take the bus to Los Alamos and she will go to Alamogordo to stay with my parents. It will give us a chance to refine our cover stories."

"That does make better sense than staying in Colorado Springs. OK, we'll do it, if you feel you can delay having your jaw looked at for several hours. If it gets worst, we'll go to the hospital in Albuquerque and have it treated."

On the bus, Laura and Lola went over the details of Carmen's cover story, stressing all the things about her fabricated life with Lola in New York. She agreed to say she was Lola's mother privately to her sister María, but to all others she was her aunt and María was her mother. To Henry she had to say Lola lived with her in Europe. By the time they arrived in Albuquerque, they had reviewed, hopefully, all the pertinent details with Carmen. They, then, put her on a bus to Alamogordo. Carmen had brought cash and jewels with her from the Fated Reality, so, Lola was not concerned about her solvency if anything should go wrong. The money she brought from the other reality was identical with that of this reality. However, some bills were duplicates but no one could say they were counterfeit, because they made them with the identical plates in different realities. The jewels were of the highest quality, purchased for her by her husband in Europe, and would afford her a comfortable living for many years.

Riding on the bus to Los Alamos the women decided they would say they were abducted in front of the Capistrano restaurant that evening the KILOGEN warheads were stolen. They would say they were told General Haig's car would be sent to pick them up. Instead, they would say, third world mercenaries abducted them, and took them to a shack somewhere in the mountains past Mescalero. The mercenaries would offer them for sale to Russia or any third world country that would pay the price. They would say they didn't know where the KILOGEN warheads were but heard the mercenaries say they would truck them out of the country through Mexico, when things cooled down.

Lola would have to undergo a comprehensive physical exam on her face and head, when they went to the hospital in Los Alamos. During that exam, they would probably discover her microchip implant. This being the case, they decided to take advantage of that likely discovery, and make the microchip's presence immediately known to the authorities. They would claim that their captives placed the microchips behind their ears so they could be easily found if they tried to escape. They would then demand to have them removed. This way, the microchips would help lend credence to their cover story without forcing them to reveal anything about the Fated Reality.

Arriving at the Hospital in Los Alamos, Laura asked the hospital administrator to call the police, immediately. When they arrived, she told them who they were and that they were held captive by third world mercenaries for more than two months in a shack somewhere above Mescalero. The police knew they were missing and called the FBI and General Haig. She further demanded that the hospital surgeon remove the microchips placed behind their ears by their captives. They told her they would do so after the FBI arrived. Within an hour, the hospital lobby was flooded with FBI, CIA, military investigators and reporters.

Lola had to have her jaw wired because it was broken in two places. After they set her jawbone, they removed the microchip from behind her ear and later had a locksmith remove the handcuff bracelet from her wrist. Later, a surgeon removed the microchip from behind Laura's left ear. They gave the handcuff bracelet and microchips to the FBI who sent them to a government lab for study. Both women were undergoing comprehensive physical exams at the request of the government and were sharing the same hospital room.

The hospital had notified the families the day before, and both families, including the fiancés, were in the hospital waiting room. Maria introduced Aunt Carmen to Henry and Kurt, and then to the Claremont's. When Carmen was off to the side with Henry, she told him about her home in Spain, and the fabrication about the time Lola had spent there with her. She described events there in both Spanish and English and he could see that Lola picked up her Castilian accent in Spanish from her aunt. Because of that conversation, he thought he completely understood, now, the woman he was going to marry.

The families discussed what happened to their daughters, and pledged to force the government to release them from any responsibilities or obligations, they might have. The work they were doing was obviously not worth the risk and they would do their best to convince the women to quit their jobs. The families knew from the newspaper stories that foreign agents abducted the women, and they nearly lost their lives escaping from their captors. The doctors told them, Lola had to have her jaw wired because it had been broken in two places. And both women had to have some type of chip removed from behind their ears that was placed there by their captors. Henry said he would retain the best legal firm in the country if the government did not allow the women to resign, immediately. Kurt said they would have to let them leave, if they so choose, because it would be a violation of their constitutional rights.

About a half hour later, they allowed the families to see the women. The women were overwhelmed with joy when they saw their families come through the door and tears began to flow. Everyone hugged the girls, even members of the other's family. After things settled down a bit, Laura spoke.

"People. We are simply ecstatic to see all of you. For a while, we thought we would never see you again. I know I speak for Lola when I say we hope we never have to work on that HAVE-FIELD Program again."

"What is a HAVE-FIELD Program?" her mother asked.

"HAVE-FIELD is the white world code name for the black world program we have been working on."

"What is the black world, dear?"

"I can't say anymore about it, Mom, because I would violate the agreement I signed with the US government."

"Joan, I'll explain it later to you. But, first let me ask. Laura, do you intend to keep working at the Los Alamos National Laboratory?" her father asked.

"After what we've been through, both of us would like to get out of the black world and work at a university in some unclassified field. Then, settle down with the men that we love."

After hearing that remark, Kurt spoke up.

"What do you mean, you would like to leave? You are going to leave and no one can stop you."

"We have to get released from the project before we can leave," Laura responded, thinking about the way it had to be done in the Fated Reality.

"Who told you that? I looked into this a few months ago, and you require no such release from that project. You're in the United States and you can quit whenever you want," Kurt said, adamantly.

"He's right, girls, you can quit anytime you want," Henry responded.

The guys then went over to their women and hugged them tightly.

Lola's father, not satisfied with the explanation the FBI agent had given them, decided to ask the girls a few questions of his own.

"Laura, would you mind telling us how Lola got her jaw broken?"

"We were trying to escape and Lola and I were struggling frantically with two of our captors. A third was trying to put her handcuffs on her. They were going to take us by truck out of the country through Mexico and we knew if let them cuff us; there would be no chance of escape, later. They were very big guys and one of them punched her so hard in the face that she dropped like a limp rag to the ground. Somehow I grabbed one of their guns and shot them."

Hearing how hard they hit Lola, her father and mother ran to her and hugged her.

Seeing how her description pained all those in the room, Laura said, "Perhaps that was too graphic. Maybe I shouldn't continue."

"No, no, Laura, go on, we have to know the truth," Lola's father said, with the rest of those in the room nodding their approval.

After an hour of discussion about the ordeal the women had to endure, the group finally decided to leave and give Lola some rest. Laura walked the group to the elevator and María and Carmen stayed a moment to talk to Lola alone.

"Lola, honey, I want you to know how grateful we all are for finding Carmen for us. She told us all about how she raised you in New York and the time she spent in Spain with her husband. I want you to know that you are a daughter to both of us. She told me you didn't want us to tell Henry she's your mother, because of what we told him years ago about you being educated in Europe. Don't worry as far as anyone knows she's your aunt and I'm your mother."

"Thanks," Lola whispered to both of them, thinking her existence in the Fated Reality will never have to be revealed to her family.

Kissing Lola good by, Carmen winked at her and whispered.

"Lola, everything here is like you described. Leaving the Fated Reality was the right thing to do. Now, get some rest, we'll talk more when you get better."

Henry and Kurt were standing alone outside the hospital, talking.

"You know, Kurt, they should try to leave on good terms because they will still need some government protection for a while. Those responsible for their abduction may not have given up yet. They know the women still possess knowledge that is much sought after."

"What would you suggest we do about that?"

"Well, it may sound over cautious. Nevertheless, I think we should go back in there and tell them about our concerns and tell them they should change their names when they leave those jobs."

"Henry, you're absolutely right, and I know just the guys who can change their names for them," Kurt responded, smiling.

The men laughed as they started back to the women's room. When they got back in the room, they told the women their concerns. The women really did not have the same concerns the men did, because no one in this reality really wanted them. However, if they wanted things to end properly, they would have to pretend to be concerned, both for their boyfriends and for the government.

"Guys, we share your concerns, but how can we solve the problem," Laura said, speaking for herself and Lola.

"You can start by changing your names and a simple way of doing that is to marry us. That would at least stop the name recognition part of the problem," Henry said, smiling but meaning what he said.

The women smiled at each other. They knew the guys were trying to help with what they thought was a serious problem.

"Well Lola, that's one way to get an offer of marriage out of a couple of college professors. Do you think we should take them up on it?"

Lola tried to smile, but nodded her head instead, the anesthetic was wearing off and she felt pain with every word she uttered.

"Guys, I'm finished with the tests they were giving me and I can leave when I get dressed. Why don't you wait in the lobby? Maybe, we can talk a bit over a cup of coffee, before I go back to our apartment. Lola is going to have to stay another day or so until the doctors are sure no complications are likely to occur."

When the men left the room, Laura quickly dressed and told Lola she would see her tomorrow.

Arriving in the lobby Laura saw the men talking to each other by the window over looking the parking lot. When they saw her, they greeted her with smiles and together they all went to the coffee shop. After Henry paid the cashier for their coffee, the group sat at a table by the window and Laura told them of her and Lola's plans.

"Lola and I are going to get debriefed in a few days by General Haig himself. After that, we'll be wrapping things up in Los Alamos and leaving the National Laboratories for good. I want to work again in university research. And somewhere along the way I want to settle down with Kurt and I'm sure Lola wants to do the same with Henry."

"Are you sure that she really wants that?" Henry asked.

"Well, Lola has told me that many times over the last few months and, as for me, if I didn't feel that way before, I certainly do now. You guys will never know what we had to go through to get back here. Nevertheless, our thoughts of you were like beacons guiding us."

Kurt squeezed her hand when she said that.

"Can you tell us more of what happened to you while you held captives?" Henry asked. "We know you were holding back a bit in front of your parents."

Laura gave them a more detailed summary of what happened during their captivity, and what she and Lola planed to tell the authorities, but said nothing about the Fated Reality. She told the men a carefully fabricated version of their ordeal, starting with their abduction in front of the Capistrano Restaurant. When she finished, the men seem to be satisfied with what they heard. But, they warned her not to let General Haig talk them into accepting another position in the National Laboratories.

General Haig, his Los Alamos staff, and the FBI debriefed the women a few days later. Laura did the speaking because it was still very uncomfortable for Lola to speak with her jaw wired closed.

"Sir, they abducted us in front of the Capistrano restaurant that evening the KILOGEN warheads were stolen. We were informed earlier, by phone, that the General was arriving that evening and would send a car for us. He was arriving too late for dinner, but, we were told, he would have his car meet us at the Capistrano restaurant after we finished eating. When we got into the car, we found third world mercenaries were abducting us. At least that's what they told us. They handcuffed us and took us to a shack that was in the mountains above Mescalero, but we couldn't be sure."

"Did they say anything about the KILOGEN warheads."

"Yes, Sir, they did. The KILOGEN warheads and even us were going to be put up for sale to any country that would pay the price they were asking. We didn't know where the KILOGEN warheads were but we heard one of them mention they would truck them out of the country through Mexico when things cooled down."

"When did they implant those microchips in your heads?" the General asked.

"Sir, they sent some medical guy to the shack where they were keeping us, a few days after we got there. It seemed like he chloroformed us and then implanted them. The incisions healed in a few days and we hardly knew they were there."

"Our Lab says they're a very advanced design and have functions on them we don't understand. However, it appears they could activate them when they wished and track the signal they emit," the General informed the women.

"That handcuff bracelet we took from Dr. Gonzalez seems foreign made. Did you see anything else that would help us identify them?" an FBI agent asked.

"No."

"How long did they keep you there?"

"For about two and a half months. Once, I heard one of them say they were negotiating the best price for us."

"How did you get away?"

"They were tired of guarding us and got a little careless. When they let us go behind the shack to urinate, we saw an opportunity to escape. Lola and I began struggling with two of our captors. A third one came and was trying to put handcuffs on her. We knew they were going to take us out of the country by truck through Mexico. We also knew if let them cuff us, there would be no chance of escape, later. They were very big guys and one of them punched her so hard in the face that she immediately fell to the ground, unconscious. I ran to her aid and managed to grab one of their guns in the struggle, and shot all the three of them. When Lola regained consciousness, I tried to get the handcuff off her wrist. I found some handcuff keys but couldn't find the key for the one on her wrist. We knew it might cause a problem later, so I cut off the dangling part with an ax that the men used to cut firewood."

"I guess we know the rest, Dr. Claremont. However, we're curious about something. We tried to find the shack in which they held you captive. But, all we could find were some old World War II buildings up there. Was that where they kept you?"

The women had to be careful about what they said at this point, because their story could come unraveled by a small inconsistency at this stage of the debriefing. Lola leaned over and whispered something to Laura.

"Sir, I can't tell for sure, but Dr. Gonzalez just reminded me of something we saw in the shack in which we were kept. Hanging on the wall was an old calendar that had a 1943 date on it. So, I think the building must have been there at least since World War II, maybe it is the same one your people found."

The women knew both realities were on the same timeline back then, so if the shacks were still there in this reality, the calendar also might still be there. If it were, it would completely corroborate their story. To the FBI and the Military types present at the debriefing, every major event had to hang together; otherwise, the case would remain open. And, the women wanted, desperately, for this case to close tightly around their cover story.

When the General and the staff heard the women describe that old calendar, they knew the their captors must have kept them there. There were no signs of dead bodies or other things that the women might have left. Nevertheless, there were tire marks made by all terrain vehicles. The General and the FBI caucused at that point, after thanking the women for their cooperation. During the caucus, they decided some of the women's captors must have returned, disposed of the guard's bodies, and removed anything that might lead to their capture.

The General later decided that the women had made their contribution to the national defense of the country by setting up the KILOGEN pilot production line. He felt the Los Alamos crew could produce the KILOGEN warheads without any further help from the women. He then agreed to release to them from any responsibility on the HAVE-FIELD Program, but only after they documented their notes on the design of the KILOGEN devices. He asked the FBI to shadow them for a year to make sure foreign agents did not try to abduct them again.

———————————

The women were deliriously happy with the way things had turned out. They could finally live the lives they felt they deserved after saving the Fated Reality from imminent disaster. They were quite sure the Synthesizer in the other reality had melted down and with it the keys to this reality permanently destroyed. They knew that even if Farnsworth rebuilt the synthesizer by copying their design, he could never make it deliver KILOGEN weapons in that reality. Even if he tried and failed, he was smart enough to think of some ruse that would get him off the hook. They knew he would never reveal anything about Alternate Reality because the authorities in his reality would never believe any explanation that involved time travel. The original cover story he had concocted, and supported for his own purposes, had become too well established to be undone. In any case, NATO and the Soviet Bloc in the Fated Reality would have to come to terms with each other. Otherwise, the world they existed in would end in nuclear holocaust because the time travelers did not intend to intervene, again.

Chapter 14

Arriving in Washington for his meeting with General Haig, Harold Farnsworth was apprehensive because he feared they would ask him to rebuild the Synthesizer. The principle inventors were gone, and reconstructing the new version of the Synthesizer would be difficult. All the recent design notes the women had made were in the old one's computer and the meltdown destroyed them. He was not exactly without a design capability because he had an electronic copy of the original Synthesizer design. In addition, he had on hand the remaining members of the Time Crease Team. However, he did not want to attempt such a formidable task under the spotlight of General Haig.

Entering General Haig's office Farnsworth sensed that this meeting was going be a lot more than a rehash of what happened two weeks ago. The sense of urgency was so thick that one could cut it with a knife. The General lost no time in getting to the reason for the meeting.

"Farnsworth, we have called you here to inform you that the order to move your entire facility to Alamogordo is still in effect. We will house you and the remaining Time Crease Team at the Holloman Base, in the officer's quarters. We will make facilities, on the Base, available to you for the reconstruction of your laboratory, there. In the new laboratory, you are to reconstruct the Weapon Synthesizer that Drs. Claremont and Gonzalez have designed. This arrangement will be in effect until the end of the Time Crease Program. It's the only way we can ensure the safe completion of this project."

"But, Sir, the design of that Synthesizer was destroyed in the meltdown. Without those scientists it could take a year or more to retrace their steps."

"You mean to tell me you have no idea how to proceed on this project without those scientists. Do you realize they are probably in the hands of the Soviets right now, being forced to work on building a Weapon Synthesizer? If you can't get the job done I'll remove you and get somebody who can."

Farnsworth could see he probably could not talk his way out of this assignment. The General was dead serious and he would dismiss him in disgrace if he refused to work on the project or even worst court martial him.

"Sir, I didn't mean to imply we can't do it, but just that we can't respond in a month or so. The Time Crease Team only has three members left. The other laboratory scientists are busy on high priority projects. Besides, they won't be much use, anyway, because they are not up to speed on the Time Crease technology."

"Farnsworth, perhaps I didn't make myself clear. This is a national emergency and the Time Crease Project has the highest national priority. You no longer have to worry about the other laboratory projects; you are now assigned full time to the Time Crease Program. Now get your Time Crease staff and their equipment down to Holloman and start working on that Weapon Synthesizer! The President ordered me to have the Time Crease Team rebuild the Weapon Synthesize and, by god, we are going to do it!" General Haig ordered in rough militaristic tones.

The General seemed half crazed and blind to any rational explanations of why they must delay the project. Farnsworth knew now he had to tackle this Herculean task and the price of failure would be extremely high. The meeting with the General and the Joint Chiefs went on and on. Each staff member had Farnsworth walk him through some detail of moving the Time Crease equipment to the Holloman Base. They gave him the authority to bring on anyone in the nation that he might find useful on the project. They also gave him priority access to any parts or equipment made in the country. Finally, they gave him two weeks to report to them with a plan and milestones that would accomplish the objectives of the program.

Flying back to Colorado Springs Farnsworth laid out his overall strategy to achieve the objectives the Joint Chiefs had forced him to accept. He thought he would first try to reconstruct the old Synthesizer that Laura had built. He had an electronic copy of its design in the Laboratory's database. He would rely on the old Team's third in command, Hillary James, to head the new effort. The two bright junior members of the old team, Veronica Richards and Claude Harris would be placed at her disposal. He could choose any other person that he deemed necessary from the Chronometry Laboratory's general staff. However, the core of the new team would comprise Drs. James, Richards and Harris, because they were the only ones that really knew what the Alternate Reality Team had accomplished. The original team had designed a version of the Synthesizer that could deliver weapons in the Fated Reality from its own timeline. Why couldn't the remaining members work from the old Claremont design notes and extend them to build the desired Weapon Synthesizer? These thoughts gave him confidence that the new project would succeed.

Returning from Washington, Harold Farnsworth immediately called a meeting of the regrouped Time Crease Team. He chose to limit the attendees to the core members, which were Drs. James, Richards, and Harris, because he had things to say that only those people familiar with the original Mission should hear. When the three core members of the team arrived at his office, Farnsworth greeted them enthusiastically and then asked them to be seated at his conference table.

"Time Crease scientists, General Haig had summoned me to Washington last week for a top secret meeting. When I met with him there, he directed me to form a new Time Crease Project Organization. Given that directive, I selected you to work on the Core Team, and the three of you will serve as its nucleus. You will be responsible for the supervision of any new members that we acquire. We can acquire these new members from the Chron Lab's general staff or from anywhere in the country, if we deem it necessary. We selected you, because you are the only people familiar enough with the work of Claremont and Gonzalez to bring the new project to fruition."

"Excuse me, Dr. Farnsworth, has the government given up on finding Drs. Claremont and Gonzalez?" Hillary James asked.

"I don't think they have given up, but as time goes by, the conclusion is that they are either dead or somewhere in the Soviet Union. If they're not dead, we can assume they're being forced to build a Weapon Synthesizer for them."

"Is it possible they escaped to the Alternate Reality?" Veronica Richards asked.

"Anything is possible. Nevertheless, as I cautioned the original Team when they were here, we are never to mention the Alternate Reality outside this office. If that story were to get out, it would either cause them to doubt our sanity or lead them to think we were part of some conspiracy. If they suspected a conspiracy, then they would accuse us of treason. They might even conclude we are Soviet spies on a mission to sabotage the efforts of our esteemed colleagues. We just don't know how they will react to that Alternate Reality story. Our best strategy will be to do as directed. So let me go on."

"Does the government seriously think we can reproduce the new Claremont design?" Claude Harris asked, wondering if he misunderstood what Dr. Farnsworth was alluding to.

"Not only do they expect us to do just that, but they expect us to do it in less than a year."

Farnsworth could see their faces drop after that statement and quickly continued.

"The task is not as formidable as it might seem, because we have an electronic copy of the design of the original Synthesizer. And, you also have your own notes on the new Claremont design."

"That still may not be enough, Harold. Without their leadership we will just get into endless debates on how to proceed and who's in charge," Hillary responded.

"Nonsense, we'll just regroup and things will begin to fall into place. Now, this is how I plan to reorganize. Hillary will be the new Team Leader and Veronica will be her second in command. Claude will take Hillary's Chief of Staff position. All other people in the new organization will fall under that chain of command. We will take this thing one step at a time and build the original Synthesizer first. By the time we finish building it, we will be very familiar with its principles. Then, we will be ready to modify the design so that it could deliver weapons in our reality from our own timeline."

The approach outline by Farnsworth seemed reasonable to the new Core Team and they decided to accept the challenge. Farnsworth then formed the new project around them. They brought scientists from other projects on board, and even brought people from other laboratories to work on the program. Then, they brought the entire new Time Crease Team and all their lab equipment to the Holloman Base. The Team itself, they housed in the officers' quarters on that Base.

Over the next ten months, the Time Crease Team labored ceaselessly and managed to reproduce the original version of the Space-Time Transitional Synthesizer and its associated Bifurcation Locator. With this phase of the program complete, they were ready to modify the old design so that it could deliver weapons to points on their own timeline. They knew it was a difficult problem, but if the Claremont Team was able to solve it, so would they. They postulated, over the next few months, theory after theory that was supposed to access their timeline at some point in the near future. The Core Team tested each new postulation by pushing small objects into the aperture of the Synthesizer and observing if they appeared at some designated point in the near future. Every experiment failed. Of course, the objects they pushed into the aperture would appear at the designated coordinates, but not in their reality.

Failure after failure occurred. Finally, in desperation Farnsworth called a secret meeting of the Core Team. The Team went for a long walk around the drill field near their quarters. Dr. Farnsworth began assessing the situation.

"Team. We have been trying to modify that replica of the original Synthesizer for the past two months and each of our modifications failed to produce the desired results."

"Harold, maybe we are approaching this wrong. Maybe we should go back and try to reformulate the entire theory," Hillary suggested.

"No, that could take months or even years. Even then, we might not discover the break through the Claremont Team came up with. We don't have the luxury of time, if we don't come up with something soon they're going to know we failed," Farnsworth said, sounding very concerned.

"What could they do to us? Dismiss us. We've done our best," Veronica said, becoming somewhat indignant.

"She's right. We are doing our best. We are scientists and not concerned about experimental failure because that is how science advances," Claude quickly added.

"You two are only in your late twenties and have been in the scientific community all your adult lives. You're among our brightest and best that's why you were selected for this assignment in the first place. However, this protected environment shields you from the outside world and as such, you find it hard to perceive how the government views failure during a national emergency. As a minimum, they would consider us amateurish frauds, too inept to carry on the great work of the Claremont Team. They would then summarily drummed us out of the scientific community. And, at the worst, they would accuse us of treason for not revealing the true mission of the Claremont Team. If the truth came out, the government would still consider Claremont and Gonzalez the true heroes of this doomed reality. Washington would think that way, because they risked, or maybe gave, their lives to save it. And after all is said and done, they would still consider us unworthy to take their places."

"Young people, Harold and I are in our late forties, and have been through many a crisis with government officials. We know the consequences of failure. Now, with that being said, where do we go from here? Harold, I detected there was some question about the Claremont Team's fate when you made that remark. What do you think really happened to them? I've worked with you long enough to know you were alluding to something," Hillary said, wanting to get at the real purpose of this meeting.

"Well, Laura and Lola were certainly loyal patriots, dedicated both to science and their country. Look how they risked their lives to save this reality. Others may not have even tried to come back, but not only did they come back, they placed themselves at great risk to avoid being captured by the KGB agents."

"But, they eventually captured them, didn't they?" Veronica asked.

"I'm not sure they were. In fact I'm quite sure they were not."

That revelation astounded the other members of the team, especially the younger ones.

"Do you have any proof of that, Harold?" Hillary asked, expressing the thoughts of the others, too.

"Only inferential proof. During the investigation I discovered their time travel suits were missing. While they could have burned in the fire that resulted after the Synthesizer melted down, I found no trace of them. That fire was not very hot, and the suits and helmets were heat resistant, they should have survived."

"Did you report that to the authorities?" Claude asked.

"Of course not. How would I explain where they went? I certainly wasn't going to tell them about the Alternate Reality. They would have me committed."

"Maybe the KGB agents took the suits along with the women," Veronica suggested.

"That's remotely possible, but I think not because the KGB wouldn't know what they were looking for and our Team leaders would not have volunteered that information. My Guess is that during the shootout with the KGB agents, they were not hit by the gunfire and had taken cover. In any case, I think the women were not seriously injured and fled to the Synthesizer Chamber. Once there, they locked the door and put on their time travel suits. The guard that recovered from his injuries said the Synthesizer was already fired up and the women were doing experiments before Lola left the Chamber to get something. In any case, when they got back to the Chamber, they probably felt it was only a matter of time before the KGB would break down the door and capture them. In their desperation, my guess is they probably punched in some coordinates in the Alternate Reality and returned there sometime after they had left. As we all know, they are very clever and are probably working now on a way to get back again."

The Lab Head's conjectures somewhat amazed the Team, but they thought he was probably right. His explanation did seem more plausible than the official one about the Claremont Team's abduction.

"If it's true what your saying, Harold, maybe they will return soon and show us how to modify the Synthesizer," Hillary said.

"I don't think we should hold our breath. They might not ever get back because so many things could go wrong. It took them ten years in that reality just to get in a position to return. This time it's going to be harder for them and they may fail. No, we have to take some action ourselves."

"How do you suppose we do that? Go to the Alternate Reality," Hillary asked, half facetiously.

"You may be joking but that's exactly what I'm thinking."

The Team could see the Lab Head was deadly serious by the way he said that. They then stopped walking around the drill grounds and sat around him in the empty reviewing stand. He now had their undivided attention.

"Team, from what we just said only a fool would miss the opportunity that now presents itself. Let me tell you my thoughts on how to get out of this dilemma. I want to take the Core Team and go to the Alternate Reality, and find Laura and Lola. The evidence suggests they did go back, and if we can find them, I'm sure they will show us how to modify the Synthesizer. We can help them rebuild the version they used to return here, and together we can save this reality, again, from self destruction," Farnsworth said.

"Dr. Farnsworth that sounds like we're grasping at straws. We don't even know for sure they are in the Alternate Reality. Even if they are, how can we be sure they will want to return or even help us? Why do we all have to go? Why don't you just go and the rest of us will cover for you?" Veronica asked, thinking what he was proposing was scary and even crazy.

"Guys, I know it sounds like we are desperate, but we really are. If we don't come up with the Weapon Synthesizer soon there will be no options left. You asked, "How do we know they are there?" We don't for sure, but we do have to get out of here. If we go there and can't find them we'll just have to improvise, they had to do that when they first entered that reality. Why do we all have to go? Because, if I leave any of you here, the authorities will eventually force you to tell all you know and then dispose of you like some kind of scientific trash. The situation here is deadly serious and they're not going to let you play around with that Synthesizer while waiting for me to return."

"He's right people, they are not going to believe us even if we tell them the truth. They certainly won't let us hang around here waiting for him to return. They'll just remove us, and if we are not shot for treason, they will send us on some kind of forced work detail. Let's all get out of here, while we still have the chance," Hillary implored the two young members of the Team.

The young people did not like the way they were perverting their scientific ideals, but by now, they were aware of the consequences of failure. Perhaps, not as acutely as Drs. Farnsworth and James, but were aware enough to hear out what their Lab Head had in mind.

"OK, people, before we are anywhere near ready to go to the Alternate Reality we have to develop a very detailed plan. We have to anticipate every possible problem that we might encounter. I suggest we pay very close attention to what the Claremont Team had told us about their experiences in the Alternate Reality; that includes creating a cover story and obtaining foolproof identification papers."

"Oh boy, that sounds complicated," Claude remarked, not sure he wanted to hear the rest.

"It is complicated and going to get more complicated. First, we have to deal with the de-aging process, which immediately brings us to when we want to synthesize in the Alternate Reality."

"Well, Harold, I think we better arrive there soon after we estimate Laura and Lola have returned. I say this because if we let too much time go by too many things can change and we would have a much bigger problem finding them," Hillary injected.

"Your right, I think it should be a few months after they arrived. The problem is determining when that was."

"Dr. Farnsworth, didn't Laura say her and Lola left that reality sometime in October of 1993? My guess is that they probably went back within a few months of that time. If I were she, I would have done that because I wouldn't want too much time to have elapsed from when I was last seen in that reality. Things would be too difficult to explain otherwise," Veronica commented, starting to become interested in the planning process.

"Good reasoning, Veronica. With that information, we should set our date of entry to be sometime in the spring of '94. That sends us back seventeen years on the alternate timeline."

"Harold, we have to be careful when calculating the de-aging factor. We have been modifying the space-time circuitry to allow us to access our timeline for weapon delivery. The de-aging factor has been reduced by a factor of two. So, we are going to de-age eight years," Hillary injected.

"That's OK. Hillary, Veronica and Claude will be about nineteen or twenty in that reality and we'll be around forty at that time. Those ages will fit nicely into our cover story."

"Cover story? What cover story?" Claude asked.

"Guys, we have to be able to identify ourselves in that reality. Remember the problems Laura and Lola ran into. They had to establish who they were and needed the proper identification papers. We can't afford to be coming up with identities spontaneously. We have to have everything in place before we go to that reality."

"Dr. Farnsworth, where are we going to enter? The Synthesizer Chamber is now here on the Holloman Base. We can't go to the Garden of the Gods like the Claremont Team did. It's too far out of the range of the Synthesizer and we have not been successful in extending its range," Veronica said.

The Team thought about the apparent dilemma they were facing. They could not synthesize in the middle of the Holloman Base because they did not know what the government was doing at that facility in the other reality. They needed some place like the Garden of the Gods, a national treasure that they probably preserved in the other reality, too. After thinking about their dilemma for a few minutes, an idea struck Farnsworth.

"I think I have the solution to our all our problems including the cover story. Why don't we enter as a family on a vacation in the Southwest exploring the White Sands National Monument? It's more than likely still preserved in that reality and we can synthesize in a remote part of the White Sands gypsum desert. No one is likely to discover us there while we recover from the time travel comas. We'll be traveling under the name of Farnsworth. Hillary will be my wife and you two will be our college age children."

"Dr. Farnsworth, do we know where to look for them?" Veronica asked.

"Laura told me they had an apartment in Los Alamos and we'll head there when we walk out of the White Sands National Monument. They are prominent scientist in that reality who went to MIT and NMSU. I'm sure we can find them if they are there. If not, we'll just have to improvise like they did. Now, let's all get back to the Laboratory, we have a myriad of details to work out before we can put this plan into place."

The Core Team's meeting ended on that note and the members went back to the Synthesizer Chamber on the Base to contemplate the plan that just evolved.

By the middle of July of 2011, it was becoming obvious to General Haig that the new Time Crease Team would not deliver the Weapon Synthesizer, as originally scheduled. They were already a month past the date Farnsworth agreed it would take to make the Synthesizer. The General knew they had built the new version but all the experimental tests conducted with the device had failed. He decided it was time to lean harder on Farnsworth, because he feared the Soviets might have one built by now. And that could change the balance of power. They summoned Farnsworth to Washington to brief the General on what was affecting the schedule. Upon receiving that request, Farnsworth put the Core Team on a schedule to complete their escape plans rapidly, just in case the General decided to convene a fact-finding committee. He knew such a move would be a fast-moving precursor to the Team's removal and unpredictable circumstances would follow.

Arriving in Washington at the General's office, they quickly ushered Farnsworth into a conference room for the meeting. The General and the Joint Chiefs were waiting for him.

"Farnsworth, you must be aware of why I had you brought here. The Time Crease Program is floundering. What exactly is the problem?" General Haig asked, his voice sounding very gruff and stern.

"Sir, many unforeseen problems arose. We are just now getting them resolved," Farnsworth answered, his voice shaking.

"Stop talking in generalities. I want specifics. The Soviets are probably ahead of us by now and your failures are placing the nation at risk. Now tell us exactly what is impeding your process. For chrissake, the Claremont Team broke ground for you; why the hell can't you simply reproduce their work?" the General asked, already tired of Farnsworth's excuses.

"Well, Sir, the Claremont Team had some sort of breakthrough during the latter part of their research. Their notes on that procedure were lost in the fire that resulted after the meltdown. We've been having trouble duplicating their efforts in that area, but we are making progress."

"Making progress? Every test you conducted has failed. Do you call that making progress? I think your team is lost in the steps of the procedure the Claremont Team had outlined for you and you are not able to follow their lead. I think it's time to bring a new team in that will be equal to the task."

That statement by the General made Farnsworth swallow hard and his stomach began to knot. He knew he must come up with something fast because there might not be a fact-finding committee. They might remove him and his team that very day.

"Sir, we have fixed all the problems and are ready to make our final series of tests in a few days. Delay any team changes until the results from those tests are in. Then make any changes you wish, but don't throw away a year's work for the sake of a few more days."

"All right Farnsworth, you have another week to show us you have achieved the goals of the Weapon Synthesizer Program. If you fail to demonstrate the weapon delivery capability, we will form a fact-finding committee and its findings will be used to formulate the next course of action. Dismissed!"

Returning to the Holloman Base in New Mexico, Farnsworth quickly informed the Team about the pressure that the General was exerting on him. From what Farnsworth related to them they knew now they had less than a week to get the Synthesizer ready for their departure.

The members of the Team worked through a checklist of tasks that had to be completed. Farnsworth worked on securing the Synthesizer. He did not want the authorities or anyone else to get access to it or its databases so he inserted special passwords for each member of the Team. The passwords were a long series of numbers and letters that would be all but impossible to crack. In addition, if the authorities made any systematic trial and error attempts, the Synthesizer would enter a timed sequence of stages that would ultimately lead to its meltdown.

Next, Farnsworth instructed the guards at the Synthesizer's Chamber door not to let anyone interrupt the critical experiments they were performing. He told them the experiments would be done in two hours sessions. Even though the Team would lock the Chamber door from the inside, the guards could gain access with special passkeys. However, when they left, he felt reasonably assured their departure would be undisturbed.

After a few more days of preparation, the Core Team completed its countdown and was assembled in the Synthesizer Chamber for the last time. They had turned on the Synthesizer and it was going through its warm-up cycle. The Synthesizer's timer was set for fifteen minutes after it finished its warm-up cycle and then it would shut down. If they did not return within two days from the Alternate Reality, it would automatically enter the timed sequence that led to meltdown. This would occur unless it was tampered with, in the interim. Tampering with it, either by attempting to find a password or by bypassing the control circuitry, would cause the Synthesizer to enter the timed sequence that leads to its meltdown. However, these precautions were not of concern to the Team. Because, after they accomplished their business in the other reality, they would return a half-hour after they left, with the solution to the Weapon Synthesizer problem. The guards and the authorities in this reality would be none the wiser and they would have achieved the objectives of the new Time Crease Program.

After donning their time travel suits, Farnsworth punched in the space-time coordinates of the point of entry in the White Sands National Monument. He set the differential spatial coordinates of each member to be twenty feet apart. He did this, so they would not fall on top of each other when they entered the Alternate Reality. After the others entered the aperture, Farnsworth quickly made a last minute check on things in the Chamber and noticed they had not locked the Chamber's door. After taking care of that detail, he approached the fiery aperture and the proximity forces rapidly drew him in.

Chapter 15

Turning her head, slowly, things began to gradually come into focus as Veronica Richards regained consciousness. Her head throbbed with some kind of strange pain as she tried to raise it. Through the visor on her helmet, she could see the shape of a huge sand dune looming up to the right of her. As she removed her helmet, the bright sunlight reflecting from the white gypsum dune made her eyes close tightly, then, squinting, she gradually opened them. Why were the dunes so huge, nothing she read about White Sands mentioned this extreme type of landscape? As she started to move, she noticed how loose her suit fit. She wondered if stepping through that aperture caused it to stretch. These things went through her mind as she attempted to sit-up. Finally reaching the sitting position, she noticed a kid with light brown hair. He wore loose-fitting pants, which he had rolled up, and he was walking around the flat area partially enclosed by the dunes. She thought, what the hell was a kid doing out here and where were her team members. The kid suddenly realized that she was sitting up came running over to her.

"Veronica, you finally came out of the time travel coma. How do you feel?"

Veronica, still squinting a little, saw he had blue eyes, and something about them made her think he looked familiar, but she could not quite place him.

"Who are you? How do you know my name?"

"Veronica, it's Claude Harris. Don't you recognize me?"

"Claude? My god, you look like kid. What happened to you?"

"You mean what happened to us. Pickup that helmet and look at your reflection in its visor, but first get out of that suit."

Claude then helped Veronica out of her time travel suit. Getting to her feet, she noticed she was a few inches shorter than the kid. How could that be, she thought? Then Claude handed her the helmet. As she studied her reflection in the visor, she saw a little dark haired girl with big brown eyes staring back at her. While the image was a little distorted, she could see it was that of a child, perhaps eleven or twelve years of age. The image so overwhelmed her that she had to grab onto Claude's shoulder to steady herself. He walked her over to the shade of a dune and sat her and himself down on the sand. After her headache subsided and she regained her composure, she began asking questions.

"Claude, what happened to us? Where are Drs. Farnsworth and James?"

"I suspect something was wrong with our de-aging calculations. We went back the full seventeen years."

"My god, Claude, I'll bet it was that factor of two in the de-aging equations. Laura had derived those formulas from General Relativity concepts and those equations are interrelated with the spatial formulas. I'll bet Dr. James made an error in transcribing those notes and never caught it. The factor of two must go with the spatial part of the formulas. Not with the de-aging equations."

"Veronica, you may have also unraveled the mystery about what happened to Drs. Farnsworth and James. If the factor of two you're talking about doesn't go with the de-aging formulas, it must be a multiplying factor in the differential coordinates. Assuming my memory of that derivation is correct, the twenty-foot spacing, Dr. Farnsworth used in setting our differential coordinates, really turned out to be forty feet. Veronica, if I'm correct, Drs. Farnsworth and James were synthesized about forty and eighty feet, respectively, under that huge gypsum dune!"

"Oh, my god, if that's the case they're probably dead. We've been in a coma for more than two days and couldn't have survived being buried alive for that long. This is terrible. Maybe, the suits offered them some protection."

"I doubt it, Veronica, they are heat resistant but are not oxygenated."

"Claude, what are we going to do? Should we try to dig them out? Veronica responded, becoming more frightened and confused as she thought about the fate of their colleagues and their own dilemma.

"We're not expending any energy digging forty feet into that hard packed dune. They're dead and we best spend our time thinking about how we can get ourselves out of this mess."

The two confused children sat back down in the lengthening shadow of a large dune and began to reexamine their situation. After a half hour of inconclusive and sometimes irrational discussion, they began to formulate a plan for survival in the Alternate Reality.

"Claude, let's reconsider some of the more constructive things we just said. I believe we should adapt that cover story Farnsworth came up with to our current situation and still pretend for the time being to be their children."

"You know it might work. If we pretended to be Farnsworth's kids, here on vacation viewing the White Sands National Monument, we could say we are visiting our Aunt Laura. We could say we had the bus drop us off here before we went on to Los Alamos."

"That's not a bad idea, but we don't even know if a bus comes here?"

"Look, let's just keep that idea as the baseline of our cover story and improvise as we go along. There must be some kind of entrance to this place off the highway. I walked out that narrow passageway between those dunes over there and found what appeared to be a plowed road. They must plow the sand off the roads in here for the tourists to use in this reality. I climbed on top of that dune, while you were still in that space-time coma, and saw some people and cars in the distance. Let's just follow that road out of here before it gets dark."

"OK, let's do that and be Farnsworth's kids here on vacation visiting our Aunt Laura. But, first let's get out those survival kits and make these clothes fit a little better."

The time travelers proceeded to cut off the legs and sleeves of their pants, shirts and jackets. Then, they cut strips of cloth from the cutoff legs and used them as belts to hold up their pants and to close their jackets. Before they started to walk out, they took the backpacks they had on their suits and put their survival kits in them, then buried their suits and helmets.

Following the road plowed in the sand, they soon came to a concession stand at the entrance of the White Sands National Monument. To their surprise, they saw that they didn't look too much different from the children of the other tourists milling around the concession stand. Many kids were wearing baggy clothes that looked like they did not fit. They saw many buses waiting outside. Finally, they decided to ask one of the drivers how to get to Los Alamos.

"Sir, could you tell me if a bus is leaving here for Los Alamos."

"Son, these are tour buses out of El Paso and not available for public transportation. But, there is one that stops here from Las Cruces and continues on to Alamogordo. It comes by every hour until seven in the evening. Are you kids lost or something?

"No, Sir, we're not. We're just here on vacation and staying with an aunt. Thank you for the information," Veronica answered, assuming a courteous but a matter of fact demeanor.

When the bus from Las Cruces came, they used money brought from the Fated Reality to pay their fare. After boarding the bus, they settled back in their seats and watched the cars and scenery go by. The number and variety of the automobiles approaching and passing them quickly caught the attention of the kids. They marveled over the many different makes and models, none of which resembled the ones in the Fated Reality.

Entering Alamogordo, the strange sights amazed the wide-eyed children. The sign advertising, motels, and little brightly lit restaurants were everywhere. None of this advertising or food availability existed in the Fated Reality. They accepted scarcity and rationing there, as a way of life. When they had first heard Laura and Lola describe the abundance in this reality they thought they must have been exaggerating. However, even with the limited exposure they now had, they could see their old Team Leaders were actually understating the huge differences between the two realities. And, as their old Team Leaders mentioned, the money they brought from the other reality still appeared to be useful in this one. When they finally arrived at the bus station in Alamogordo, they walked down the street to one of those little brightly lit restaurants before taking the bus to Los Alamos. The menu of the restaurant was displayed in bold letters above an open window to the kitchen area. Hamburger sandwiches of all kinds were being shoved through the widow at a high rate. They watched as something called fries, were dumped into a large metal bin from mesh metal baskets and then scooped into little boxes. Although, the lines of people waiting to order their selections were long, the children were shocked to discover how short a wait there actually was. They were sitting down and eating the burgers and fries in a matter of minutes.

Laura was in her apartment in Los Alamos and deeply engrossed in her thoughts as she packed for her move to Las Cruces. A lot had happened since she and Lola resigned their positions at the Los Alamos National Laboratory last December. She had gone back to New Jersey and had taken a research position at Rutgers University. Lola had gone back to NMSU and returned to her position in the Electrodynamics Laboratory.

The women had been writing papers and collaborating on the possibility of enlarging space-time singularities or wormholes, as the scientific community called them. They knew the Synthesizer they had developed was actually based on the same physical principles. They submitted their ideas to various government agencies to do research in subatomic space, which is filled with a substance called Quantum Foam. In the subspace of Quantum Foam, minute wormholes appear spontaneously. Enlarging one of these tiny wormholes for human entrance and keeping it open long enough to pass through requires a huge amount of negative energy. Laura had designed a practical means of generating large amounts of negative energy when she invented the Space-Time Transitional Synthesizer in the Fated Reality. The proposals the women had made to the government agencies were concerned with developing an energy converter. Their unique converter would produce the huge amounts of negative energy required to enlarge a subatomic wormhole. They so impressed the government's scientific community with their ideas that they gave the women a grant to build the energy converter. When they finally awarded the grant, they decided the work would be done at NMSU's Electrodynamics Laboratory. The women and Henry, after many discussions, finally had convinced Kurt to take a position in the NMSU's Physics Department. That way, Kurt and Laura could work at the same institution while she worked on the energy converter.

The ringing phone suddenly brought Laura out of her thoughts. When she answered it, the voice of a child asking for Dr. Laura Claremont, puzzled her.
"Hello. This is Dr. Claremont."
"Thank God it's you," the child's voice responded.
"Who is this?"
"It's Veronica Richards."
"I don't know any child by that name. Do I know your parents?"
"Oh, Laura, it's your old Time Crease team member, Veronica Richards."
Suddenly things began to come into focus.
"Dr. Veronica Richards from the Fated Reality? Is that you?"
"Yes."
Laura's mind began to race, as she thought: *Oh my god, they're here! Or,*

maybe Lola's playing some kind of joke on me. Certainly, no one else in this reality would even know Veronica's name. No, she had never done anything like that before, and I don't believe she's becoming a comedian, now. I had better find out what the hell happened.

"You sound like a child."

"Oh, Laura, it's a long story and a tragic one. I'm at the Los Alamos bus station with Claude Harris. We're exhausted and confused, could you please come and get us?"

"OK, stay put. I'll be right there."

Those disturbing revelations sent Laura running out of her apartment. As she drove to the bus terminal, she began to surmise what had happened. She concluded that they had reconstructed the old Synthesizer and something had gone wrong when they came to this reality. Why didn't she destroy all the notes and memos on that old design when she had a chance? After cursing herself for not doing that, all kinds of bizarre scenarios went through her head. They included the other reality invading this one, to the capture of her second in command, Lola Gonzalez.

Arriving at the bus terminal, two kids in dirty, baggy clothes came running up to her and threw their arms around her.

"Laura, thank God you are here. Something terrible has happened," both kids blurted out almost simultaneously.

"All right, calm down. You can tell me all about it when we get to my apartment. Too many people are staring and listening to us here."

When they got into Laura's minivan, the kids were shocked by the luxury it afforded. In the Fated Reality only cars with designs dating back to 1962 were available, even the new ones had similar design characteristics.

"Laura, you must be very important in this reality to rate a vehicle like this," Claude remarked, as he looked around the minivan.

"Guys, there is an abundance of consumer goods including cars in this reality. Even an ordinary person can afford a nice vehicle."

"Laura, Dr. Farnsworth and Dr. James are dead," Veronica, blurted out.

Laura could see the fear on their faces and could tell they needed to say what happened, right then.

"All right, why don't you give me a brief summary of what happened, now. Later, after you're cleaned up and rested, you can give me all the details."

"Laura, the authorities in the Fated Reality forced Farnsworth and what was left of your old team to build a new Synthesizer. We copied your old design but couldn't modify the design so that it could deliver weapons in our reality. You know the price of failure there. We became desperate and concocted a plan to escape and find you and Lola. We thought together we could help you rebuild the Synthesizer here and then we could all return to the Fated Reality. We felt you could show us how to modify the old design to make it deliver weapons from the Fated Reality's timeline."

Laura knew that was impossible because it violated the causality principle, but chose not to inform these young time travelers of that fact at this time.

"Who else went through the aperture with you?"

"Only Drs. Farnsworth and James. Dr. Farnsworth called us the Core Team because we were the only ones familiar with the design of the Synthesizer and its original purpose."

"Then you four were the only ones who knew about the Alternate Reality?

"Yes, everyone else, including the authorities, thought you built a Weapon Synthesizer and used it to deliver those KILOGEN devices," Veronica answered with childlike sincerity

"Are you sure Dr. Farnsworth stepped into the aperture?"

"We are very certain because he was right behind us," Claude answered also with childlike innocence.

"One more question before we go up to my apartment. Why do you think Farnsworth and James are dead? Laura asked as she pulled into the apartment house parking lot."

"They were not in sight when we awoke from our time travel comas and we think we know why. We think a factor of two was introduced into your de-aging formulas when we tried to modify the Synthesizer. We thought we would only de-age by half the time differential. But, now, we think it must have been a multiplying factor, not a fractional factor, and it should be applied to the differential coordinates not the de-age formulas. If that's true, it means that the twenty-foot spacing Dr. Farnsworth used in setting our differential coordinates turned out in reality to be forty feet. If those suppositions were correct, we concluded, Drs. Farnsworth and James synthesized forty to eighty feet under a huge gypsum dune that was near us," Veronica explained.

"If you had studied the theory of the de-aging effect carefully, you would have realized the effect is always linearly dependent on the time deferential. Therefore, its constant of proportionality cannot change. The only possible place a scale factor error can occur, is in the spatial differential coordinates."

"You must think we're stupid," Veronica said, as tears appeared in her eyes and even in Claude's.

That response by her younger team members made Laura suspect there may be some effect on the brain when going back in time to one's pre-adolescence. Even though much of the neural development is preserved, the brain might revert to childlike behavior under certain circumstances. She guessed that the further back one goes into one's pre-adolescence, the more childlike one's behavior becomes.

"No, Guys, I didn't mean it that way. Everyone can make mistakes but some are more lethal than others. OK, enough questions and answers for now, let's go up to my apartment. You can get cleaned up and I'll run out and get some takeout food. The kids did not know what takeout food was but they were too exhausted to ask any more questions and just followed her obediently to the apartment.

When they got to the apartment, she gave them each a pair of her pajamas and showed them where the bathroom was. Then she left for the Capistrano restaurant to get some takeout food.

While in the car she called Lola on her cell phone. Lola's phone rang and finally the answering machine picked up. Laura left the message "We have Visitors, return my call ASAP". Before Laura could hang up, Lola was on the phone.

"Visitors? What visitors?

"People from out of our past are here in this reality."

"Laura, stop being facetious, what's going on? I'm just getting ready to go out. Henry is taking me to a play."

"I'm not joking. We have visitors from the Fated Reality and they're in my apartment right now."

Laura quickly related the story about how Veronica and Claude got here. And, how, Harold Farnsworth and Hillary James died in a miscalculation associated with the space-time formulas. Those revelations completely stunned Lola. Laura could hear Henry in the background asking her what was wrong and Lola tell him there was some glitch with their grant. She told him she would have to go to Los Alamos and sort out the details with Laura, but she did not think there was any long-term damage.

"Nice cover up ART2," Laura inserted, now being half facetious.

"God, I thought those designations and that whole nightmare was over, but I guess the next phase has just begun. I'll be over the first thing in the morning. ART2 out. Lola replied, also being half facetious.

When Laura returned to the apartment the kids had showered and were waiting for her, dressed in the pajamas she gave them. They were extremely tired. So, she fed them the takeout food, then, put Veronica in Lola's old bed, Claude on the sofa and went to bed herself.

The following morning, while the newly reunited members of Time Crease Team were having breakfast, its other charter member let herself into the apartment. When Lola came into the kitchen, the appearance of Veronica and Claude startled her. Her old subordinates ran to her and started hugging her. They were acting like children. She did not know quite how to respond, so she kissed them both on the cheek and gave them a hug. Over breakfast, the kids revealed all the frightening details of their escape from the Fated Reality. After two hours of discussion, Laura put a stop to the conversation.

"OK, guys, I guess we heard enough for now. Why don't you go into the other room and put on the jeans and shirts I put on the sofa for you? Put on your old combat boots for now and stuff some paper into those things, they're very loose. Lola and I are going to take you down to Sears and get you some clothes." The kids went off to the other room to get dressed and the women continued their conversation over another cup of coffee.

"Laura, we have a problem and, if we're not careful, it could ruin everything for us here."

"Yes, and as I see it, it breaks down into two related problems. The first is what to do with the kids and second is what to do about that Synthesizer still back in the Fated Reality. The kids say it will meltdown if someone tampers with it. Also, if they don't return within two days after they left, it will melt down anyway."

"You know, Laura, two days is a long time in that reality and they're excellent at cracking codes and gaining entrance to computers. Maybe we should rebuild our Synthesizer and destroy that one before the guards in the other reality enter the chamber. It's the only way to guarantee they won't come here."

"Do you really think they could figure out what's going on and shut down the destruct sequence in two days?"

"They don't have to figure what's going on in two days, Laura, only shut down the destruct sequence. Then, they will have forever to figure what the Synthesizer really does."

"I guess you're right. We'll have to destroy it. But, let's not sweat that now. We still have our Federal Grant and with it a permanent solution to that problem if we need it."

"I think I see what you're saying about the synthesizer. However, rather than second guessing each other about the kids, tell me briefly what you have in mind, before they come back."

"Lola, as you can see, de-aging has left Veronica and Claude with most of their neural development still intact. However, going back to pre-adolescence has put them in that nonlinear state we often talked about in the other reality. I'm not talking about physical appearances, but also about maturity issues. I'm sure you noticed. They exhibit childlike behavior. They are children, albeit extremely intelligent children, but still children. They will have to grow up in this reality and they're going to need our protection and guidance."

"Are you saying we are going to have to raise them? My God, how are we going to fit them in with our guys? You and I are both planning to get married in the fall."

"I know, but we're going to have to work something out. We can't leave them on their own for a variety of reasons, apart from the moral ones."

"OK, Laura, I get your point, let's think about it. It's going to take one hell of a cover story to fit them into our lives. Now, what do you want to do about that synthesizer? You agreed, it has to be destroyed, but you seemed to be implying something else when you said our grant would offer a permanent solution. I don't want to go back there again."

"Neither do I. Going back there won't help change the mind set of that world. We already put them in a holding pattern and its up to them to work out their problems or perish. No, we won't go back. What I have in mind is to rebuild a version of the Synthesizer with some of our federal grant money. Then, send a small explosive device back to that Synthesizer Chamber, and destroy that thing a few minutes after the Core Team left in 2011."

"I agree, but we shouldn't say anything to the kids about that. They think we're all going go back to modify that old Synthesizer and make it deliver weapons in that reality."

"We couldn't make it do that even if we wanted to. It would require us to change the laws of physics. We'll need a few years to construct the new version of the Synthesizer that I have in mind. So, the kids will have plenty of time to adapt to this reality. Once they do, they won't want to return to that dismal world, anyway."

A few minutes later, the conversation ended when the kids returned to the kitchen dressed in the clothes Laura gave them.

"That's better guys, now let's go and do some shopping," Laura said, as she and Lola put the dirty dishes in the sink.

Arriving at the shopping mall, the women and the two kids headed for Sears.

"My God! I can't get over the variety of products in the stores. There is such abundance here. But, I'll bet your ration coupons don't allow you to buy very many of these things," Veronica commented, her eyes wide open in amazement.

"Guys, we don't have ration coupons in this reality, all you need is money," Lola informed the kids.

After that remark, the women took the kids into children's department at Sears. Having to shop in the children's department for clothes embarrassed the kids. Seeing their embarrassment, Laura quickly informed them of their status.

"Guys, that's the way it's going to be for several years until you grow up.

"Several years? I thought we were going back to the other reality when we get through building the new Synthesizer," Claude replied, appalled by the several years remark.

"Look. It took us ten years to get back the first time. While it won't take that long this time, it's still going to take four or five years. We have to build it secretively out of spare parts from other projects. And, no one must know we are doing it. Is that clear?" Laura explained planting the seeds for the cover story they would have to create.

"I think so," Claude answered; beginning to realize their stay in this reality would be a long one.

"What Laura is saying is that we are going to need a good cover story to explain your existence in this reality, while we accomplish our long term goals. Laura and I can't accomplish these alone. We will need your full cooperation."

"We will certainly give you our full cooperation. We were your subordinates and team members in the other reality and we still are in this one"

"All right. Now that you have brought up the subject, let's take the things we bought and go and sit on one of those benches. So, we can discuss what Lola and I mean by 'full cooperation'."

When the group put down their packages and were seated, Laura began to delineate the terms of an agreement they would all have to accept.

"First of all, you must clearly understand the situation you are in. Here, you are children, even though you have the minds of educated scientists. They will expect in this society, you to still be under some type of parental supervision. We must have a cover story that, completely and unquestionably, explains every detail of your relationship to us. You must attend school with children your age, at least for a while."

"Why can't we just stay with you, out of sight in your apartment, and work quietly on the assignments you give us?"

"Someone would discover you. And, when they reported you to the authorities, we would be arrested for child neglect and the state would take you from us. If that happened, our plans would be destroyed and we would be forced by law to stay apart. Laura and I had to become college students and blend into society in this reality. You must do the same before you can officially work with us. It took us four years to get our degrees and four more to establish ourselves in the scientific community here. You're mentally very intelligent adults and can probably breeze through the academic requirements in this reality. And, like us, be through with college in four or five years. Then you can work with us full time and help us achieve our goals. However, unless you can convince the educators in this society that they should allow you to accelerate through the system, none of what I just said will happen."

"Oh, Lola, I think we can easily do all that, but I don't think it'll take that long," Veronica said, thinking the women were exaggerating a bit.

"Lola, let me make a few remarks. You must understand the social situation you are in. Lola and I have been integrated into this society, not only from a scientific standpoint, but also in a social way. We have had to play the part of adult females with normal desires and feelings. Otherwise, people would think something was wrong with us and that was the last thing we needed. We had to cultivate relationships with members of the opposite sex, and now each of us is seriously involved with a man. We both intend to get married this fall."

"My god, do they know about us?" Claude asked.

"No, and they don't know that we are from the Fated Reality, and you must never tell them."

"Does that mean your not going back to the Fated Reality?"

"No, it just means we haven't told them yet. We are concerned that if they do find out prematurely, we may never be able accomplish our goals. You see they are very important men at the institution where we do our research and where we plan secretively to build the Synthesizer. In fact, one heads the prestigious laboratory where our work will be done."

"My god, this is more complicated than I thought. Gee, I never realized the things you and Lola had to do to accomplish what you did. Or for that matter, what you still have to do to accomplish what is ahead," Veronica remarked.

"Well, we have been quite open with you, but as members of our Time Crease Team we know you will play your part in accomplishing this difficult mission. Incidentally, don't mention the term 'Time Crease' to anyone or to our men when you meet them."

"When are we going to meet your fiancés?" Claude asked, intrigued by the plot the women were weaving.

"You will be meeting them in a few days, but only after Lola and I have developed the proper cover story to explain your relationship to us."

"We could pretend to be your children or something like that," Claude responded.

"Perhaps more like a relative of some kind, but we are going to have to work out what type and all the nuances of the relationships. However, we'll discuss that later, right now we have to finish shopping," Laura said.

After buying the visitors complete wardrobes, the women took them out to dinner and then back to the apartment. There they could relax and fill in the details of their cover story.

Chapter 16

Returning to the apartment, the newly reunited Time Crease Team began discussing various scenarios that would allow a smooth integration of its younger members into the women's lives. To help generate ideas the women had the kids take out the credentials that Farnsworth had them bring to the Alternate Reality. They had each had two birth certificates and a driver's license. One birth certificate had the surname Farnsworth on it, with Harold and Hillary as parents. It indicated it was issued by the San Francisco Department of Vital Statistics. It looked authentic enough because Farnsworth used a copy of his own birth certificate as a template to forge it. The kids also had copies of their own birth certificates from the Fated Reality. One was Veronica's and said she was born in Florida. The other was Claude's and said he was born in Massachusetts. All the birth certificates showed the kids were twenty-eight years of age. Clearly, they were not directly useful and the drivers' licenses were also of no value, given the apparent ages of the children.

The women rejected cover stories with the children as their relatives, because they could not withstand serious scrutiny. They realized they would need a vastly more complex ruse to deceive their families and more importantly, their men. Because the cover story was taking more time than anticipated, Lola decided to stay at the apartment with Laura and the kids for a few more days. Laura had to explain to Kurt her reason for not finishing her packing and coming to Las Cruces as planned. Both women explained to their fiancés that they had to stay in Los Alamos for several more days. They claimed they had to handle some alleged conflict of interest problems that concerned their new research grant and the work they had done at the Los Alamos National Laboratory. The men accepted their explanations but warned them not to get involved with those black world people again.

After sleeping on their problem for a night, the women gradually began to fabricate a cover story they were sure was going to hang together. As the women and the kids sat in the living room of the apartment a day later, Laura began to restate what they had come up with.

"I guess what we have agreed upon, so far, is to have Veronica and Claude be the adopted children of the Farnsworth family. First, we will carefully change the year of their births on their Farnsworth birth certificates and have them copied on high quality document paper. The date changes are easily done with stick-on numbers. They have all we need at that business supply store down the street. However, I want the originals destroyed when we are finished, because they have a way of turning up again when least expected."

"OK, now let's go over how we know you women and why we have come to you for help," Veronica suggested.

"First of all, let me make something clear. We all agree that coming forth with any revelations about the Fated Reality would be counterproductive. The only purpose such revelations would serve, would be to make our families and men think we had taken leave of our senses. Now, to make them accept the reasons why we want to care for these children, we must have two levels of deception. They must be such that if or when the first level becomes unbelievable, the second level is believable and a logical follow-on from the first. To lend plausibility to the cover story, Lola and I must include something about our families and something the men already believe happened to us twelve years ago. Consequently, we will build on their belief that we met in Europe nearly twelve years ago. She was there traveling with her Aunt and I was there with a group of college girls touring France and Germany. Actually, my counterpart in this Reality was there, doing just that and somehow met her demise when she and another girl went behind the Iron Curtain on a dare. In any case, the families and the men already think we were abducted and somehow we turned up in a coma a year later in Colorado Springs. When we recovered, we appeared to have no recollection of what happened during the year we were supposedly missing. It is upon those facts, real or contrived for the purposes at hand, that we will build the second part of our cover story."

"I can understand why we are trying to mesh things with what occurred twelve years ago, but why the two levels of deception?" Claude asked.

"We need the two levels because Laura and I need to establish why we were hiding something if the first level of deception fails. Don't you remember how Central Intelligence did it in the Fated Reality? They were experts at this sort of thing in that world of lethal spying and deception. As part of our training in the Fated Reality's Special Forces Reserve, they taught us how to uncover such practices. Nevertheless, let's continue. As we said yesterday, Laura introduced me to Hillary James in Europe and we have been friends since then. We renewed our friendship when we discovered her working on a black program at the Lawrence Livermore National Laboratory in California. She had married a man by the name of Harold Farnsworth and was living with him and the two children they adopted, near San Jose. We got friendly with Hillary's family and quite fond of the children, probably because of their apparent intellect. A tragedy occurred in that family while we were working in Los Alamos and we never learned about it until the children showed up at our apartment. We will say their parents had died when their single engine plane apparently crashed over the ocean near Monterey. The children somehow survived the crash and made their way by bus to Los Alamos to find Laura and I and ask for help. The authorities believe the entire family perished in the crash. You guys now want to live with us, and we feel it is our responsibility to take you in, because your mother would expect us to do just that."

"But, why is that part of our cover story not enough? Why do we need a second part?" Veronica asked.

The women could see that their younger associates were very inexperienced at this sort of thing. Perhaps, in the de-aging process they became a bit more gullible than they would be as adults. In either case, the women felt they must take the time to explain the subtle nuances to them.

"That story may fool some people but probably not our men. They are extremely intelligent guys and will soon find holes in it. They may choose to ignore the inconsistencies but in case they don't, we must have a backup story that will excuse us for making up that tale. Lola and I have come up with just the thing to make them believe we used that story to hide a dark secret from our past. We are going to say, if they confront us with inconsistencies, that we have been hiding something we did in Europe twelve years ago. We will say we were young girls seeking adventure in France and West Germany when someone dared us to sneak behind the Iron Curtain into East Germany. We nearly made it into Berlin but were caught by the East German police. An American Business man in West Berlin visited us in jail. He told us, he could get us out if we agreed to the proposition a wealthy benefactor was willing to extend. The benefactor was willing to pay all the necessary bribes to get us out of East Germany and safely back home, if we would agree to bear children for him. His wife could not have children and he was desperate for bloodline heirs. For reasons not disclosed to us, they did not want to adopt and were making this offer. They were living in Europe at the time and able to affect our release. We will say we were desperate and very frightened and the hopelessness of our situation made us accept the proposition. Then, we will say we were kept in a chateau in France until they released us. It was there that we gave birth to Veronica and Claude."

"How are you going to tie that part to the first part of the cover story?" Claude asked.

"After the children were born, I'm going to say the family had sent Laura and I back to the United States by private plane. The plane landed in Colorado Springs. They took us to the Garden of the Gods where they had us dress in spacesuits. They wanted us to appear as if we were involved in some kind of college prank. Then they had someone render us unconscious, so it seemed as if we were comatose. The Farnsworths knew it was unlikely that we would come forward with the true story because of the embarrassment it would cause our families and us. To be sure we were living up to our part of the bargain, the Farnsworths have kept track of us all these years. Apparently, when Farnsworth's plane crashed, the father died and the mother lasted for three months before succumbing to her injuries. During that time, she told the children the family had lost their petroleum refineries during the OPEC oil crisis and with it their fortune. She told them about their birth mothers and how they were now highly regarded scientists. The children were told to seek us out and came to Los Alamos. We will then say, we made up the first part of the story because we still did not want to reveal the embarrassing details of a long forgotten mistake. In addition, we will say; we have convinced the children that the first part of the cover story would be a better way to blend them into our lives and would cause everyone less embarrassment, including them.

After hearing the elaborate two-tier cover story, they realized it was naive of them to think that entering the Alternate Reality, and blending in successfully, would be an easy task. They could see if they did not pay close attention to what the Team Leaders were saying, their mission could easily fail. They felt like children learning a lesson from vastly more experienced parents. In fact, it would not be hard accepting the guidance of these "mothers."

The women spent the next day repeatedly going over each minute detail of the cover story with the children, making sure all potential questions had consistent answers. They even downloaded a set of birth certificates from a genealogy web page that had some vital statistics from a town in southern France. They placed the names Veronica Gonzalez and Claude Claremont on them, along with the appropriate dates of birth. They then printed document quality copies to lend credence to the second part of their cover story, if required. Later, they would the figure out a way to officially authenticate the birth certificates they had just made.

Before the women departed for Las Cruces, they showed Veronica and Claude where the town library was located. It was on a street a few blocks away from the apartment building. They told them to go there each day in their absence and read all that they could about the Alternate Reality. They gave them money and stocked food in the apartment's refrigerator for them. The women had the children commit to memory their addresses and phone numbers in Las Cruces and the names of all members of their families and fiancés before they left. They were not concerned about leaving them alone for a few days, because, after all, they were twenty-eight years old, mentally. Aside from their physical size, they were capable of handling almost any situation that might arise.

Arriving in Las Cruces, the women found Kurt and Henry waiting for them in Laura's new apartment. The men had been speculating for the past four days about what had detained the women in Las Alamos. When they finished hugging each other, the men started asking questions.

"Henry and I were becoming concerned. We imagined the government officials were trying to induce you to return to work at the Los Alamos National Laboratory again."

"Oh, it was nothing like that," Laura assured them.

"Well, what the hell were you doing up there for four days. Did you have that many things to pack?" Henry asked.

"No, but we did get the surprise of our lives," Laura responded.

"What could be so surprising in Los Alamos, except perhaps, if there was a problem at the National Laboratory," Kurt asked.

"I think we better tell them, Lola. We had visitors. Two children from California arrived on our doorstep and asked to be taken in."

"Two children? What two children?" The men asked, repeating each other's question.

"Remember six months ago when we returned after that ordeal with the terrorists, you asked us if we had ever met twelve years before in Europe. We told you then we had, but didn't elaborate. Well, at that time Laura introduced me to one of the friends with whom she was traveling. Her name was Hillary James. I had become quite friendly with her and Laura. A few years ago, we renewed our friendship with her when we discovered her working on a black program at the Lawrence Livermore National Laboratory in California. She had married a man by the name of Harold Farnsworth and was living with him near San Jose with the two children they had adopted. In short, we got quite friendly with Hillary's family and quite fond of her children. Unexpectedly, four days ago, the kids showed up in Los Alamos with a frightening tale about a tragedy that recently occurred in their family. Apparently, their parents had died when their single engine plane crashed over the ocean near Monterey. The children somehow survived the crash and made their way by bus, in torn and tattered clothes, to Los Alamos to find Laura and me. The kids were frightened and hungry when they appeared on our doorstep and Laura took them in. Then she called me."

"That's why you ran out as if you had seen a ghost," Henry remarked.

"Yes, dear. I didn't want to say anything until I found out all the details. When I got there, Laura and I questioned the kids in depth and found out the authorities believe the entire family perished in the crash. After much discussion, they informed us that they wanted to come and live with us. They begged us not to go to the authorities because they didn't want to be sent to a foster home. After four days of agonizing discussions we finally decided it was our responsibility to take care of them, because their mother would expect us to do just that."

"How old are those children?" Kurt asked.

"They are eleven years old. There is a boy, Claude, and a girl, Veronica. The kids say they were adopted by their parents."

"You are going to the authorities, aren't you?" Henry asked, suspecting the women were getting involved with something in which they should not be involved.

"No, we are not going to the authorities, because it would break the kids' hearts. They are probably right; they would be put in a foster home in another state. And, if they did that, getting custody of them wouldn't be easy for us. Besides, no one knows they're alive," Laura responded, trying to avoid discussing the legal ramifications.

"Henry is right. You have to go to the authorities. You can't do this just because you think their mother would wish it."

"We don't have to do any such thing. We're not letting Hillary's children be put in foster homes. We have discussed this ad nauseam with each other and Lola is going to take Veronica and I'm going to take Claude."

"You can't do that. Don't we have something to say about it?" Kurt snapped back with Henry agreeing.

Henry could see Lola's dark eyes glare at him and he quickly remarked.

"Hey, we were supposed to go out to dinner. Why don't Kurt and I go out to get something and bring it home? It will give us a chance to clear our heads and when we get back we can eat and discuss this calmly on full stomachs."

"That sounds like a good idea. Lola what should we have, Mexican food?"

"No, we had that two days in a row with the kids. Why don't you pick up some of those Chinese dinners?"

The men left immediately for the Chinese takeout dinners without calling ahead. After they left, the women started assessing the situation.

"Laura, this isn't going well. Do you think that insisting that the kids come with us, before the guys even met them, was the right thing to do?"

"Well, at least it's bringing this thing to a head, fast. I think we're going to get to phase two of the cover story a lot quicker than we planned. The guys are very sharp and I don't believe they bought that explanation."

As they drove to the Chinese Restaurant, Kurt and Henry were involved in a serious conversation about what the women had just revealed.

"You know, Henry, something is fishy about the story they are telling us. Why are they so adamant about taking those kids in? They never even spoke about having children of their own, much less adopting some."

"I agree. Something is wrong with that story. It just does not hang together. I suspect they are leaving a lot out, but I can't put my finger on it."

"Look, it's obvious they're apprehensive and very uptight. Let's just calmly discuss it with them, maybe ask a few questions. Let's not force them into choosing between those kids and us right now. We should at least find out the whole story before we make any demands or say something we'll be sorry for."

The two couples ate the takeout food in relative silence for about twenty minutes until Henry finally spoke.

"Ladies, Kurt and I have been thinking about what you told us and find some of what you said very difficult to understand. You seem to be saying that children of a friend of yours came to you saying that their parents perished in a plane crash. Then pleaded with you to take them in and become their new parents. They asked you not to go to the authorities because they feared being placed in a foster home. Hearing their impassioned request, you immediately granted their wishes. Then, you come prancing in here expecting Kurt and me to just accept your unilateral decisions and happily form families with each of us taking one of those children. Doesn't that sound the least bit strange to you?"

The women knew he was right and what seemed to be a good cover story did appear quite absurd when viewed from that perspective. The usually very resourceful women, now thought they had made a serious blunder. Of course, every other story they had contrived had seemed even more ridiculous. The irony of the whole thing was that the truth was the most unbelievable. Trying to explain the existence of visitors from another reality, including themselves, had led to a hopelessly entangled tale of half-truths and lies. These same thoughts went through their minds as they stared into space trying to think of a way to respond to Henry's question.

Seeing the women staring in silence with frightened, troubled expressions on their faces caused Kurt to respond.

"What Henry is trying to say is that perhaps you haven't told us the whole story."

After a long pause, Laura finally looked at Lola and broke the silence.

"You're right, we haven't told you the whole story and it's too late to tell you now. Lola, I think it's best if we go back to Los Alamos and sort this thing out. It's our problem not theirs."

Lola knew what Laura was alluding to and nodded her agreement as she followed Laura out the door. The men sat there dumbfounded and just stared as the door closed behind the women.

The women had driven down from Los Alamos in Laura's minivan and their things were still in the car, so there was nothing to pack. They quickly got into the minivan and drove off.

As the women drove, bouncing one idea after another off each other, they realized they had nearly driven to Alamogordo. In their confusion, they had taken route 70, instead of route 25 to Los Alamos. They had driven more than an hour out of their way and decided to stop for a cup of coffee, before cutting back to route 25.

Veronica and Claude were watching television when they heard a key turning in the apartment door's lock. They were a little apprehensive because they did not expect the Team Leaders to be back so soon. It was nearly eleven and not knowing what to expect both went into the kitchen to hide. When the door opened, they heard strange male voices.

"Laura, Lola are you here?"

"There not at home," a child's voice replied.

When the men walked into the kitchen, they saw two frighten children, one holding a knife and the other a stick that looked like a mop handle.

"Take it easy, we're friends of Laura and Lola. Have they arrived yet?" Henry said, looking intently at the children.

"No."

"You must be Veronica and this must be Claude," Kurt said, realizing who the kids must be and trying to break the tension that was building.

That remarked did ease things a bit.

"Who are you?" Veronica asked.

"I'm Lola's fiancé, Henry Vega, and he's Kurt Peyser, Laura's fiancé"

The children put down their weapons, and went to the men and introduced themselves. Then they asked the men to come into the living room where they could sit and talk.

"Are you supposed to meet Laura and Lola here? Claude asked, wondering if the women had changed their plans.

"Actually, they came to Las Cruces and told us about two children that suddenly appeared on their doorstep," Kurt said.

"They told us about you, too. But, where are they now?" Veronica responded, not wanting to say too much, either, until she found out what happened.

"They were coming back here, maybe they stopped for something," Henry replied.

"Why didn't they come back with you? Did you have a disagreement of some kind?" Claude said, sensing there was something wrong.

"I guess you might call it that. When they arrived, they told us about two children that had showed up in Los Alamos with a frightening tale about a tragedy that recently occurred in their family. Apparently, their parents had died when their single engine plane crashed over the ocean near Monterey. They told us that the children had somehow survived the crash and made their way to Los Alamos to find them. After much discussion, they told us they wanted to assume responsibility for you because they were good friends with your mother. When we told them that might not be in your best interest, they became upset and started to quarrel with us," Kurt explained.

"I suppose you weren't very receptive to them taking care of us, were you?" Veronica replied.

"It's not that we weren't very receptive, but felt that they were not telling us the whole story. Even you can probably see that the story lacks many important details," Henry said, trying to draw the kids out a little further.

The children then asked if the men wanted a soft drink but when they refused one, the kids went to the kitchen to get themselves a one.

"Kurt, these kids are very clever. They're trying to determine if we objected to them and they know we are trying to get at what Lola and Laura are hiding. Let's keep the conversation going, and maybe we'll get our questions answered."

In the kitchen, the kids were also discussing the situation.

"You know, Veronica, the Team Leaders gave them the first part of our cover story and they didn't accept it on face value, as the leaders predicted. Maybe, they're letting their fiancés get here first so we can deliver part two for them."

"Do you really think so? I guess it's obvious that the men are trying to find out more."

"Look, even if the team leaders didn't plan it this way, I sense the time is right for part two. So, let's reveal it to them, just remember to relate the details like kids would do," Claude responded. He realized at this moment, they could be more convincing than even their esteemed team leaders.

Returning to the living room, the kids picked up the discussion where it was left off.

"Dr. Vega, you are quite correct the story Laura and Lola told you did lack many important details. In some areas, the story was incorrect. But, in talking it over with Veronica in the kitchen, we feel it's in 'our best interest' as you put it, to tell you the whole story. We know our mothers might not like it, but, we also feel we have to know where we stand," Claude said.

"Mothers??? Did you say mothers?" the confused men asked, in unisons.

"Claude, let me start because Mom spoke to me more about this than to you. Our mother told us a story about two young girls on an adventure in France twelve years ago. Apparently, someone dared them to sneak behind the Iron Curtain into East Germany. When they foolishly acted upon that dare, the East German police caught them. A man, who visited them in jail, told them he could help if they would agree to a proposal that a wealthy benefactor was willing to extend. The benefactor was willing to pay all the necessary bribes to get them out of East Germany, if they would agree to bear children for the benefactor. His wife could not have children and he wanted actual bloodline heirs. My mother told us they were desperate and very frighten. Finally, they agreed to the proposition. They were kept in a chateau in southern France where they gave birth to my brother and me."

The astounded men looked at each other in disbelief, but soon realized this story was beginning to explain all the mystery surrounding the disappearance of the women twelve years ago. It also explained their reluctance to describe what happened to them during that year. It angered the men to think of the mental anguish the women had to suffer all these years. It even bothered them more, because the women still thought they had to hide from them, their foolish decision to act on that dare.

"We're glad you shared that with us, but tell us how you came to seek them out," Kurt said.

"OK, Veronica, let me tell them how we found our birth mothers. After we were born, our parents sent Laura and Lola to the United States by private plane. The plane landed in Colorado Springs and from there, they were taken to the Garden of the Gods. Someone had given them an injection of something, and they were later found unconscious. They didn't come forward then because of the embarrassment it would cause them and their families. Our parents kept track of them all these years to make sure they were keeping their part of the bargain. Four months ago, our father's plane crashed and our father died. Our mother lived for three months before succumbing to her injuries. During that time, she told us they had lost their petroleum refineries and with them, their fortune. She, then, told us the story we just told you about our birth mothers. She said they were, now, highly respected scientists living in Los Alamos and told us to seek them out when she died because she was sure they would help us."

The men sat there for a few moments in deep thought, trying to fathom what they had just been told. They knew the story must be true, not only because it fit the facts as they knew them, but because it was spontaneous. There was no way for the women to know they would show up at their apartment at this time. They themselves were uncertain at first about coming here, but now they were happy they had. They were certain they now knew why the women would try to keep this terrible episode in their lives from them. This impromptu visit probably had saved their relationships with the women before either they or their proud ladies foolishly decided to separate.

"Gentleman, we hope our being truthful hasn't hurt our mothers' relationships with you and I hope they forgive us for telling you what they were trying to hide. Now, please excuse us, it's getting very late and we're tired," Veronica said, rubbing her eyes.

"Sure, go ahead to bed, we'll take it from here. We'll wait in the living room until they arrive," Kurt said with Henry nodding in agreement.

After the kids went upstairs to bed, the men continued to discuss the situation. Among other things, they commented that Veronica looked like Lola, and Claude resembled Laura. They concluded during their conversation that the kids had even inherited their mothers' keen intellects.

A half hour later the women entered the apartment and were shocked to see the men sitting on the sofa. Laura tried to say something but the men stood up and hugged them. Then Kurt quickly whispered, "The kids are sleeping" and said they were taking them to an all-night diner for a cup of coffee. In the car, the women tried, again, to speak but the men asked them to refrain from speaking until they were at the diner. When they were all comfortably seated in one of the diner's booths, Henry began speaking.

"Ladies, the children have told us everything about what happen to you twelve years ago in Europe.

The women's faces dropped as they exchanged glances with each other.

"Oh, my god, they didn't tell you about that, did they?" Laura uttered, thinking the kids really blew it for them.

"Let us explain and then we'll get out of your lives," Lola said. She thought, they would simply tell the men they had lied about everything and then quietly release them from any marital plans they had made.

"You're not going anywhere. You don't think our feelings for you are so shallow that we would run off at the mention of an indiscretion you made twelve years ago, do you? A couple of very young and foolish college girls acted on impulse a long time ago and paid dearly for their indiscretion. They don't have to keep paying for it again and again."

"Henry expressed our feelings very succinctly, now, let's put all of that behind us and plan on how to introduce our new children to our families."

The women began to realize the kids might have actually helped. The men were trying to ease their apparent discomfort and seemed to believe the second part of their cover story, as told by the children. The realization that the kids may have saved their relationships prompted Lola to say.

"Our families will never understand and they will be so embarrassed by the way we behaved ourselves. Especially mine, you know how Hispanics are about that sort of thing, Henry."

"Your families do not have to know about what had happened in Europe twelve years ago. The kids could still be the children of your deceased best friend, who have come to live with you," Kurt said quickly, with Henry nodding.

"Kurt and I talked the whole thing over and agreed that we would be delighted to accept the kids into our families when we're married. We think that Veronica should be in the Vega family and Claude should be in the Peyser family."

With that remark the girls grabbed the guys hands, then leaning over the table, nearly knocking over the coffee cups, kissed them long and passionately. Laura then remarked in low tones.

"A few hours ago things looked so bleak because Lola and I thought our past would destroy any chance we might have had for a happy life here with you. But, thanks to the way you have understood our problem, our wildest dreams might still come true."

"What do you mean 'might' they will come true, right Kurt?"

Kurt nodded. Then, the conversation shifted to how best explain the children to their families. And, finally, how legally to handle their adoption

---

The women were ecstatic with the way things were evolving in the ensuing years. The kids were in private schools for the gifted in England and were acclimating well to this reality. They no longer expressed any interest in completing their mission. The women's research project was going well and the design of the new Space-Time Transitional Synthesizer was progressing as planned. They had saved the Fated Reality from imminent disaster, but the synthesizer left in tact, even for a few days, in that reality still worried them. Common sense told them they had more than fulfilled any obligations they had in the past to that reality. It further told them, they must destroy the keys to this world that were left behind otherwise more dangerous visitors would soon arrive.

Printed in the United States
60632LVS00003B/313